FEARLESS AT HEART

A KINCAIDS OF PINE HARBOUR NOVEL

ZOE YORK

For a twenty-year-old girl who was both sure and not sure at the same time; I'm forever grateful

For twenty years, Seth Kincaid has kept his visits to his home town brief. He's not avoiding January Howe, exactly —he's giving his high school girlfriend space. But that distance evaporates when she takes over her family's marina for the summer. Which means every time he flies his floatplane into the harbour, she's there, and the temptation to fall into her sunny smile and forget about the past is stronger than ever. He can't resist lending a hand, though. Not when she needs the help.

January has a lot on her plate. She's temporarily raising her niece and nephew while her sister is overseas, and running the family business, too. The last thing she needs is the dangerous risk of pretending a fling with Seth could be simple. Except the grown man version of the boy she once dated is…perfectly easy. He helps with the kids, no questions asked, and then once they're asleep, satisfies her in ways her eighteen-year-old self couldn't have imagined.

But two decades of distance is a shadow layered on top of complicated, long-ago memories.

Whatever this temporary magic spell they are under, it can only be for the summer. Any chance of something else between them evaporated the day Seth joined the Air Force—and broke her teenage heart.

1
____

Seth Kincaid had a crappy social life—nonexistent, truthfully, especially during the winter—but leaving early from the only party he'd been invited to in six months had to take some kind of self-sabotaging award. Especially because his alternate plan was firing up his computer and digging into a review of the business plan for Fly North Aviation.

It had been a mistake to go out tonight. What he'd been doing was running away from his feelings, a Kincaid classic choice, because tomorrow he was going home to Pine Harbour. And that required a certain amount of emotional armour that would only come from diving into his work and finding reassurance in his life choices to this point.

"You're heading out already?" Teegan Matthews, who had invited him, noticed him reaching for his coat, and uncurled herself from the arms of her wife Linda, and followed him through the kitchen.

"I have an early morning tomorrow," he said, not making eye contact with her.

He liked Teegan a lot. They'd bonded over both being pilots, both ex-military, and both…well, antisocial. Except Teegan wasn't that anti-social, since she was throwing a party for her neighbours. That was Linda's influence.

"More people are coming." She hitched her thumbs in the back pockets of her jeans and rocked back on her heels.

His eyes flared in surprise. "Like, someone you wanted me to meet?"

She winced.

They weren't that close. He shook his head. "Sorry, gotta head."

She sighed. "Can't blame a girl for trying."

That made him smirk. "You just want someone to go on flyfishing double dates."

"Would you?"

"No."

She laughed, but it definitely sounded like a *don't you want to get laid?* kind of laugh.

And…no. Not really.

He let himself out the side door and wrapped his scarf around his neck. After two weeks of warmer-than-usual spring weather, it was cold tonight, with a sharp wind blowing in off the lake.

Tomorrow, he'd get in his float plane and fly south. Both towns were on Lake Huron, but Blind River felt worlds apart from Pine Harbour. He had made that deliberate choice four years ago, when he released from the Air Force and started his northern air ferry business. Close to home, but only by air. Close enough to visit, and close enough to leave after a meal with his brothers.

Twenty years ago, he'd made a decision—a series of decisions—that made it hard now to go back. It didn't stop him. It just made the whole thing more fraught every time.

Focus on work. He had a new summer season to gear up for, his busiest yet.

As the wind picked up, he let himself into his house. A non-descript two-bedroom bungalow on the edge of town, it was a decent base for work, and that was pretty much all Seth cared about. There wasn't a lot to do, but Sudbury and Sault Saint Marie were both reasonable drives, and he had an airplane. He could fly wherever he wanted to go.

The problem was, he didn't want to go anywhere.

It hadn't always been this way. When he was in the Air Force, he had enjoyed the personal travel. He'd also enjoyed the occasional no-strings-attached fun with discreet colleagues, and that had stopped when he got out of the military, too.

Because he bought a plane and a house, and poured himself into this next stage of his life. Because he invested everything he had in a ten-year plan, and that first year, it had really seemed like it wouldn't get off the ground.

The soul-deep shame he felt that year dragged him right back to high school, to that feeling of not being smart enough to get into university, to that fear that he would never amount to anything impressive. The middle kid, the troubled bad boy.

Back then, it had been January Howe who had saved his ass. And then he'd fucked that up, too, by falling head-over-dick in lust with her, in that wild and reckless teenage way.

While he waited for his computer to boot up, he pulled up the group text chat with his brothers, to text them a reminder of his departure time. He truly did love flying home to have breakfast with them, private angst aside.

The reason for tomorrow's visit was his brother's wedding, later this summer. Will wanted to convene a wedding planning committee, a subcommittee to the primary committee of Will and his fiancée, Catie. A Bromittee, he called it, to plan a few surprises for his bride.

It was vaguely nauseating, but mostly benign and secretly a bit cute.

And there was no breakfast quite like diner breakfast at Mac's.

So when Will texted to see if the lake was landable, and did Seth want to fly south for a spontaneous gathering because Adam and Owen—both first responders—had a rare Saturday morning off together, there was only one answer.

Seth: I'm in
Will: Great! I'll email everyone the group planning document
Seth: And I'm out
Will: I'm joking!
Adam: Is he, though?
Josh: Definitely not, but I've blocked his email address so I'm safe
Owen: This is the first big family wedding, you guys, play nice

Big brother, playing Dad, as always. Seth rolled his eyes as he reread those text messages from earlier, then fired off a quick follow-up message.

Seth: Sunrise is at 7:29 tomorrow, I'll be departing promptly at 7:30 Seth: Should be landing around 8:15

————

THE NEXT MORNING, he slowly glided to a stop next to the dock at Howe's Marina, then hopped out and tied up his plane.

The small marina sat in the centre of the harbour's curve, at the T-junction of Main Street and Old Whiskey Harbour Road, which snaked along the shoreline. On the other side of the intersection, hidden by the marina at the moment, was his brother Josh's garage. Once upon a time, the harbour had been a vibrant hub, though that had faded in recent years.

As he strode toward the marina's main building to check in, memories from twenty years ago rolled through his mind. They did every time he flew into Pine Harbour.

Sneaking onto the roof late at night. Smoking a joint with January on some random sailboat the day after Seth's mom died.

The first time they had sex. The last time they had sex.

The night they broke up.

Two years of teenage hormones, shared grief, and private pain. And nobody knew about almost any of it.

Well, nobody except January, and she didn't work here anymore. Hadn't in years. She was a teacher now, at the school where Will was the principal, because Pine Harbour was just that small.

It was her sister who ran the family business now, which was why Seth felt comfortable flying home this often. He could handle seeing August, even if she did remind him of her older sister. And his own complicated feelings about this place took a back seat to flying south being the easiest way to visit his brothers—a forty-five minute flight sure beat a two-hour ferry ride with at least an hour of driving on either side.

Besides, the marina needed his business.

That's why he had signed an agreement with August last summer to run charters out of Pine Harbour at least three times a week, from early May until Labour Day. He'd been pleased with the boost to his business last year, and was actually looking forward to resuming those runs again this coming summer. He'd run the numbers again last night, to remind himself of his priorities, and his commitment to his business.

He took a deep breath as he wrapped his fingers around the handle on the door to the marina office. The bell jangled.

But it wasn't August Howe sitting behind the counter this morning. It was her daughter, Summer.

"Hey kiddo," he said as she waved politely. She had a glum look on her face. "Where's your mom?"

Summer burst into tears.

Seth held up his hands. "Whoa, I'm sorry."

From upstairs, he heard a rush of footsteps.

"Summer?" a worried voice called out.

One he recognized even after all these years.

Those approaching footsteps belonged to January, he realized in the split-second before she appeared in the doorway and froze.

"Seth?"

But he only had her attention for a split-second before she turned to her niece.

His attention stayed locked on his ex-girlfriend the whole time.

Her dirty-blonde hair was tied up in a messy bun on top of her head, pieces spilling out this way and that, and she was wearing a sleep shirt with a wineglass on it and a probably funny slogan he couldn't make out before she wrapped her arms around her niece.

Seth's gaze had tangled on her bare legs and sheepskin slippers before they disappeared behind the counter, and it took him a moment to jerk his head up and refocus on her face, ducked low to murmur reassuring words to the crying teen.

Then she took a deep breath and lifted her head. Her heart-shaped face—more beautiful than ever—had a careful and hard-to-read expression firmly in place, her gaze landing somewhere just north of his shoulder. "I was expecting you next month."

Ah. So this surprise was one-sided. He flinched. "I'm sorry, is August…?"

January nodded, still not quite looking at him. "She's fine. She's just…overseas. Summer misses her." She glanced back at her niece. "I guess that's why you snuck down here?"

Overseas?

The young teen nodded solemnly. "I thought I could help out. I saw Seth's plane land and thought I'd come down and check him in."

January winced. "Thanks, honey. Not your job. It's my job now. I just need to stay on top of the calendar."

"I didn't have a booking," Seth said in a rush, trying to smooth over the hurt feelings and ignore the hammering of his pulse in his neck at the same time. The marina was never full, but especially not full in the spring, before most boats were put in the water. "Your sister is overseas?"

The object of his high school affections, and the woman whose heart he broke at least twice when his brain wasn't yet fully formed, nodded again. "Yep. An opportunity came up with the Forces for her to do a tour in Lebanon, and we all agreed she should grab it. A once in a lifetime opportunity for her, a wonderful adventure."

That last part sounded practiced. He recognized the patter, and saw through the brave front. August was a long-time military reservist, serving as a clerk in the same army unit two of Seth's brothers were in.

A tour overseas would be an exciting opportunity for her. He knew that pull better than most. But it would be hard on her family, especially her kids. A tough call. The deciding factor to go would have been more than adventure.

It would have been the infusion of some much-needed cash for the marina. Through his brothers, Seth knew the Howe sisters were in a hard spot with the property. They had been ever since their dad died and it turned out his estate was nothing but debt. He'd joined the air force for similar reasons. The military bonuses when he went overseas had been something he could send back home for his brothers—and then set himself up with his plane when he got out.

But a tour was usually six months, sometimes longer.

Which explained Summer's tears.

And threw a curveball into Seth's plans for the summer. "For how long?"

"She'll be back in September." January crossed her arms over her chest.

Seth took two more steps to the counter. Close enough he could see the way her sleep shirt rode high on her thighs. "So the marina…"

She squared her shoulders, her back straightening as if readying for battle. "Oh, we're still open for business."

"Summer's in charge?" He was grasping at straws now.

The thirteen-year-old giggled.

January gave him a half-smile in apology, but it didn't touch his deep desire to cling to denial. "She'll be a big help. But it's me. I'm now the operator of this marina for the summer."

When was he going to be informed of that change in the plan? His gut roiled. "You're a teacher."

Her eyebrow curved up. Was she surprised that he knew her job? Or was she annoyed that he was questioning her decision to step in here? He wasn't doing that. He was just…

He didn't know what he was doing.

"I'm taking a sabbatical from the school. Just while Augie is gone."

He nodded dumbly.

Her expression shifted, turned vaguely…defensive. "I knew we'd be seeing each other… I just didn't realize it would be this early in the season. It's been a long time."

Not long enough for those memories to find a box to live in, though. "It sure has."

"You start in May, right? Three times a week, same as last year?" Now January's eyes had a sharp glint to them. *You better not cancel that contract*, they warned.

He wouldn't.

It would feel like walking on fire every time he stepped through that door, but he wasn't going to yank the business out from under her. "End of April is the first chartered flight, I expect. Today is just a personal trip to see my brothers for breakfast. I just need a day slip."

Summer rang him up, and he paid her for the use of a berth.

The whole time, January watched carefully, like she wasn't wearing a light cotton sleep shirt that, sure, covered the same amount of skin as a dress, but she had *slept in it*. How often this summer would he see her like this? Early morning just-woke-up touchable, but very much off-limits?

Would every conversation between them be observed by a sad teenager? Would January even want to talk to him if they were alone? Or would it be all business, thanks so much, here's your receipt?

"Will that be everything?" Her voice was cool.

He nodded resolutely and stepped back. So yes. It would be like that. All right. "I'll be back in a few hours." He stopped at the door. He needed some coffee. And a punching bag. "Sorry I made you cry, Summer."

"It's okay." She sniffled, so no, it wasn't.

He held her gaze for a moment longer, waiting until her smile firmed up, then he nodded and turned his attention to January, who had come around to the side of the counter. "I'll see you next month, then."

She nodded.

It was impossible not to look down at her bare legs, to feel a pulse of something both familiar and foreign at the same time.

She cleared her throat. "I will be more professionally dressed at that point."

He took his time dragging his gaze back up to meet hers, and felt himself shrug. That was better. A little cocky brashness never hurt as a bit of armour. "Don't do that on my accord."

When she blushed, the apples of her cheeks darkening in a pleasing way that felt good, too. Like maybe he wasn't the only one reeling at the realization this summer was about to be a dangerous walk down memory lane.

———

JANUARY SAGGED against the counter as soon as Seth left. She ignored the curious gaze of her niece and focused on the wild, rampaging feelings inside her. Oh, she needed to get a handle on those for sure. She stared out the window at the lake, grey and a little choppy today. All she could actually see was the dock system straight ahead, where Seth's plane was tied up, but she could feel the dilapidated motel to the south and the small beach to the north framing the marina.

Was that what he noticed on his way in? How old and small and rundown Pine Harbour looked?

We're trying, she wanted to tell him. *We're making the harbour better, one small bit of change at a time.*

Summer hopped off her stool. "Seth is cute."

"Excuse me?"

"For you." Summer grinned, clearly enjoying the rise she was getting out of January. "He's nice, too."

Was he nice, now? January wouldn't know. Once upon a time, he'd been deeply kind. And then he left.

Unaware of the turmoil rioting through January, Summer continued. "Mom says you dated him in high school."

When had August told her daughter about that? "That was a long time ago."

Whew, this conversation was raw. Her niece had no idea how shook January was, how unexpectedly stripped bare she felt.

She'd known she would see him. *In five weeks.* And it was embarrassing that she was still trying to convince herself she'd have been ready. There was no preparation thorough enough for the cocky smile and searing, unreadable look he gave her on the way out.

"He was flirting with you."

No, he was putting up a strong offence. "Seth was not flirting with me. He was…"

"Looking at your legs."

She squinted, trying to figure out all the layers in what had just happened. "Judging my outfit."

Summer shrugged. "I don't understand grown-ups. It doesn't have to be that complicated."

Oh, but it did.

It was really important that January be on guard now.

She'd thought she had weeks still. Had planned on sending him a professional email introducing herself as the temporary manager of the marina.

August had offered to explain the situation herself, but January had put her sister off. *I'll do it.* And then she didn't do it.

Not her finest hour. Her history with Seth had never been January operating at her best, so why would she think the present would be any different? And August didn't know the half of it.

Dating.

Ha.

No, they hadn't dated in high school. They'd secretly fucked, and fought, and loved, and cried, and shared all sorts of secrets. All while she was his math tutor and he was the scrawny but brawny guy who waited for her at the end of the day to walk her home.

Except for when they weren't speaking to each other, which happened a few times, and stretched on for weeks. She couldn't even remember what those quarrels had been about. Mutual panic about getting too close, of course she knew in hindsight. That was what it had *really* been about, every time. But what pretence had they grabbed on to? Maybe jealousy, although he'd never really looked at another girl, not the way he'd looked at her.

Stop thinking about him.

She couldn't indulge in those memories.

For the next six months, January's whole focus had to be the kids and the marina. She'd promised her sister she would hold down the fort.

It was more complicated than Summer could ever know.

"Hey," she said, dragging herself back to the present more determinedly this time. "I bet it's almost time for your mom to call."

Summer's gaze darted to the new clock on the wall. There were two of them now, side by side. Summer and her brother Levi had painstakingly painted two labels. One said Pine Harbour, and the other said Beirut.

A way for the kids to keep track of where their mom was in her day, and a constant reminder to January of her singular focus for the summer. August needed January to step up and take care of everything while she went overseas with the Canadian Forces—a lifelong dream to serve in a foreign operation, one she'd thought she would never realize. That she'd been given this opportunity now, when January could help with the kids, was a stroke of luck. The Howe sisters didn't get many of those.

According to August's itinerary, she'd be in briefings after arriving, and get access to her private quarters mid-afternoon local time. It was almost eight in the morning in Pine Harbour, which made it two in the afternoon in Lebanon.

January knew that August's tour of duty—as a financial clerk supporting a training centre—was as safe as overseas missions went. But the day before, when they'd dropped her off at the Air Force base in Trenton, the kids had been overwhelmed by the sea of green and the quiet intensity of a departing group of soldiers. They just saw the uniforms and it all become even more real on a whole new level.

The drive back had been rough.

It would be better when they could video call with her and see that she was settled in her temporary home on the other side of the world.

Another hour, maybe.

She just had to stay focused on the countdowns that mattered. One or two hours until they could see their mom again.

Four weeks until the marina officially opened for the season. Four weeks in which she could shower them with her undivided attention. Fourteen weeks until the end of the school year. The summer holiday break would be something to look forward to. *Keep them looking ahead.* Twenty-six weeks until August came home.

Her sister had given her a mission, and January wasn't going to fail.

She'd streamlined and simplified the marina operations for the summer. No weekend barbeque offerings, only coffee in the office. For food, people could order delivery, and she had all the local offerings posted on a bulletin board. Her top priority was the kids.

They were going to make it through those twenty-six weeks strong and focused and as happy as a teenager and a pre-teen could be. And a grown woman, too. January was going to get through this summer, and the challenges of Mr. Long-Buried Memories being back in her life, and come out the other side stronger than ever.

They might need a giant wall calendar to celebrate every single hard-fought week of success, but they were *all* going to be in one piece when their favourite person returned.

2

THE PARKING LOT at Mac's Diner was full when Seth and Josh arrived, but their brothers had already scored the booth in the corner, so they skirted around the people waiting.

"Morning," Owen said, passing over a menu. "Did you see January and the kids at the marina? How are they doing?"

I made Summer cry probably wasn't the thing to lead with. He grunted something about them hanging in there, then pretended to be absorbed in the options on the menu. His mind was still reeling, though, and the words swam on the page.

Of course his brothers all knew that August was gone. Why hadn't it come up in conversation?

Because Owen and Will are smart enough to know you don't like to talk about January, and Josh and Adam were too young to know what was going on back in the day.

He could name it, and still feel blindsided at the same time.

The waitress appeared with a carafe of coffee. "Know what you want, fellas?"

Everyone else did, so Seth waited until they'd all ordered, and then just said, "Same," to the last order before his.

He'd eat whatever was put in front of him.

"How's business?" Adam asked.

Seth refocused his gaze on his youngest brother. "Good, yeah. Bookings are happening already."

"It's great that you can fly out of the harbour so often. Especially this summer, with the wedding and all."

And all covered a wide swath of everything Seth was missing by not living here. Owen, the oldest, had a new baby, a little girl with his wife Kerry. Will, the second oldest, was getting married at the end of the summer. Adam was married, too, jumping the queue a bit, not that Seth would ever have gotten out of his way if he'd waited.

At least Josh, the second youngest, was in a similar life place to Seth. Single, focused on building his own business.

But Josh had moved home. He might have relationship demons in his past, but they weren't *here* in Pine Harbour.

No, Seth was the secret coward around this table. He was the only one who had spent the eight-minute drive up from the harbour and across town to the diner thinking about how much it would disrupt his business plan to somehow just *not* fly out of Pine Harbour this summer.

And he couldn't do it.

Not to himself, and not to the Howe sisters.

"Did you all have a chance to look at the wedding calendar I shared with you?"

Seth winced. "No."

Will waved his hand. "That's fine. While we're waiting for food, let's put the important dates in our phones."

"If we do it manually, maybe we'll remember them," Josh joked.

Owen grumbled something about wanting everyone to take this seriously, and Seth pulled out his phone, but he was already running on autopilot again.

He would take it seriously. Later. After he'd gotten his head around the fact his summer wasn't going to look anything like he thought it would—and the hot, uncomfortable feelings that licked up his spine because of the change in plans.

Every time he tried to drag his focus back to the conversation at hand, those feelings roiled again. And that only made him feel worse. His brothers were his whole life. He'd sacrificed a lot for them, and in turn, they had always been his safe harbour. They never pushed him too hard to come home, and when he did, they dropped everything to see him.

They accepted him as he was, shuttered and hard to connect with. How he needed to be to construct his life in a productive way.

Once they finished eating, Owen invited everyone back to his place to catch up with his wife Kerry and see their daughter Lila. Seth loved his nieces—Owen also had a grown daughter, Becca, who had a son of her own now— and usually grabbed every opportunity for baby snuggles, but today his heart wasn't in it.

Which made him feel like an absolute heel, so he went anyway, but when Josh said he didn't want to stay long, Seth grabbed the excuse with both hands. "I need to get back sooner than later," he said, not that anyone was paying that close attention. "Busy week ahead."

A stretch. He had two days of flying planned, which was his usual schedule in the winter and spring. It was enough to keep his business afloat, and summer—when he flew at least five days a week—was when he made big strides towards his goals.

That was where he needed to pin his focus. It didn't matter who he saw at the office when he checked in at Howe's Marina. What mattered was the growing customer base here on the peninsula for flights north. If he played his cards right, he could expand his business to include another plane in a year or two. Start partnering with the premium tourist locations, because they would want his business instead of the other way around.

How's business? It was great, and yet it still felt fledgling. It wasn't where he wanted it to be.

Back at the garage, he bid Josh a quick goodbye, then went straight to his plane. It wasn't his usual practice to stop at the marina office before departing, and while his footsteps slowed as he neared the door, he kept going.

He would treat January the same way he treated August.

That his thoughts about her were wildly different... well, that was his problem to work out.

An hour later, after getting the plane ready and a clear, easy flight back, he landed in Blind River and tied up his plane.

This was a familiar routine. Go through his post-flight checklist, then stroll up the dock. Nod at the Fly North Aviation sign at the shed. That sign meant so much to him. Planting it in the ground had been the best day of his life. He never got tired of seeing the red letters, the gleaming white wood. *Operated by Kincaid Air Ferry.* Four years into a ten-year plan, and he was on fucking track.

Then he got in his truck and started going through the mental catalogue of what the rest of his week looked like. He had two flights booked, supply runs to fly-in lodges, no passengers. And he needed to do a grocery run to the Sault or Sudbury at some point.

Not for the first time since he'd departed Pine Harbour, his thoughts drifted to January. His plan to survive the summer would hinge on his ability to treat one sister exactly the same as he did the other. With professional courtesy, and professional distance.

Good luck with that, he thought. Then he turned up the radio to distract himself.

When he pulled onto his street, he saw Linda and Teegan sitting on their front porch, bundled up in toques and polar fleece, drinking beer. They waved, he waved back, and then he parked in his driveaway and went into his house.

He'd done enough socializing this weekend to last quite a while.

And he wasn't up for Teegan making small talk about whatever friend of hers she'd wanted to introduce him to last night.

"You just want someone to go on flyfishing double dates."

"Would you?"

"No."

He didn't do that.

There *had* been a female helicopter pilot when he'd been stationed in Colorado who he'd actually dated for a solid year, but they'd never once gone on a double date of any kind. It had strictly been a "whose house are we sleeping at tonight?" kind of deal, two or three times a week.

And when they went in different directions, he hadn't

been broken-hearted. One of the reasons he'd been attracted to her in the first place was the promise that her career would one day take her away from him, that he wouldn't have to break up with her, that it would be mutual.

Seth had experienced enough heartbreak in high school to last him a lifetime. The deaths of his parents close together, the crushing chaos in the aftermath of that as his brother Owen—only four years older—became the official guardian to Seth and their younger two brothers, Josh and Adam. Will, in his second year of university, had been just out of the age range to need a guardian—not that it stopped Owen from bossing him around. *Your job is to stay at university, graduate with fucking distinctions, and get a teaching job back in Pine Harbour.* Will had done exactly that.

For Seth, there wouldn't be any full-ride scholarships to university. So he made the fateful decision to sign a recruiting contract with the Air Force. That decision had torn him and January apart just as she'd needed him to be her pillar of strength.

But he hadn't had any other options. The recruiter had promised everything Seth had ever dreamed of. Travel, education, and multiple career paths. All paid for by the military.

The worst part was that it had all come true. He couldn't even be mad at the guy for selling him a bill of goods, like some veterans grumbled about. The Air Force had been very good to Seth. It wasn't their fault that he'd left half his heart behind in a small town halfway up the Bruce Peninsula, with the girl who had done everything in her power to make sure he got out.

They had both sacrificed a lot for that escape. He'd

spent twenty years proving over and over again it hadn't been a mistake.

He would never limp back to Pine Harbour in failure. He had a plane, a sign by the road that represented so damn much, and a ten-year plan to prove it had all been worth it.

3

____

By the middle of the following week, all the wheels had fallen off the morning getting-ready-for-school routine.

In theory, when January woke up all she had to do was double-check that the kids had sandwiches made in the fridge, and other snack components so they could pack their own lunches. Get them up and into the shower, and then they were self-sufficient to get out the door while she worked in the office downstairs.

It was the _get them up and into the shower_ part that was easier said than done. And both of them were grouchy once they were up, which she would need to manage with patience and grace.

Except she was also not really a morning person, so now she was hiding downstairs in the office, nursing her first cup of coffee for the day as she tried to get ahead on her work because she was taking some personal time once they were off to school.

Levi came downstairs, wearing mismatched socks and no shoes. "Can I have a cup of coffee?"

Her first instinct was to say no. He was eleven, he

didn't need coffee. But she hadn't been sleeping that well —ever since the unexpected Seth visit—so she'd made this pot half decaf. The closer she got to forty, the less her body needed caffeine, but she still craved the ritual. "Knock yourself out."

He poured a mug, added two heaping spoons of sugar —*sigh*—and a big splash of cream. "Why is the coffee down here?"

Because it had always been down here. Because her parents had been cheap, and having two coffee machines when one would do was not the Howe way. "It's a long story."

He carried his mug carefully to the counter where she was sitting and leaned against it. "What are your plans for the day?"

She gave him a fond smile. He was trying on all these adult-esque conversation starters lately, and she really loved it. "I'm going to see someone about a house."

"Why?"

"Because I can't live here forever, we'd trip on each other."

Last fall, two things happened at the same time. January decided to sell her house—a little cottage that had been her starter home, that she'd poured her heart and soul into for more than a decade—and build something bigger. A new place that would be her forever home. It had coincided with yet another breakup of a casual relationship that had gone nowhere, and she'd realized that she'd been waiting to find "the right guy" before moving into a nicer place, and now forty was right around the corner, and she didn't want to wait any longer.

And August was told she might have an opportunity to go overseas.

A plan clicked into place. January sold her house, put the proceeds into a bank account she didn't look at or think about, and moved into the marina. They had family meetings with the kids, and talked about what it might be like for Aunt January to be the only grown-up for six months, and once everyone was on board, August signed on to the tour to Lebanon.

It had been a lot of fun to live with August and the kids. She hadn't been naive enough to think it would continue being nothing but fun once her sister left, of course, and she also knew that when August returned, she would want to be close to moving into her own place.

Aunt January as a house guest was a temporary fixture.

Which meant it was time to think about using that locked-away bank account for its intended purpose.

That decision was harder today, after spending the morning looking at the marina books, than it would have been a week or a month earlier.

"Levi, you didn't pack your lunch," Summer screeched from upstairs.

January winced as she glanced at the clock. "Go," she said with a sigh. "Be quick."

But Summer was already tearing down the stairs, carrying both of their backpacks.

"We're going to be late, you little brat."

"Language, Summer." January bit back an added reminder that her niece was the one who woke up late—again. And January herself had lost track of time, too. "I'll drive you to school," she said, smoothing the ruffled feathers. "I have a meeting, so I was going to put up the 'Back in Ten Minutes' sign anyway."

The sign was a running joke with their regular marina customers. It had August's cell phone number on it, and she put it up instead of hanging a closed sign. It had zero grounding in reality. The sign could mean the marina was closed for the afternoon, or that she literally was just dashing up to Main Street for a coffee and a treat from *Bake Sale!*

January was confident that the marina wouldn't have any urgent walk-in customers on an early spring Wednesday at nine in the morning.

And she had to see a woman about a house. Or the idea of a house.

"Shoes on, Levi. Let's go, let's go…" She grabbed her purse and keys, double-checked she had August's cell phone—because everyone knew that number, and her sister couldn't take it with her anyway—and hung up the "Back in Ten" sign.

At the school, she made the kids get out a block away from the turning circle and walk in, because the kiss and ride line was a teacher's worst nightmare, and then she headed back to Main Street.

Unlike the marina, the main drag was hopping today. Officially the population of Pine Harbour was only six hundred people, but new businesses like *Bake Sale!* were increasing the town's presence with other residents on the peninsula.

January parked just down from the bakery, then texted Catie Berton, Pine Harbour's only hairdresser-slash-real estate agent.

January: Grabbing breakfast and my third coffee of the day, what do you want?
Catie: I'll meet you there.

While she waited, she catalogued her rioting thoughts.

One layer to the strangeness that was her life—both Catie and Isla were in love with Kincaid brothers. Isla had married Adam, the youngest, and Catie was engaged to Will—who was also January's boss at the school.

Small town life was never not complicated.

She'd always been able to partition the Kincaids Who Lived in Pine Harbour from the One Who Did Not, but that partition seemed flimsy this morning.

There was something surreal about two of her closest friends in town being *his* sisters-in-law. She could only hope they didn't pick up on her strange mood. Neither of them had known January and Seth as a couple. Catie had been too many years behind them at school to connect the dots, and Isla was a very recent arrival in Pine Harbour.

"How's it going?" Catie materialized in front of her, her straight blonde hair swinging around her head as she bobbed to get January's attention. "Earth to the home buyer."

She took a deep breath. Right. Her mission for the morning. "Hey. Whew, yeah. That's me."

"Let's get some breakfast into you, no need to be hangry on top of the nerves." Catie held open the door of the bakery.

Inside, Catie's soon-to-be sister-in-law, Isla Petersen was on the phone, so her part-time staff person Bailey Patel was behind the counter. The younger woman was a Pine Harbour native like January. In fact, in her first year of teaching, January had Bailey as a student. Now they were friends, and co-conspirators of sorts with Catie and Isla, intent on modernizing the Pine Harbour business community.

"What can I get you this morning?"

January scanned the chalkboard. "I'll have a cinnamon iced coffee."

"Ooh, that sounds good. Two of those," Catie said. "And those butter tarts…"

January smiled as Catie oohed and ahhed over today's offerings. Other than Isla's special twenty-five cent chocolate chip cookies, the offerings at *Bake Sale!* changed every week.

Isla's phone call ended, and she greeted them, then helped two more customers that arrived while Bailey was making their drinks.

It was a perfectly ordinary morning, except for the fact she was maybe going to sign a contract to build a house in an hour or two. And she was worried about the marina maybe not having enough cash flow to survive the summer. Plus there was the countdown-to-the-return-of-Seth chaos.

The other three women were talking about the ongoing politics of parking management. Catie and Isla were firmly in the camp of not charging downtown visitors for street parking, and had managed to convince the powers-that-be that an annual fundraising event would be a more effective way of covering the costs of maintaining parking spots than charging customers at the meter.

That didn't stop it being an ongoing item at town meetings, though.

Bailey rolled her eyes when Isla told them it was going to be on the next agenda—again. "We can bring flasks to this meeting, right? We'll turn 'parking lot issues' into a drinking game."

"Lemons to lemonade." Catie tapped her chin. "Do you think we could cover the parking budget by setting up a cash bar at the town meeting?"

"Half of the budget goes to enforcing the parking fees, anyway," January muttered. She had less patience for the debate than her friends did.

Or maybe that was just the disrupted sleep talking.

"Preaching to the converted," Isla said. "But sometimes you just have to laugh."

"So you don't cry," Catie added.

Bailey slid their iced coffees across the bar. "Let me distract you with something delicious."

"Cheers to that." January lifted her cup and took a long, glorious sip.

"Oh!" Catie snapped her fingers. "Before January and I leave, Will wanted me to double-check that you all got the wedding calendar invite? Did you accept it and did it synch properly to your phones?"

January and Isla shared an amused look. "Yes," said the baker, schooling her features. "It was very detailed."

Catie looked very proud of that. Nothing like two Type A personalities getting married to make everyone else feel like a disorganized hot mess. January was very familiar with Will's aggressively organized ways, though, and she'd learned to triage his instructions into what he needed her to do, what he'd like on top of that, and what was really just his own to-do list being shared in a communal way, so everyone was on the same page.

"Come on," January said, nodding to the door. "Let's go stare at some dirt."

———

"Now is the time to sign," Catie said as January squinted at the empty lot.

She knew it was the right call. She'd wanted this for

almost a year. But it was just so much money. A mortgage for the rest of her working life. She blew a raspberry. "Don't pressure me!"

Catie laughed. "You wanted me to say that. Specifically, if I can quote your text message, because you needed a bit of pressure."

January took a long sip of her iced coffee. "Right. Good point. Thanks for putting up with my indecision."

"Do you want to talk it out?"

No, because she hadn't talked about the marina's cash flow problems with August yet. Her sister might have a different perspective on it that January wasn't considering.

But from where she stood right now, it seemed as if it was going to be hard not to dip into her house savings over the summer.

On the other hand, locking that money up into a contract on a new build would remove that temptation to invest in the marina when she'd made a commitment to herself a long time ago to never, ever do that. And if she waited much longer, the price of building could go up and she could get priced out of the market.

She blew another raspberry, this time at the universe for rushing her into a decision, and turned in a slow circle. She really did love this neighbourhood. Will lived just down the street. Although not for long. "Will has decided to move into your place?"

Catie nodded. "It has too much sentimental value for me. Do you want to buy his place? It's an informal Kincaid Inn right now, but he doesn't want to hang on to it forever."

January shook her head. She wanted something that was wholly her own. And if she poked hard enough at this fresh wave of nerves, it was triggered just as much by

Seth's return to her life as it was the precariousness of the marina.

Maybe eighty percent Seth, twenty percent money pit business. By the fall, when the house would be built, she'd be back to the security of her teaching job. And at that point, moving in to the new house would feel amazing.

Ignore the what if *pangs the bad boy pilot brings up.* It was easier said than done, but an important reminder that the grass was not greener on the other side of the lake.

She'd done this dance before. The first time she'd wondered if this was what she was meant to do with her life had been after teacher's college, when she returned and found the town so quiet, so staid, that she wasn't sure how she'd survive.

But then she made friends. Got a boyfriend, and some hobbies, and started to re-discover the peninsula as an adult. There had been a lot to like—love—so when an old house by the lake came up for sale and she could actually afford it, she made an offer.

And then the doubt reared its head for a second time.

It wasn't a coincidence that at the same time, Seth had just returned to Canada from Afghanistan the first time. The comparisonitis when she looked at her own life was yikes. She'd only gone to university in Toronto for four years, and then came back. He'd literally flown around the world, saving lives. While she bought a house in desperate need of love, and thought about getting a dog?

She'd decided against the dog.

But she'd bet on the house, and it had been good for her. And then she met a guy who had a dog. Had even planned on marrying him, until she realized she was more attached to the dog than the man.

Another eight years passed before the doubt returned.

Now there was another real estate deal in front of her, and those same quivering fears were back. Seth's business was booming. Why couldn't they do the same thing with the marina? Was this town the problem?

I love this town.

She really did. Fiercely. It wasn't the town. It was the marina, it was the ghost of her father, and the legacy of all of his bad decisions.

And why did she even care? The marina was not—would not—be her whole life.

She didn't want that.

But August did, for her own complicated reasons, so January would keep it afloat until her sister got back. Six years ago, her sister had sacrificed a lot to take it on, and now it was January's turn. Even though she was the older of the two by almost three years, it had been August who always held their family together. After their mother died when they were in high school, after the more recent loss of their father, and even when August's ex-husband abruptly left for the west coast, not long after she took over the marina.

Romantic love was not the Howe family's strongest suit. August, with the broken marriage and deadbeat dad custody issues. January had that mistake of a failed engagement under her belt. Plus Seth, if she counted her high school experience, which she didn't. They'd never loved each other, not like grown-ups do.

And their parents, too, had been a hot mess of hot and cold feelings. It was no wonder the Howe sisters fell for emotionally unavailable men. The irresistible pull of wanting something that could never be was all that had ever been modelled for them.

What did it say about them that they clung to their

father's legacy, the marina, even after he was gone? After they discovered the maxed-out mortgage?

August could have found full-time work with the army. January had a career as a teacher. And yet here she was, taking a leave of absence from that job to keep the marina open all summer, to cling to memories she wasn't even sure were real.

"Okay, I'm ready—" She stopped as her phone rang. A quick glance at the screen told her it was the school calling. "Sorry, one second. Hello?"

"Hi January. Is this a good time to talk?"

She winced. Levi's teacher.

Catie waved her off, pulling out her own phone.

January took a deep breath. "Sure. Yes. What's going on?"

"It's about Levi."

January had made this phone call herself hundreds of times over the years. She sighed and closed her eyes. "Homework?"

"He's behind on a few assignments."

"Yeah. I'm sorry that slipped through the gaps. I'll follow up with him tonight."

"Thanks. I'll send you an email, too, but I just wanted to touch base over the phone first."

"I appreciate that. How's he doing in class, otherwise?"

"He misses his mom, that's pretty clear. He's been…quiet."

Damn it. "Okay."

"He's a smart kid. And I do understand that it's been a rocky month."

"Yeah, no, I get it. Thanks for the call." She hung up and nodded to Catie, but the nerves were back.

Maybe she shouldn't focus on the house until August

was back. Once the builder started, there would be a lot of decisions that would pull her attention away from the kids.

And then there's Seth.

Yeah, that was one too many things to worry about at once. She wasn't going to see him again for a month. Maybe by then her life would be a little more organized.

Or at the very least, she'd have figured out how to get the kids out the door on time.

"I need to talk to my sister," she finally said out loud. An unexpected calm, a perfect kind of *rightness* followed. Yes, of course she did. August was her person, through thick and thin.

They had each other's backs, and the marina wasn't their father's any longer.

It was August's now.

Maybe it was time for January to re-evaluate what mattered most.

4

"No, absolutely not." August leaned into the webcam on her computer. "You should build the house, Janie. If the marina needs money infused over the summer, it will come out of my army pay."

"But that's the nest egg for the kids college fund."

"Maybe I'll be ready to sell the marina when it comes time for them to go to college," her sister said.

January ignored a pulse of panic. Maybe August *should* sell the marina when the kids were old enough. "Would you want to?"

"I don't know. But I *do* know that you sold your house for one reason and one reason only—to build your dream home. That money doesn't come near the marina."

She rubbed her forehead and glanced to the other half of her computer screen, where the master spreadsheet was open. "Okay, but I see us barely breaking even. How did you afford to pull this manager salary every month?"

Her sister didn't reply.

January snapped her attention back to the video call. "Augie?"

"I don't need it every month."

"Augie!"

"What?"

"Why would you want the business to pay me more than it has realistically paid you?"

"Because you're doing this as a massive favour to me, and I do it as a labour of love."

She wanted to argue that point, but it wasn't untrue. Damn it. "Well, my first act as manager is giving myself a temporary pay cut. I'd feel better if we kept some of that money in the accounts in case of emergency."

"But we have insurance and my pay—"

"Should be as much yours as my house money is mine."

August laughed. "We're both kind of stubborn, aren't we?"

"Mmm." January glanced at the door to the stairway upstairs. It was ajar. "Hang on." She closed the door, then took her seat again. "Listen, I wanted to talk to you about something else."

"Is everything okay?"

"Yeah. No. Yes. It's not about the marina." Not really.

"What's going on?"

"Something happened last week, and I didn't tell you about it at the time because you had just landed and I didn't know how I felt about it, but I've decided I don't want to tell Catie or Isla—for reasons—so…"

"What *is* it?" August leaned closer to the screen. "You're all flustered. That's not like you."

"Mmm." January made a face. "So, Seth flew into town unexpectedly."

"Personal trip?"

"Yeah." The casual way August reacted? That's how

January should have, too. Twenty years later, Seth should be nothing to her.

But secrets had a way of hooking in deep and not letting go.

Because from the outside, he was just a guy she dated for a while in high school. Casually. No big declarations of love. More than a few declarations of *this is not love*, which had stung at the time, but had also been true.

She'd leaned into those boundaries when things got tough. Had found a kind of strength in knowing he was just a fellow horny teen, not a great love she could lose. And even when things got more serious than either expected, and they had to make hard decisions framed by heartbreak and tears, he'd been a good friend to her.

All good things end, though. And in the winter before graduation, when she got a fat envelope accepting her into the University of Toronto, Seth walked into a recruiting office and sealed their fate as heading in separate directions.

"He was surprised to see me because I hadn't emailed him yet about the..." She stuck her tongue out at her sister. "Temporary change in management. And it was harder than I expected. But I should have known it would be weird. Maybe that's why I didn't email him? I don't know. Anyway..." She took a deep breath. "I wasn't honest with you when I said it was going to be fine. It *is going to be fine*. But it may be rocky, and I'm worried he may try to shorten the contract on us or something like that."

August frowned. "Why? You guys are ancient history. You haven't mentioned his name once in more than a decade. And wasn't he the one who broke up with you?"

Shot straight to the heart. "It was complicated."

"Well, I will email him and make it clear we expect him to—"

"I was pregnant." The words fired out of her like gun shots. Three sharp snaps. The last word blurring into one fast syllable. *Pregnt.*

But August heard it no problem. Her eyes went wide, then soft. "In high school?"

"Yeah." January blinked away a tear that wouldn't fall. She didn't cry over it. It wasn't that kind of a feeling. It wasn't *sadness* she felt, just a strange hollowness. Like the crater in the aftermath of a meteor strike. "We didn't tell anyone."

"Oh, sweetie."

"It was a long time ago. But when we broke up—and yeah, he let everyone think it was him, but we both knew we were going in different directions, had even before I found out I was pregnant—it was just too much. I wanted to stay together until the end of the summer, and he needed to leave right after graduation, and it just… Seeing him in person was hard. For both of us. He was pretty clearly rocked that I didn't tell him in advance that I would be there. Not that I knew he was coming. Oh and I was in my pyjamas when he showed up, looking like an absolute hot mess."

"Did he look extra fine?"

"Of course he did."

"What a jerk." August smiled fondly. "Are you okay?"

No recriminations. No *why didn't you tell me sooner*. Just pure love, which had always been their way. January took a deep breath. "Yeah. I am. I will be."

"Can I ask a question?"

"About Seth?"

"Yes."

Another direct hit. But it was better to get all of these feelings out now, with Augie, rather than in dribs and drabs over the summer—or worse, in front of Seth. "Sure."

"Is he the one who got away?"

"No. He's…more like the one who left town on mutually agreed upon and deeply bittersweet terms."

"And now he's back."

Oh. No. January saw where her sister was going, and that had to be cut off immediately. "For the summer. He'll leave again. He always does."

"He left once, a long time ago. That's not *always*. Maybe things will be different this time."

January shook her head. "You don't come back from something like that."

"Why not? What happened?"

Nothing. And everything. "Remember that weekend I got in shit for going away with him and not telling Dad where we went?"

"Yeah."

"That was the weekend I had my abortion. We skipped school on the Friday. Seth borrowed someone's truck and took me to Hamilton. I had the procedure, and then we stayed in a hotel for two nights. He held me in the shower. It was…brutal. And good, too. I mean, he was very sweet the whole time. So much better to have him as a support than to go through it alone."

"You let Dad think that you were partying."

"I wasn't going to tell him the truth."

August scrubbed her hand over her mouth. "No, I guess you wouldn't. I'm sorry. I wish I'd known."

Her sister was fifteen at the time. No way was January dumping that kind of real-life heaviness on her little sister, so soon after their mother died.

"It was our secret. And we dealt with it the best we could, and then we went our separate ways."

"Until now."

She nodded.

"How did you manage to not see him at all last summer?"

January winced. Not her finest moment. "I added his flights to my calendar as summer school."

"You didn't teach summer school last year?" August looked both impressed and aggrieved. "You lying little witch."

"I didn't want to see him if I had a choice about it! He's dodged me all these years, I thought it was for the best if I continued the tradition."

"And then I had to go and take this job."

"It's fine."

"I'm not sure it is." Her sister rocked back, then exhaled loudly. "Wow. So how was it, really, seeing him after all this time?"

"It was a lot."

She gently nodded. "It was probably heavy for him, too."

That sucker punch in the feels landed differently. Because now that she had said it out loud, this secret that only one other person in the whole world carried for her, it didn't carry as much weight as it did in her head all those years.

Which meant she should probably say something to Seth, too. Maybe not immediately—she'd follow his lead a bit—but if there was an opening to tell him that she'd told August and it felt good, she would take it.

"But even so, he's not going to cancel the contract."

August shook her head. "No way. He's a good guy, he wouldn't."

Her sister was being perfectly reasonable.

Except when it came to matters of the heart, reason didn't always win out. "If he does, we'll make up for it somehow. If you're paying me top dollar to be the marina manager, I should probably make myself useful and find a new revenue source."

August snorted. "I'm paying you medium dollar at best. Pace yourself. It's going to be a long summer."

———

FOUR WEEKS LATER, January's alarm went off at six-fifteen in the morning. She dragged herself out of bed and into the shower. Today was Seth Day.

That wasn't how she'd marked it down in the calendar, of course. It was recorded as *Kincaid Air Ferry Charter Service Begins.* But for more than a month, while she'd been playing Full Time Amazing Aunt out loud, figuring out a bedtime routine that didn't take hours and the vagaries of the pre-teen palate, she'd also secretly been counting down the days until she saw him again.

Old habits die hard.

Seth Kincaid. Her first kiss, her first fuck, her first phone call when her mother had a stroke, her first break-up, her first—

The list was long.

She knocked on Summer's door first, then Levi's. "Time to get up," she called out.

No answer. She had ten minutes before she needed to open the office for Seth's clients.

She'd packed their lunches almost every day over the last month, but she really didn't have time this morning.

She tried Summer's door handle, but it was locked. She knocked again, hollered both of their names, then gave up —for now—and went downstairs. The first rule of being an aunt with temporary custody was pick your battles.

The second rule was, keep texting the little monsters a running countdown to when they had to get out the door.

Downstairs, she made coffee and texted a picture of the machine to both kids.

January: Come and get it.

After she told August that Levi had asked for coffee, and confessed that she thought it might be a helpful lure to pull him through the morning routine, her sister had emailed the paediatrician and copied January. A half hour later, they got an amused reply back that a half cup was fine, as long as Levi didn't exhibit any signs of anxiety after drinking it.

January had doubled-down on "a doctor said it's fine," and their mornings got significantly better when at least one of the two kids had something special to look forward to.

Not that either of them replied this morning.

She set a timer on her phone for five minutes. Maybe if she took a picture of Seth after he arrived and texted it to Summer, the teen would come running down.

You just want an excuse to take a picture of your ex when he shows up.

No. Did she? Maybe. Probably not.

Possibly.

If she did, it was harmless. So much water under that

bridge, a boat full of nope could float with ease. There was zero chance of Seth being anything other than a handsome man she held at arm's length for very good reason, so she could admire the way he'd matured into his looks.

She'd known that he had, of course. Photos had crossed her timelines, and his brothers had all turned into good-looking men.

But after she'd gotten over the shock of their first in-person meeting after all this time, she'd slowly realized that their meeting that morning had seared a new image of him into her mind. She kept replaying the way he looked as he'd paused at the door, glancing back at her. Long legs, still denim-clad and shoved into Doc Martens. Tight hips, only slightly less narrow than in high school. But from the waist up, he was quite different now. Thicker. Stronger. Like he'd been to war and borne some scars, toughened up around them and turned a bit burly.

The close-cropped beard was new, too.

It all looked good on him.

And she'd been standing there in her *every day is wine day* pyjamas. She could still feel the visceral wave of shock and embarrassment as he'd glanced down at her legs and back up again.

Not today.

Today she was dressed like a grown-up. Black trousers, a silky tank top, and a blue cardigan on top. One of her favourite teaching outfits. Professional and pretty.

She unlocked the office door, texted the kids a GIF from a horror movie, and settled in behind the desk.

5

SETH CIRCLED the harbour twice before landing his plane. He took his time strolling up the dock, too. Almost like he needed to prove to himself that he was in no rush to see January again. But their last meeting had lingered in his thoughts.

He wanted to see her again. Was looking forward to it.

No rush.

Nothing to look forward to. *Chill, Kincaid.* Oh, he was chill. He was ice.

Pausing for a moment—one last demonstration to himself that all of this was a choice, and he was fully in control of his feelings—he put on a casually devastating smile and opened the door.

January was behind the counter, a mug of coffee in one hand, the other propped on her hip. He took in a few things at once.

She'd dressed up. Or...gotten dressed. Like a professional.

Nice top.

Nice hair.

Nice glittering smile, just as insincerely casual as his own.

Nice tits in that top, too. That helped him focus on what he was here to do. "Morning."

"Welcome back." To the town, to the business, to her life, but only in this incidental way. "None of your passengers have arrived yet, but we're prepared for them. Coffee's on, if you'd like a cup?"

He glanced over to the machine. Next to it was a neat tray of white mugs just like the one she was holding. "Sure. Thanks."

He'd planned to check in, then go across to the garage and wake up Josh. Instead, he found himself filling a mug and adding a splash of cream.

When he turned back to the counter, January was deeply absorbed in something on the computer.

He took another good, long look at her. Even after twenty years, she was still familiar to him. The way her thick hair grew in all different directions, so even when tamed into a ponytail, she had fine baby strands going this way and that at her brow and temple and around her ears. She wore more earrings now than she did back then. Had two cartilage piercings up top, too.

His private little rebel.

She'd always been a good girl, eager to work hard and get ahead…but also wanted to sneak out at night and mess around with the bad boy. He'd been more than happy to oblige.

His grip tightened on his mug as his brain went to wondering who filled that role for her now. *None of your business.* He'd burned that bridge when he joined the Air Force.

Without looking up from her computer, she broke the silence. "Two flights this week? And three next week?"

"That's right."

"It'll be good to see the parking lot full so early in the year." She flicked her gaze up to look at him, but only for a moment. "Thank you for the business."

"It's good for both of us. I get to see my family more often."

She nodded. That had been something they'd bonded over. Where other teens seemed disinterested in their families, Seth and January had both clung to their siblings. And each other, at least for a little while.

Losing his parents had pushed him to grow up fast. Those last two years of high school had been non-stop grown-up decisions for him.

For both of them.

"Good coffee."

"Thanks."

It was like they were strangers. After all that they'd once gone through, now they shared silence with a ticking clock.

Seth glanced up.

Two clicking clocks, slightly out of synch. His heart softened at the labeled plaques beneath the timepieces. "How's August doing?"

"Good. She has a pool, so…" January shrugged. "What did Will say on her Facebook post the other day? *Tour experiences may vary?* She misses the kids, but she's having the time of her life."

The reminder that Seth's brothers were all connected to January on social media stung a little. For no good reason. But the Will impression was bang on.

Of course it would be. She worked with his brother, too.

How did you avoid this woman for twenty years?

Very, very carefully.

"He's just salty because the infantry always gets the dusty, dangerous tours of duty. Your sister's smart. Clerks have it almost as good as the Air Force."

That got her attention. Her gaze finally connected with his, bright curiosity hitting him like a laser beam perfectly calibrated to sear beneath his skin.

Why did he want her attention, again?

He raised his mug and took a long slug of the hot coffee.

"You had a pool?"

He shrugged. "I spent two years in Colorado."

"That's pretty cushy."

"It was a highlight."

"And now you're in Blind River?" She framed it like a question, but he was pretty sure she knew the answer was yes.

Interesting. She'd kept some tabs on him, then.

"No pool."

She smiled. "A freezing cold lake is almost as good."

"There's those two weeks in August when it's almost swimmable."

"A lot has happened in twenty years, huh?" So she was naming the elephant in the room.

He nodded. "Yep."

"It's been nice to see your plane in the last few years. When you fly in."

And then out again, almost as quickly. His getaway vehicle of choice.

Her expression shifted, softened, then firmed into a

mask of some sort. Her voice changed, too. "It's good to see you now."

Was it, though? If she needed to carefully guard how she said that?

Behind him, the door opened, and his first passenger for the day strolled in. Seth moved to the side and watched as January took his license plate details and charged him for parking, then went through the spiel about valuables and what time Seth would be loading them onto the plane.

"And that's your pilot," she gestured.

Seth waved. "Hey."

"Morning." The passenger went outside, and they were alone again.

"Oh, I wanted to mention—our fuel provider can get aviation fuel." She said it quickly, the words coming out in a practiced rush. Then a pause, and further explanation added more slowly. "August mentioned that it came up in a discussion with you, but she didn't have a chance to organize it before she left."

"Great." He scrubbed his hand over his jaw. He didn't want to ask them to take on risk on his behalf. "Only if it's not expensive for you to add that as a service."

She shook her head. "Other pilots might appreciate it, too. If we can get known as a place to stop and fuel up, that would be great."

"We can be picky about—" He cut himself off as another passenger arrived. Two down, two to go. He finished his coffee, then set the mug on the tray marked for dirty cups.

He wanted to finish the conversation about the fuel, but he had to get his pre-departure flight check done, too.

She turned back to him as soon as she finished with that customer. "You were saying about the fuel?"

"We can be picky. Marinas aren't ideal—no reflection on you, but boat fuel isn't great for planes and we like to serve ourselves if possible."

"Okay, that's good to know."

"I use an app to track where avfuel is available."

"What's that called?" She scribbled it down on a notepad when he told her, and then the third and fourth passengers arrived.

Time for him to leave.

January waved a quick goodbye as he headed outside. It itched him, that the conversation had been rushed. There'd been that long run of silence when he'd first arrived, and then suddenly they were talking, and *then* there wasn't time to finish it.

Maybe he would email her about the fuel. Business account to business account.

He greeted his passengers again dockside, then did his full walk around—a crawl around at times, as he carefully dodged under the wings and along the floats—which was always a good, entertaining way to start a flight. "All right folks, let's do a quick safety orientation, then we'll get under way. The weather today looks great, should be a fun trip north."

He ran through a quick orientation to the plane, reminding them how to get in and which parts they could touch and which parts were off-limits as "no-push, no-pull, and no-step" zones. Then it was the emergency routines, the locations of their personal flotation devices should they need it, and how to exit the plane in an emergency. "And finally, once I push off from the dock, we're going to start moving, there's none of this taxiing to a runway and then waiting business, got it? I get in and we're off."

Most of the time, his customers were big fans of flying, and these folks were no different. They were friendly and had questions about the plane, questions about his Air Force service, and once they were in the air, questions about the flight time.

Every single one was so common, he had a standard patter. His priority when flying was vigilance for the craft first, customer care second, but it was an important second-spot consideration for him.

It hadn't been when he started. For the first year that he operated as Kincaid Air, he mostly worked on referrals from a couple of pilot friends who were too busy, or who wanted to take some time off. And he got repeat customers from lodges wanting supply runs, but he didn't retain as many charter clients as he wanted to. Building his own customer database and establishing a brand had seemed like administrative drudgery compared to getting in his plane and pointing it in the direction of a hard-to-get-to lake.

But as he entered his second year of business, and his savings from his time in the military started to dwindle, he got more serious. He renamed the business, leased part of a dock, and got a real website.

That year, he grew both his referral and repeat flights as well as his "I found you on Google" customer base.

The following year, thirty percent of his business came from repeat customers, and Seth officially had a business plan.

Now he was four years in to a ten-year plan, and the expansion to Pine Harbour felt good. He had to be vigilant that he didn't let nostalgia consume him, though. His ten-year plan didn't include moving home full time. In the winter, flights out of Pine Harbour wouldn't be possible.

And he couldn't risk losing the business growth he'd forged already.

But after a month of worrying over what it would be like to see January three mornings a week, today hadn't been half bad.

He thought of the silky blouse under her tight little cardigan.

Not half bad at all.

———

TWO DAYS LATER, January watched Seth's plane make a graceful circle of the harbour as he prepared to land. Then she headed downstairs to let him in, but she wasn't alone. Levi had woken up early for once, eager to see the plane land. So when Seth stepped into the office, after that awkward moment where their eyes met and she forced herself not to look away, he poured himself a coffee and let Levi pepper him with questions.

January logged into the computer and dove into work. She tried her best not to sneak too many sideways glances. It might still be hard to hold his gaze, but it was far too easy to stare at him when he wasn't looking.

He had faint lines on his face now, around his mouth and at the corners of his eyes, that made her wonder whether he'd spent the last twenty years laughing or frowning—or both.

Her Seth had been relentlessly uncaring about almost everything. Too cool to be affected, too chill to bother.

She'd loved that about him, had craved his balancing energy to her overachiever tendencies. Had spent the next two decades bouncing back and forth between wanting to replace him as her gold-standard for a romantic partner—

never able to do that, not even close, even with their heart-breaking history—and being determined to go in the opposite direction and find someone more like herself. And that ping pong-ing approach to dating hadn't done her any favours, which is why she was staring at another email from Catie, quietly encouraging her to sign the house building contract before someone else did.

"Maybe your aunt could look it up for us."

She jerked her head to the side at the rough intrusion of Seth's voice. Both he and Levi were looking at her. Levi in his usual, nosy eleven-year-old way, Seth with a carefully guarded perusal.

"What's that?"

"Is a meerkat the same as a mongoose?" Levi beamed up at Seth. "We're playing twenty questions and he maybe got it in five guesses—or six—depending on the answer."

"That's pretty fast." She clicked on a browser window and searched up the answer. "Meerkats are a part of the mongoose family. So it's one specific kind of mongoose."

"Six answers, then." Seth shook his head and smiled at them both, but his attention lingered on January's face. "Still respectable."

"Very," she murmured.

He dropped that assessing gaze to her mouth. She reached for her mug, suddenly eager for something to put between them, but it was empty.

She shoved off her stool and moved around them to get more coffee. Out the window she spotted Seth's last customer arriving. "That's your final guy," she chirped.

"My cue to leave, then." He said something under his breath to Levi, who giggled. All of the Kincaid brothers were great with kids, so of course Seth was, too.

She ignored the dull ache that bloomed in her chest.

That ache had no business in her body. *That* was pure foolishness. Instead she briskly tossed two sugar cubes into her mug and poured hot coffee over them, watching them carefully as they started to dissolve, and then were submerged.

Cream next, just a splash.

And then a spoon to stir it all together, but she only got as far as sliding it into the mug when his footsteps paused behind her—just for a second, a hitch in his step more than a full pause—and that dull ache pulsed like a fever spasm. Then he brushed past. Not close enough to touch, but she felt the size of him moving the air, and then he was at the door.

This time he didn't stop and look back.

And once he was outside, striding toward the dock, the quiet countdown clock in her mind reset. Another forty-eight hours until his third and final charter for the week.

She lifted her mug to her mouth and took a long, slow sip as she watched him do his welcome spiel for his customers. He looked relaxed, happy, and confident. It was hard to picture *her* Seth owning an airplane. Operating a business. Being responsible.

But that's why he'd joined the Air Force. Because growing up fast in Pine Harbour was a dead-end street for a kid like Seth.

She frowned. The man he'd turned into definitely hadn't made the mistakes that kid had feared. He'd done just fine for himself. A plane like that? She dragged in a rough breath, then finished the last big slug of coffee.

She could still feel that micro-pause, when he'd been right behind her and she'd *felt his presence,* and there had been that dull ache, which she'd drowned in coffee.

Semi-successfully, so that meant she needed another one now. Extra-large. Full-caff.

"You got a wife?"

"No, sir." Seth checked the wind gauge once more. No luck on that front. It was an unseasonably still day. The glassy surface on the lake below him was hard to land on, and tough to take off from, too. He'd have to make his own waves.

"Lucky son of a gun. Mine won't stop giving me grief about these trips."

That sounded like a problem that would be solved with a bit of basic communication—both ways—but what did Seth know about marriage? Vague recollections of his parents' relationship, and very recent observations of his brothers falling in love.

Honeymoon phases weren't reliable sources of data, but he was pretty sure Owen, Will, and Adam would never complain to a stranger about their wives' opinions of their hobbies. And he was doubly sure that those opinions wouldn't be grief-laden.

It reminded him of a meme he'd seen on the internet a few times. *Are the straights okay?* Meaning, the people who seem hell bent on defending marriage as *their* God-given unique special status didn't always seem to…like being married?

The old ball and chain.

Seth couldn't imagine sharing his life with a whole other person at the best of times, but why the hell would you want to do that with someone you didn't like?

He supposed that was part of what kept him in brisk

business. It was rare for him to take couples or families anywhere. His clientele was heavily skewed toward one demographic—the type of guy who wanted to know everything about Seth's military service and live vicariously through his life as a bush pilot now.

Seth never spoiled their fun. Yeah, his life was pretty good. Exactly what he'd always wanted, in fact. But he didn't have anyone at home wanting to spend more time with him. Nobody except his computer, which he was overdue for a date with, because he still hadn't done April's month end accounting.

And that's what he should be thinking about as he landed the plane. Accounting, the business, and keeping his customers happy.

Speaking of which… "Folks, I'm just finishing my visual check of the lake, and we're good to land. This will be our final approach to the lodge. Looks like a nice day up here for you all."

He reduced his speed, checked his instruments, and sank into the routine. Patience was everything in a landing. Every part of flying was deeply satisfying for Seth, but setting down perfectly on the lake? Nothing better.

"Have a great week, yep, thank you. Watch your step there. Perfect. Got everything? Great." And then they were off, strolling toward the lodge with their gear, and he was all by himself. He took his time doing the check of the plane. Next week he'd have pickups to fly back, but today he was on his own. Just him and the sky, exactly as he liked it.

But instead of the usual peace he found in the air, he found himself rehashing the morning. The pulse of nerves as he landed in Pine Harbour. The self-talk that he didn't care. The tug deep in his chest as he stepped inside and saw January.

She'd picked another pretty outfit again. A dark red v-neck top with sleeves that ended at her elbows, and she'd decorated her wrists with silver bangles on both arms. How many more encounters before he stopped being surprised that she wasn't wearing jeans and a hoodie, her reliable everyday high school outfit?

His thoughts tumbled back twenty years. The earnest way she'd glared at him for not doing his homework. The way she'd take his hand and drag him up to her room, promising it was easy, it wouldn't take that long, if he'd just sit down with the textbook and do the work.

He'd gone along with it because he'd liked the feel of her fingers holding tight to his. Because her hair always smelled good and her neck looked soft and kissable.

And the first time he'd gotten his hands under her sweatshirt and discovered that January Howe had gotten busty over the winter? He'd practically exploded in his pants.

Even in high school, her tits had been incredible. Soft, full, and a little heavy.

Never had she displayed them the way she did now. The single men of Pine Harbour were fucking lucky.

If she liked being looked at.

Stop thinking about her tits. He checked his altimeter, then did a visual scan around him. No other aircraft in the sky. No clouds, either.

It would be an easy flight home if he kept his mind where it mattered. He had April's month end to finish, and a customer newsletter to send out. Fuel prices to check, then a bit of market research. Who had raised their prices over last year? Was anyone offering a multi-trip discount?

It was popular with some of the bigger companies, but Seth preferred to offer the fairest price he could to every customer.

On the other hand, it could be good to reward loyalty.

This was his least favourite part of owning his own business. Marketing always felt like a gut call between two or more equally valid options. He could weed out the bad ideas, but the good ones? There were many. Which path would take his business where he wanted it to go?

There was no handbook for that.

It was one of the rare times he missed the military. The regimented order of everything.

Seth had flourished in basic training. Had done so well that it didn't matter that he wasn't actually cut out for the more academic courses at the Royal Military College. Once he admitted he'd graduated high in his class with the help of January, the school arranged for tutors for him. And not wanting to let her down, not that she would ever know, he applied himself exactly as he did for her. As if she were still taking him by the hand and dragging him to her room. Although he never made out with any of his RMC tutors.

His thoughts leapt back to the passenger asking if Seth had a wife. No. And he never would.

If Seth were ever going to fall in love, it would have happened already. It would have been January, back in high school. And he hadn't loved her then, because he'd been able to walk away from her even when he knew it broke her heart.

6

SETH SETTLED into a decent routine over the following week as his summer schedule kicked into high gear. Now he was ferrying customers back at the end of the trips as well, so he had passengers in both directions. And his weekly charter out of Blind River started, too. He was in the air five days a week, and loving it.

He wasn't loving his brief interactions with January, though. But either he couldn't find the right way to start a conversation when they were alone or someone—or something—else would interrupt them when they finally got into it. Their conversations rarely passed the polite, surface level stuff.

And every time he saw her, he felt on edge.

One afternoon, he was just about to take off from a hunting lodge on a fly-in lake up north when he decided to check his email one last time. Why not take advantage of the lodge's satellite internet service? The cell service map was spotty at best almost all the way back to Blind River.

And as soon as he clicked into his inbox, he saw

January's name. An email from her would have pinged his attention no matter what, but the urgent subject line ratcheted up his alarm.

From: January Howe
To: Seth Kincaid
Subject: SERVICE INTERRUPTION ALERT

Seth, a storm blew in this morning after you left and we had some damage to the outer floating dock. It is no longer secure. We aren't the only ones affected, though, and the marine repair company can't come out until Friday. At this time, I'm not sure we can safely host...

He kept reading, his brow furrowed. This kind of thing happened on the lake, and it wasn't the end of the world. But it sounded like she was getting shoved to the bottom of the repair list, which was bullshit.

The first solution his brain went to—charging to the rescue—was probably not the best option, so he kept thinking. An alternate plan was finding a different pickup location for Friday. But the marina's parking lot was ideally located, safe, and affordable for his customers.

He could also just move the passenger loading to the beach in the harbour. It was a bit rustic, but he could sell it. He'd learned that, with a flex of his chest muscles and the right kind of smile, most people forgave him almost anything, including less than ideal boarding conditions.

Yeah, that was what he'd do.

His thumb hovered over the reply button. He'd email her and tell her it was fine, and good luck. He'd be there on Friday, and would work around the damage.

But he didn't actually tap that out.

His brow furrowed tighter, that first instinctive response getting louder at the back of his mind.

He didn't want to insert himself into a solution, but now that he knew about it, he couldn't very well just let it go.

The internet connection wasn't strong enough at the lake edge to make a phone call, so he sent two text messages to his brothers instead, then checked the forecast. The storm was long gone now, and he could make it back to Pine Harbour before dark. Whether he liked it or not, polite distance was no longer an option. Not if January's dock was going to get repaired in an expeditious manner.

The urgent tug inside him to fly to Pine Harbour was strictly professional, he told himself as he readied the plane for lift-off.

It might come at a personal risk—not something his brain wanted to look at closely *at all*—but his business and hers both required that dock to be safely repaired. Whether she liked it or not, Seth was going to be a part of the solution.

January was on a video call with August on her computer—and on hold with the insurance company on her phone—when Will walked into the marina office, a large and heavy-looking bag slung over his shoulder.

"Want to say hi to Will?" she asked her sister.

Will set the bag down at the door and ambled over to the counter. "Look at those sweet digs!"

August pivoted her laptop around, giving him the tour. "How are you? I hear wedding plans are well under way."

"Sorry you'll miss it."

"Save me a piece of fruit cake," August said.

They razzed each other about military service a bit, then August changed the subject back to the dock repair. It was late in Lebanon, dark out August's window, and her sister needed to get to bed. "See if the insurance company will authorize another repair company. There's a list of them in the binder…"

January pulled it out from under the counter.

"That one. And if you don't get anywhere tonight, send me an email and I'll follow up with them in writing."

"I'll be fine."

August looked over at Will. "Tell her to listen to me?"

"Listen to your sister."

"How often do you listen to your brothers?" She raised her eyebrow. "Or any of your teachers?"

Will made a face at her, then looked at August. "It's almost like she's forgotten that I'm her favourite boss."

"You are my only boss," January snapped. Her neck was tight. Then she sighed and wiggled her phone, the tinny sound of hold music barely audible. "Sorry. I'm in a forty-minute queue and counting. I called them when the kids came down to talk to their mom, and I'm *still* on hold. What are you doing here? Not that I'm not happy to see you. It's been a while."

He clapped her on the shoulder. "Well, good news is, I'm here to help. Adam's on his way, too."

On the computer, August waved. "In that case, I'm going to bed."

"Night, Augie." January ended the video call and turned to Will. "What kind of help?" She glanced out the window, wincing at the view of the dock slapping against the water. The storm had passed, but the wind had stayed. *Keep breathing.* One of the things her sister had done well in the last couple of years was ensure they had good insurance—even if it cost a pretty penny. And August had also built some good systems around how to manage damage like this. Templated emails January just had to copy and paste, a checklist of who to call and in what order.

It could be way worse. This could have happened later in the season, when they actually had boats tied up to that outer dock.

Keep breathing.

"The dock repair." Will frowned. "Seth didn't email you?"

That was when she heard the plane. "Uh...no." She hung up the phone, connecting with the insurance company again suddenly a low priority, and pushed away from the counter, rounding past Will to head outside.

He followed just in time to see Seth set down on the choppy surface. Instead of trying to pull into the marina around the damaged floating dock that formed the outer perimeter, he pointed the nose of the plane toward the beach just north of them—and then, when he was metres away from the shore, he turned the plane around, the back end of it now pointing to shore. The wind pushed it in a way that made January cover her mouth, holding in a muted squeak of panic.

But it worked, and the floats bumped up onto the sandy shore. After the propellers stopped spinning, Seth hopped out and gave them a sharp wave before grabbing rope and tying up the plane, the rope stretching all the way to a tree.

And then, like he did this all the time, he hung a couple of red flags on the ropes that now crisscrossed the beach.

She turned to Will and repeated, "Dock repair?"

Seth strode toward them quickly, nodding first at January, very briefly, then turning his attention to his brother. "You got the gear?"

"Yeah. Adam's on his way, too."

"What do you think?" Then without waiting for Will to answer, he pointed to the bag. "I'll have to take a look, eh?"

Will nodded. It was like they had had a whole conversation in two one-sided questions.

Seth disappeared into the office, returning wearing a wet suit. She blinked in disbelief as he methodically checked the gear Will had brought over, then hoisted an oxygen tank onto his back and waded into the stormy lake.

"Will," she breathed…

"He's fine." He gave her a weird look. "He didn't tell you he was coming back to help?"

"Maybe I missed an email." She shivered, even though it wasn't that cold. "Thank you."

"Any time." That confused frown deepened. "You could have called me."

"No," she protested. "We have professional companies to do this sort of thing."

"Seth said they weren't coming until Friday." And the way Will said that, neither of the Kincaid brothers thought that was acceptable.

January had been frustrated, too, but there were other marinas that needed repairs as well. And she hadn't known how to push back. "Yeah."

"You have a business to run!" Will shook his head. "No, we can get this done faster."

"We?"

"Jan, you're a friend and a neighbour. Why wouldn't you think we'd help you?"

But she wasn't either of those things to Seth. Not anymore. Not for a very long time. So no, she didn't think he'd help.

Although they were business partners of a sort. While she looked on that as a form of charity—he was giving her much-needed business—he did have a vested interest in the marina being fully repaired as soon as possible.

She shouldn't try to guess at his motives. Seth had always been hard to read and full of surprises. Once upon a time, she'd looked at him and made some assumptions. He'd been an outsider, a bad boy, a pothead. He'd seemed pretty simple and straightforward when she started tutoring him, but she'd realized he was putting on a careful front. His father's death had rocked him, and he was just trying to survive. But he proved to have a lot of depth and layers.

And as they got to know each other, he turned out to be the only person who really *saw* her. He figured out that she didn't know how to carve out a bit of fun from a life otherwise built for study.

In the most unexpected way, he turned into her best friend.

Through two of the hardest years of her life, he'd been her closest person, and then he left her.

She'd understood the choice at the time, had supported it and helped him make it happen, but for the last twenty years, she had imagined that curious and complicated boy finding his way in the world.

Never had she imagined he'd one day be back in Pine Harbour, running part of his business from here. It was like they'd come full circle, back to the marina, but everything had changed.

———

SETH LIKED BEING underwater almost as much as he liked being high in the sky. Everything had a checklist, or a countdown timer, or a manual for what to do.

Right now, he needed to get a visual assessment of the damage under the loose dock, and also inspect the posts, chains, and brackets on the other docks as well, to see if they were at risk of snapping, too.

He tried not to think about the stricken and confused look on January's face. There was no manual for that.

What are you doing here? He didn't have a deep answer for her on that score. Or for himself, either. He was figuring out if a dock could be fixed. Nothing more, nothing less.

It didn't take him long to see the problem. The dock had two systems holding it in place, and both had failed in the storm. One of the metal rods that the dock floated up and down on had snapped, probably at a rusted out point, another was bent, and some of the chains that anchored the dock had broken loose as well. The rest of the interconnected dock system looked fine for now, but they would need to do a bracket-by-bracket assessment to be sure.

Kicking away from the damaged area, he surfaced and shoved his mask off his face.

His youngest brother Adam had now joined January and Will at the water's edge, and was geared up to dive as well. "What's the verdict?"

"Two rod posts have to be replaced. That can wait for the professionals. But two chains snapped as well, and that's why the dock is flapping. We should reconnect those right now, if we can get our hands on some appropriate chain and connectors. That would secure the dock well enough to ensure it doesn't fly away—or put more stress on the rest of the dock system." He was answering Adam's question, but firing the information at January. He didn't want her to think he didn't know it was her call. "If you think that's a good plan?"

"Is it safe to do that?" She glanced back and forth between him and Adam. "I don't want you to be hurt trying to help. That would go over badly with the insurance company."

"We'll be careful. And we'll work together. Will is a very good lifeguard, too."

She worried her bottom lip back and forth between her teeth for an agonizingly long five seconds—he found himself counting—and then nodded. "Sure. If you can do that, that would be amazing. And I'll pay you, of course."

He waved that off. "Any chance you've got some chain in good condition?"

She did, in the supply room behind the marina office, so he ran through the repair strategy with Adam, practiced a few tool hand offs, and then got to work.

It didn't take long once they got started, but when the repair was finished, it was definitely too late to fly home before the sun would set.

"I'll need a berth for the night," he said, shaking the water from his hair.

January handed him a warm towel. Apparently, while he'd been under water, she'd gone inside to get a stack of dryer-fresh towels—which he appreciated, because the lake was freezing cold, even in a wet suit.

He unzipped the front of his suit and shoved it down his arms, then rolled his shoulders before wrapping himself in the towel again. Adam did the same, but January's attention stayed glued on Seth. "It worked, then?"

"Yeah, the chain will hold it well. The posts still need to be replaced, but the chains are sufficient in the short term. Don't let the kids run on it, that's all. It'll be a bit tippier than usual." He shivered.

"Oh my God, please, come inside and change, both of you." She pushed them toward the office.

They changed in the supply room, and hung up their gear to dry there instead of shoving it all in the bag wet.

Seth cracked the door open to the office. "Will, can you come back and collect the stuff tomorrow after it dries?" His brother didn't answer, so he pushed the door open the rest of the way as he tugged his t-shirt on. "Will?"

"He's outside, putting caution tape on the dock," January said. She was behind the counter, turning off her computer—and not looking at him.

Maybe because he'd just strolled in on her while he was half-dressed. He smoothed a hand down the front of his shirt, then ran the towel over his hair again. Then he held it out. "Thanks for this."

She took it, her gaze finally meeting his. "The literal least I could do."

"I'm going to move my plane over now," he said, jerking his thumb in the direction of the beach.

She nodded. The uncertain look in her eyes was back, and he wanted to reassure her that the dock was going to be okay, but it was rapidly getting dark, and then his brothers were both in the office, urging him to move the plane.

After it was tied up in a berth, he let Will drag him up the hill to Catie's for dinner, even though he wanted to stay and talk to January more. She had to get dinner sorted for the kids, anyway.

And there'd be time to talk again soon. They had all summer, after all.

Will noticed Seth's reluctance to leave the marina, though. His brother was no dummy. "You okay?"

Two short words, asking a lot of questions that Seth didn't have answers for. So he gave his brother three words of his own that he hoped were true. "I will be."

"That was good of you to come help."

"The marina's an important part of my business now. Had to do my part."

Will accepted that answer, when they walked through the door of Catie's house, his brother's attention immediately shifted to his bride-to-be. Catie was in the kitchen, dancing and stirring a pot of risotto on the stove. Will caught her in his arms, carefully made sure the wooden spoon found the spoonrest, then spun her around in a circle before covering her mouth with his.

It was hard to watch, and not because Seth wasn't happy for his brother. Of course he was.

It was just so foreign to his own life—and what his brothers lives had been until very recently. They'd been a tight knit group of bachelors for so long, even over some distance. And now one by one, they were losing their hearts to partners who were perfect for them.

And Seth kept coming home to frozen stew he'd made a month earlier.

He busied himself checking his messages as Will filled

Catie in on the last two hours. There was an email from Teegan, asking if the town he was flying out of was called Pine Harbour, because Linda—who worked as a house painter—had just accepted a two-week job working for a contractor there.

Here.

Seth chuckled to himself. "Well that's a small fucking world."

"What is?" Catie swept by him with plates.

"Jake Foster just hired my neighbour down the street to do some painting for him."

"He couldn't find anyone closer?" Will asked.

Catie shook her head. "I'm hearing about whole crews coming in from hours away. Blind River isn't the furthest." She tilted her head sideways. "Will she commute with you, Seth?"

He snorted. "I think she's staying here for the duration, but her wife might hitch a ride once or twice. Those two are almost as honeymooned up as you guys are."

Catie blushed. "Go help your brother with the salad, and I'll keep my kisses to myself until you're gone for the night."

"Don't do that on my account," he gruffed. "It's nice to see you both happy."

———

DINNER WAS FINE. Good. Great, probably, although Seth was too tangled up in his own thoughts to really appreciate the food his brother and Catie cooked.

And it *was* nice to see Will in this space, with his fiancée, just the two of them. He'd essentially moved in with Catie, as over the last year his house became a second base for their niece Becca—Owen's grown daughter—and her son Charlie when they visited. Becca and Charlie had more space there than they would at Owen's house.

And of course, Seth and Josh crashed at Will's sometimes, too.

Only Adam didn't—anymore—because he had bought his own home.

Technically Josh owned his own "home" as well, but it was an apartment above the garage he'd sunk all his savings into, and looked like the set of a snuff film. So when it got really cold in the winter, or if he just wanted modern comforts, he would roll up at the Kincaid Inn.

Something about that kept chirping at the back of Seth's mind. Which meant he was missing something clearly important, only tripping back into the conversation when Will said January's name.

"Sorry, what was that?"

"Catie just said that January's building a house down the street from my place. She signed a contract yesterday."

"Did she?" That surprised him, based on what he knew about the marina's business. But then again, she didn't work for the marina most of the time. And if Will could afford a nice house on the edge of town as a principal, surely January could as a teacher, fifteen years into her career.

It was a sharp reminder that he didn't know that much about her life—other than it was here in Pine Harbour, and his life was not.

Catie nodded as she speared a piece of cucumber from her salad. "She's wanted to build a place for a while now. It was a lot of fun working with her on the deal."

Which meant he couldn't pry, because Catie had ethical bounds around being the real estate agent.

Not that he wanted to *pry*, exactly.

Is she happy, he wanted to ask. He should have asked her that already, but he was afraid of the answer.

Did she get the life she wanted?

But as much as he loved his brothers, he couldn't ask Will that, not even after whatever Will thought he saw tonight. He'd never been able to talk to any of them about January.

He'd never been one to bare his soul in general, had always kept his feelings tightly locked up. When they were little, their mom had seen that in him, and she'd had a way of gently prompting him to share his secrets with her and her alone.

What scared him, what he dreamed of. He told her in tiny pieces, little slices of his thoughts, and she pieced them together.

And then she was gone.

The only other person he'd ever truly confided in was January. He felt so fucking hollow thinking about that, but naming it didn't make a difference. He couldn't get close to people. He'd tried. It was just how he was built.

He was emotionally unavailable, which felt like both a tired cliché and the painful truth at the same time, and that dated far enough back that there were echoes of it from every age. He'd been just shy of fifteen when Owen told him he was going to be a teen dad. Seth's only moral support effort was offering his brother a slug of booze from the bottle under his bed.

He grabbed his water glass, washed down his last bite of rice, and leaned back in his chair. "When is the house going to be built?"

Will picked up his own glass as he glanced between Seth and Catie as his fiancée answered. "She wants to take possession soon after her sister returns. Do you know the Howe sisters well?"

And Will choked on his water.

"Yeah," Seth said dryly.

Catie frowned at them both. "What am I missing?"

"Will never told you that January and I dated in high school?"

Her eyebrows hit the roof. "What? No. Tell me more."

He took a deep breath. "She was my tutor, and I fell for her—pretty hard, as teen boys do—and we were together more or less until I left for the Royal Military College." *She was the best part of his life, at the worst time of his life*, but he couldn't say that out loud, because his brothers were just as important, too, and one was across the table. "It's ancient history, and I only want the best for her. It's great news about the house."

"Smooth," Will muttered.

"Says the guy who can't swallow water properly," Seth snapped back.

Catie looked like she wanted to ask more, but decided not to, which Seth was eternally grateful for. They changed the subject to dock repair, and how hard it is to get urgent work done in general—and that brought them full circle back to the challenges in the construction industry.

Which led into dessert, and then Seth insisted on doing the dishes.

Once he finished, he told Will he was ready to crash for the night, and Will handed over his truck keys. "Leave it at the marina in the morning, and we'll collect it. Put the keys in the glovebox. Catie has a spare."

Seth was halfway to Will's house when he remembered he left his emergency bag—including his toothbrush and a spare change of clothes—on his plane. So he took a left on Main Street and headed for the harbour.

The lights were on in the residence upstairs, but the marina office was dark, so he took the path straight to the dock. He unlocked the plane, grabbed his bag, and turned around—and saw January sitting on a bench in the twilight.

"Hey," she said quietly, raising her hand.

He lifted the bag to indicate his surprise appearance, then locked the plane back up, and slowly strolled toward her. "What are you doing out here in the dark?"

"Taking a break from being a referee between two children intent on bickering over the most ridiculous things." She lifted a mug from the seat beside her. "And waiting for my chamomile tea to cool down."

He nodded.

There was a long pause, and then just before he was going to bid her goodnight, she spoke. "Listen, I wanted to say…"

When she trailed off again, Seth's hand flexed at his side. He was acutely aware of it, a response to a slight tremor, his body's well-trained response to stress. Tighten up, get under control. Keep breathing.

Why was this so hard for both of them? They were grown-ups.

That thought was enough to snap him past the feelings. By the time she found her words again, he was cool as a cucumber—until she spoke. "It's hard to see you. Here."

He hadn't expected that. He believed it without a doubt. He recognized the tone in her voice because it was note-perfect for a matching tone inside his head.

This is too hard.

How many times had he thought about leasing a

second plane and branching out sooner than his business plan suggested? Get another pilot to take these flights, and his angsty feelings about January were solved, because he'd be back in Blind River full time.

Out of sight, out of mind.

Except while it may have worked for the last twenty years, it hadn't worked for the last month.

Things had changed.

And he was fighting an internal battle not to overreact, as well. It was still his instinct, even after all these years. Run away, don't look back. That time was done, though. He wasn't going anywhere, as much as he desperately wanted to. Limits, yes. Fleeing, no.

"It's been weird, yeah. It shouldn't be this hard." he admitted gruffly. "I stayed away too long. That's probably part of it."

She looked out over the lake, visibly unsure of what to say next. Then she nodded, and a few strands of hair swung out of her loose top bun. "You've had a lot of adventures, though." And then as if she thought that needed an explainer, she added, "I've heard a bit about you, over the years. Will…he's proud of you. He can't help but share the highlights."

Seth rubbed the back of his neck. "The feeling is mutual."

"I did always like how close you guys are."

He smiled ruefully. "Speaking of…us. I should tell you that you came up at dinner tonight. I told Will's fiancée that we used to date."

"Oh?"

"She asked if I know you well."

A long pause. Then a tired laugh. "You used to, didn't you?"

"That's what I said." He sighed. "And then Will choked on his water."

"Oh." This time, her laugh was more of a giggle. "Siblings, huh?"

He pointed to the marina residence. "They aren't the only ones who have complicated relationships. Not everyone is quite as symbiotic as you and August."

"Thanks, I probably needed that reminder."

He chuckled. Was it enough to just name this as hard? Was that a good first step? Huh. He dragged in a breath. "How about you? Any adventures?"

"Not like you." A pause. "I'm happy for you. That you get to fly every day."

What should he say to that? *Thanks?*

Her smile slipped for a second, then came back brighter than before. "That's what you wanted. It worked out, then."

It had. Exactly as he'd wanted. "And you're teaching."

"Usually." This time it was her who pointed to the residence. And she stood. "I should go and check to make sure they're still alive."

He followed her to the door, and made sure she got inside, before heading to the truck.

It wasn't until he was stretched out in the quiet of Will's spare room that he realized he hadn't felt on edge at all in that conversation. They'd shared a little bittersweet truth, and it hadn't hurt nearly as much as he'd always feared.

It hadn't hurt at all.

7

THE NEXT DAY Seth took off at daybreak, before anyone at the marina was awake. He had to get up to Blind River to pick up a supply run order for a fly-in lodge. Thursdays were usually his shortest day of the week, but not today, with the extra leg of travel. It gave him a bit of thinking time, though.

There were parts of his business plan that were hollering at him to maybe get pushed up. And his to-do list kept growing, because he was spending so much of his time in the air these days.

A good problem to have.

But what he really needed was a solid weekend at home to get caught up.

He didn't get it.

Friday ended up being a longer day than planned, so Saturday became his errand running day, with a drive into the Sault for groceries, and then Sunday morning, Will texted and asked if he could fly back to Pine Harbour for dinner that night. All the other brothers were available, and Will wanted to brainstorm a new idea he had for the wedding.

Seth could have begged off. He could have joined via video.

But he found himself texting that he would attend. He had to be in Pine Harbour the next morning anyway, so he'd be saving himself a bit of flying time on his longest day.

Levi must have spotted him doing his flyover to assess the landing, because the kid was waiting on the dock. Seth tossed him the line and let him tie up the plane. Then he tipped the boy—always good form to appreciate a dockhand—and thanked him for the help.

"Do you have another flight today? I could help load people's bags." Levi grinned as they strode together toward the marina office, the kid taking two steps for every one of Seth's.

"Nope, I'm staying for the night. I'm having dinner with my brothers."

"I wish I had brothers, instead of a rotten sister." That was said with a bit of a growl.

"I like your sister."

"I like my sister, too," Levi grudgingly admitted. "Except when I don't."

"I know the feeling well. It's true for brothers, too, you know."

"Really? That's a shame."

Seth laughed out loud as he opened the office door. "Tell me about it."

January glanced up from her perch at the computer, just for a second, surprise skittering across her face. She gave a nod of acknowledgement, then quickly went back to her work, typing a bit more before he came to a stop in front of her.

"I need a berth for the night," he explained. "This is personal use, so I'll pay cash for it."

"Not after you repaired my dock, you won't," January muttered good-naturedly, waving his money away.

From upstairs, Summer yelled Levi's name, then came tumbling down the stairs. "Carson and Leesha are going to the park, want to go with them?"

Levi's grumpiness over having a sister forgotten, he nodded eagerly.

Summer turned to her aunt. "Can we?"

"Sure. Be back by six for dinner," she managed to call out before they were out the door again.

Which left them alone.

He should leave, too. Follow them out the door and head straight to his brother's garage. But it was only approaching four o'clock. He had almost two hours until they needed to be at Will's for dinner, and Josh was a cranky asshole.

And there was something different about January today. For one thing, she wasn't wearing her business clothes. Instead she was wearing a long-sleeved baseball t-shirt with a Grand Ole Opry logo on it and what looked like a pair of ragged cut-off jean shorts. And while the stress of the week before seemed to linger—in her furrowed brow, in some bright yellow Post-it notes with black marker scrawled on them—she still looked good. Really good.

The t-shirt cupped her curves, rounding over her breasts and fluttering around her waist. It was danger-ously touchable, deeply attractive, and sparked far too many questions in his head. Had she gone to Nashville herself, or with friends? Or someone special?

It was hard to deny that everything about her made him curious. The clothes she wore, the proper way she conducted herself. The music she might listen to, the trips she may have taken. Not that she gave him any clues. Not that he would give in to that curiosity. But he liked it, in a way.

"Sorry for the surprise arrival," he said, rocking back on his heels. "I'm going to Will's for dinner."

Her brows pulled tight in confusion, then she wagged her finger as understanding dawned. "Right. The Bromittee."

"You know about—" His neck burned hot. It was a small fucking town. Of course she did. Everyone knew everything about everybody at all times. "Yeah. For the wedding."

"It's really sweet how Will is into all the planning. Catie's doing her best to not be nosy, but you know how she is." And she laughed lightly.

Except Seth didn't know what she meant about Catie, not really. Not enough to know whatever January knew about her. Because Seth didn't live here and—

It's really sweet how Will is into all the planning.

January knew all about the wedding, because January would be *at* the wedding.

Because she lived here, and was close friends with Will, and of course his fiancée too. Not just *at* the wedding, but probably as looped in on the planning of it as Seth was supposed to be.

They weren't just going to see each other all summer *for work*. They were also going to attend multiple social events together. Was there enough exposure therapy in polite business transactions for him to be prepared to watch January dance all night long with some eager date? No. His curiosity did not extend that far.

On a scale of one to awful, how terrible would it be to bow out of his brother's wedding? *Disastrous.*

This hadn't been an issue before. Adam had eloped, and Owen's wedding took place in the middle of a country music festival that, to the best of his knowledge, January hadn't attended. *But you looked for her that night, didn't you?*

Besides, January wasn't that close to either of them. But Will? She'd worked with him for fifteen years.

How had Seth not seen this coming?

His pulse was hammering in his neck, and that was annoying. It was making it hard for him to think straight. "Do you know much about the wedding so far?"

Was she laughing at his ridiculous question? Her eyes were doing…something. "Not that much," she said evenly. "Just the date. And, you know, the location. The primary players and who will be making the wedding cake."

"Yeah."

"It's mostly just been the two of them. And you had that one Bro-mittee meeting."

That was not seriously a name people were calling it. Was it? It had been breakfast where Will had made them all put a bunch of dates in their phones. Seth couldn't remember any of the details. He was the worst kind of brother. "Right."

"We'll both find out more tonight, probably?"

"We will?"

"Catie's having a girls' night get together at the same time as you're having dinner at Will's. I'm going to feed the kids and run."

"Ah."

"Lots of time to get oriented to our tasks, though."

"Mmm."

"It's not until the end of the summer." She paused. "We'll have to compare notes."

All out of agreement sounds, he just nodded. That was a peace offering, he recognized it as such. She was making the more personal kind of conversations he'd been itching to have, but did it have to be about his brother's wedding?

"Although we do have to get going on the stag and doe plans," she said, her brow furrowing.

Right, that was on his calendar in July.

More dancing.

Did people take dates to those things? Did grown-up January dance? He hadn't taken her to the prom either year they were together. The only time they danced together was at their grad celebration, and fuck that had been a bittersweet night.

She tilted her head to the side, her eyes narrowing. Had her thoughts gone to the same place? The way he'd held her tight against him, too close for the liking of teachers, but he'd had to because she was quietly crying into his shoulder and there was no way in hell he was letting anyone else know that she was upset.

Her tears were his to wear, and his alone. They were his fault, after all.

"I haven't been tuned in enough to the wedding details," he admitted. "But I guess after tonight…"

"The Bro-mittee meeting," she prompted. Now she was definitely laughing at him.

He grinned reluctantly. "Yeah, after *that*, I'll know more. And I will report back."

Her lips curled playfully. "I hear there were some alternate names thrown around? Wedding Rescue Team?"

If she kept smiling at him like that, he'd let her laugh all she wanted at his expense.

"Will vetoed that one because Catie's plans are perfect and don't need to be rescued." He could remember that, apparently.

January's shoulders shook, then she exhaled happily. "Those two."

"They're pretty good together."

"Yep. And sometimes deeply annoying to everyone else with the Type A power trips." She was laughing out loud now, and to his surprise, he realized he was, too. His cheeks were warm from the strain.

"As long as we're all on the same page about that."

She winked. "Oh, we are."

On the wall, one of the clocks dinged. It was the top of the hour. He glanced over at them, noticing that it was eleven at night in Beirut. "What's the latest update from Lebanon?"

"August is doing great. The kids get to talk to her most days. And she's even getting to do some travelling on the weekends."

"That's the best part of a tour, if it's safe."

She nodded. "Yeah."

"And how about you?" His hand flexed again. He wanted to know, though. "Holding down the home fort?"

"It's— We're adjusting. You saw me last week having a little self-timeout."

"Levi's a good kid. Summer, too."

"They are. They really are. It's just...I'm not their mom."

"If Levi has any questions about what it's like to go overseas with the military, I could talk to him."

She hesitated.

"Or Will." He shook his head. "Or anyone else who he actually knows, I guess. Sorry, I don't know why I immediately jumped to thinking I'd be the right guy to talk to him."

Something peculiar crossed her face, and she frowned.

He notched his thumb over his shoulder, pointing at the door. "I'm going to get going."

Which would require moving his legs, and they were firmly planted on the floor. He couldn't stop looking at her face, at that unsure expression. At the way she nibbled on her lower lip. He wanted to gently ease her abused flesh out from between her teeth and soothe it with a soft swipe of his thumb.

Or his mouth.

Fuck.

"I'm sorry," she whispered. "That's very kind. And he seems to have latched onto you. It's just that…"

"It's fine." His voice grated.

"No, really. It's been a weird spring." She dragged in a sudden, deep breath. "I'm trying to get through this one week at a time. But I bet Levi would like that, so if you don't mind him following you around, of course, feel free to talk to him. I just…"

Again she trailed off. It was hard for her to talk to him. He got that, of course he did. It was hard for him, too.

"I'll let him know that you're someone he can approach. An old friend who went to the Air Force and who knows what his mom is doing." She nodded, as if affirming for herself that the story made sense.

It was the truth, so it would.

But not the whole truth.

An old friend.

Yeah. He needed to sink his thoughts about how soft her mouth looked deep in the middle of the lake. "Sure."

"But, uh, if you want to compare notes on the wedding? I was serious about that." Her lips curved back into a happier smile. "I'm pretty good with secrets."

They both were. "Same."

This time when her gaze flew to his face, there was nothing confusing about her expression. Bare grief, just for a second. Raw feelings he hadn't felt in a very long time slammed into him. And then a bright strength soared into place.

"I remember." Two soft words, and by the time he said them, the grief was gone.

They were dredging up the past, but they were dealing with it, too. She probably already had in better ways than he'd done.

She pushed away from the counter between them, and walked to the end of it. But instead of coming around to his side, she gestured to the stairs. "Time for me to close up."

He'd said he had to go, too. But then he didn't. Now she was telling him he'd overstayed his welcome.

With a sharp nod, he took his leave.

But he would be back. Maybe they needed more of these conversations. A little more dredging, a little more acknowledgement of the past, but a lot more of those smiles.

Making January laugh had just soared to the top of his priority list.

8
___

JANUARY TOSSED and turned all night. When dawn broke, she crawled out of bed and crept downstairs to put coffee on. It was still an hour before anyone would—

Except down on the newly repaired dock, a large body crouched next to Seth's plane. Frowning, she hurried to the window…and then sighed when she realized it was the pilot himself. It looked like he was pumping water out of the floats.

Was he always up this early? Probably *earlier* most days to get his plane ready and then fly here in time for his charter pickup.

She started the coffee maker, then ran upstairs and threw on some clothes. Jeans and a sweater, because it felt like she was losing a battle at maintaining any pretence of professionalism around Seth anyway.

Downstairs, she shoved her feet into rubber boots and filled two mugs with coffee. She fixed one with a bit of sugar and cream, and the other with double of both.

Taking a deep breath, she pushed the door open and made her way down to him. When he caught sight of her, he stopped what he was doing and gave her a slow smile. "Morning. You're up early."

She held out the mugs. "This one's a regular, that one is a double double."

He shoved the sleeves of his sweatshirt up his arms, then took the regular. "Didn't realize you offered dockside coffee service."

"It's a secret menu thing. Only on even days that start with F." And when she couldn't sleep because her brain kept going places it shouldn't. Settled, long-ago buried places. "And for people who fix my dock."

He lifted the mug in a solemn salute. "Well, thank you."

"How was the wedding planning sub-committee meeting?"

His right eyebrow curved up at her delicate phrasing. "You can call it the Bro-mittee."

"I think it might be more fun to make it extra formal?"

He snorted. "All right."

She took a sip, then sighed happily as the coffee warmed her from the inside out. "I love this time of day," she said at the same time as he said, "Will wants to plan a scavenger hunt for Catie."

"Oh!" She stepped closer, surprised and excited. "That's such a good idea."

"Will she think it's fun for an entire week? He's planning a daily clue."

"Amazing. Oh, and you know what would be hilarious?" She laughed, an idea forming in her head. She reached out to tap his arm as she said, "You should have the downtown storefronts..."

Seth grunted as her fingers slide over his forearm, and she yanked her hand back just as quickly, trying to ignore the wave of warmth that rolled over her skin from the contact.

Her heart pounded. *Keep going.* "The store displays could be clues. Bailey Patel would be a good person to coordinate that slyly."

He lifted his mug and drained it.

Silence stretched between them.

"Well, I should…" She glanced behind her. "It's time to start my daily routine of snapping at kids to get out of bed."

Another grunt.

Whatever. She turned briskly and headed back to the office.

He followed, making her very aware of his body behind hers.

"January." She stopped just short of the office.

Her name out of his mouth… She hadn't heard that in a very long time. Low, like honey. A little rasp. A tremor of what she used to think was need, until he proved that he definitely did not need her.

"I like your idea. I really do. I think we should keep talking about it."

"Your passengers will be here soon."

"Another time, then. Lunch one day."

"You're not here at lunch time." She sounded desperate now, to her own ears.

"I'm here more than I thought I would be." He hesitated. "I can make time for an old friend."

Something about how he said that made her pause and consider his offer for real. The way his voice caught on the last three words. *An old friend.* She'd said them yesterday.

It wasn't the most honest way to describe Seth, but it was true. He had been her best friend once. Could they latch onto that part of their history, and only that part, and forge a new connection?

Ignore the fact that when she touched him, nerve endings she'd long thought dormant roared back to life?

Footsteps from the parking lot broke their private moment, allowing her to escape inside as Seth greeted his first passenger with a practiced charm she barely recognized.

He only had two customers today, which meant they were halfway to him leaving already.

Inside she called up the stairs and got a sleepy acknowledgement from Summer. Good enough. She grabbed her phone and texted both of them a funny meme about aliens going to school for the first time, then turned on her computer. She had a fuel delivery today, and three boats arriving for overnight stays. Plus a phone call with the marina repair company to get them to take the chain repair off their invoice to the insurance company, because they didn't do that work, Seth did.

She pinched her nose and took a deep breath.

Then she pressed her fingertips to her lips, just for a second, and told herself she could think about Seth's forearm later. Much later.

———

SETH DIDN'T HAVE anyone to return to Pine Harbour after he dropped off his passengers, so he made it back to Blind River by lunch.

He texted Teegan as soon as he was home.

Seth: Is Linda gone this week? Let me know if you want porch company.

**Teegan: No, she leaves on Sunday. But we're both
home today, if you want to come over.**

He grabbed a few beers from the fridge and sauntered
down the road. They met him on their porch. "Ladies."

"Beer *and* a smile? Who are you and what have you
done with Seth Kincaid?" Teegan snagged a bottle, took off
the cap, and handed it to her wife. "Here you go, baby."

Linda winked at him. "Thank you."

"Maybe I just like hanging out with you."

They both screwed up their faces like, no, that didn't
compute.

He sighed and sank onto the chair they'd set out for
him. "All right, I have a favour to ask. Actually, it might be
a business proposal? Depends how much you miss
flying."

Teegan grunted.

"I'm thinking of spending more time in Pine Harbour
this summer, and want to offload at least one of my flights
from here. I can lease a second plane for the summer. So I
just need a pilot." He paused, handed Teegan a beer, then
smiled. "And I happen to know you're a damn good bush
pilot."

"Stop flirting with me," she muttered. But her eyes
were bright.

They'd never talked about this, because Seth didn't
want to get her hopes up if his business couldn't sustain it,
but it had always been his plan to offer her a job when he
was ready to expand. She worked part time as a licensed
counsellor, specializing in veterans and other survivors of
PTSD, but there wasn't a lot of demand for therapy in
Blind River.

And he knew she missed flying, but couldn't afford her

own plane. Once a month, she'd rent hours from a company in Sudbury, and he let her take his plane for short trips when he wasn't using it.

It was a good solution, no downside.

Except his friend was looking at him like he was a puzzle to solve. That might be a downside. "Why the change in plans all of a sudden?"

Because of a cup of coffee and the light trail of fingers over his skin. "It's hard to fly five days a week."

She nodded. "All right." She held out her bottle, and he tinked his against hers. "Count me in, boss."

———

THE NEXT DAY, after he did his supply run up north, he flew to Owen Sound to check out a plane for lease. And then, since he was halfway to Pine Harbour, he just kept going.

When he arrived at the marina, the "Back in Ten Minutes" sign was hanging in the window, so he texted the phone number on the sign to let January know he'd taken a berth and she should charge him for it, and headed across the road to Josh's garage.

The right-hand door of the garage was open, and he could see his brother's legs sticking out from under a vintage pickup truck.

"It's me," he called out. "Decided to drop in for the evening."

"Hey." Josh wagged his foot. "Like my new truck?"

Seth whistled. "I sure do. Are you going to restore her?"

His brother rolled out from under the truck and grabbed a rag to wipe his hands off. "Yep. She's not in the worst shape, considering she was in someone's barn for thirty years."

Seth paused mid-text to Will, asking if he could stay at the Kincaid Inn. "Thirty years?"

"I know. I spent the last week flushing and filling and replacing a few essential pieces. She's running for now, but I might end up dropping a new engine in it anyway."

"Amazing." Seth frowned at his screen. "Did you know that Will is getting new carpets installed?"

"Oh yeah, he said something about that."

"Nobody told me. I was going to crash there tonight but apparently the whole upstairs is torn apart. So…can I order us some takeout?"

"No can do," Josh said apologetically. "I have soccer practice. Want to come? We'll go to the pub after."

Seth was tempted, but he was also tired. "Do you mind if I just hang out here instead?"

"Knock yourself out." Josh went over to the wall and pulled a keychain off a hook. "Here's a key to the apartment."

"Thanks." Seth's phone vibrated as he took the key. A message from January letting him know she was back in the office, and he didn't need to worry about paying for a berth for the night.

Nonsense.

He tossed the key in the air. Suddenly less tired, but still not interested in watching a soccer game. "Thanks for the use of your couch tonight, bud."

"Couch? Can't you go sleep at Owen's or Adam's?"

Seth shrugged. "I could. But this way I'm that much closer to my plane in the morning."

Josh muttered something about a *fucking weirdo* under his breath, and Seth just laughed.

But his amusement ended abruptly when he got back across the road and heard what sounded like tears coming from upstairs. Gulping, hiccupping little boy tears, and a soothing voice.

And then the marina phone rang.

Summer appeared from the stairwell before he could step outside, as if maybe she'd been sitting on the bottom step. "Seth's here," she bellowed before answering the phone. "Howe's Marina, can you hold please?"

"That sounded very professional," he said when she tucked the handset under her chin and gave him an expectant look. "But go ahead. I just came to talk to your aunt."

"Aunt January!"

"I heard you the first time, Summer, there's no need to yell." January stepped into view and gave Seth an exhausted wave. "Hi. Sorry, we're having a lot of things happen at once."

He lifted his gaze to the ceiling. "Anything I can help with?"

"No, we're fine—"

A loud retort sounded from upstairs, a sharp bang.

"What the hell?" January pivoted fast and sprinted out of view.

Seth had a split second to decide if following her was infringing on her personal space. He decided it was worth the dice roll.

"Don't forget you have someone on hold," he said to Summer as he moved past her and up a set of stairs he hadn't climbed in twenty years.

The marina residence was a kitchen and living room over top of the office, and two split levels of bedrooms behind that. His first impression, before he found January leaning against the kitchen doorway, was that the whole place seemed brighter than he remembered.

"What happened?"

She turned, her expression defeated. "My casserole exploded."

He glanced past her. Sure enough, chunks of glass were everywhere, and what looked like a very delicious potato and cheese casserole now dripped all over the stovetop where the dish had been set down, presumably to cool. "Where's your broom?"

"No, it's fine, I've got this."

He nudged her arm gently. "Where is it?"

"Seth—"

"Let me help."

She nodded. "It's in there." She pointed to a narrow pantry in the far corner of the kitchen. "On the other side of the mine field."

"Good thing I'm wearing boots." He glanced down the hall to the living room, where Levi stood staring at them wide-eyed. "Hey, bud. We need a new dinner plan."

January waved her arm, inviting him closer, and Levi ran into her embrace. "I'm so glad you weren't in the kitchen," she murmured behind Seth as he found a path to the broom closet.

"You, too," Levi said, his voice tiny. "You just took that out of the oven."

Seth glanced back just in time to see her kiss the top of her nephew's head. The boy's face was tear-streaked still, but Seth was pretty sure that was from whatever conversation he'd overheard the tail end of when he arrived, and not the scary dinner explosion.

He grabbed the broom and dustpan and efficiently swept the floor. January came in behind him with a vacuum, and before long they had everything clear except the mess on the stove.

Seth blew out his cheeks. "How do we tackle this?"

"Oh, no, this is a me problem." She cast a glance at the fridge. "After I figure out what I can make that's fast."

He reached past her to grab a menu from a pizza place that advertised itself as new in town, ignoring the spike of pleasure he felt at the warm proximity of her body. "Listen, I was going to order pizza for dinner anyway. And I had big plans to eat it by myself over at Josh's garage. Can I double my order and share it with you and the kids?"

She groaned and ground the heels of her hands into her forehead for a second. Not the reception he'd been hoping for. But then she lifted her face. She looked tired. "Are you sure?"

Three little words that could mean a lot more than simply, was the offer sincere. But it was, and as for the rest of the layers…he'd tackle them one at a time. "Yeah," he finally said. "I'm sure."

———

JANUARY USED a couple of thick rags to scoop the worst of the mess off the stove as she listened to Seth place an order for three different pizzas. He'd asked her if there were any no-go toppings for the kids, and then just took charge, and she was so grateful for it, even though it was still surreal to have him in this kitchen again after all this time.

She had a flash of a younger Seth digging in the freezer for popsicles, then it was gone, and she was back in the present. He was leaning against her counter, one long jean-clad leg crossed over the other, as he waited patiently for the order to be confirmed.

She moved the grates on the top of the stove into the sink and grabbed two more rags.

"Twenty-five minutes." He grabbed the garbage bag she'd been using and brought it closer to her. "Here you go."

"Thank you." She spied a small piece of glass at the back of the range and carefully nudged it forward, then grabbed it with a rag. "What a mess."

"You're getting there."

She huffed weakly. "I think I'm scarred for life, though. That baking dish has never exploded before." He barked a laugh, and then she realized what she'd just said. "Wait, I mean…"

His laughter deepened, and she joined him, her sides shaking and tears forming at the corners of her eyes.

He held up his hand, trying to stop for a second. "Are you *sure*?"

She shook her head. "No," she wheezed. "I'm not sure. Maybe it did once?"

Summer appeared in the doorway, took one look at the two of them laughing their asses off, and disappeared again.

That only made January laugh harder. She gave up trying to clean the stove top and leaned against the counter next to Seth. He grinned at her. "Did that feel good?"

She nodded and drew in a long, sobering breath. "Thanks for your help. Again. The dock, and tonight… It wasn't necessary either time. And I really appreciate it."

"Yeah. Sure."

Turning her head, she looked at him more fully. "I'm sorry, I'm not being a good host. Do you want something to drink before dinner?"

He shook his head. "No, I'm fine."

"I have the stuff for a salad, we can have that with the pizza."

"Sounds good." His gaze searched her face. "Can I take over with the stove cleaning while you make that?"

No, she wanted to say. *Stop being so kind, I can only handle so much,* but she didn't think there was a limit for how much of this she could take. It was all just so strange and lovely, and she wasn't going to stop him if he wanted to help. Two months into being the sole guardian, she was over having to do everything herself. And with four months still to go, she would take the strange and wonderful reprieve for an evening.

Even if it did mean she would probably spend another sleepless night wondering what the heck it all meant.

"That would be great," she heard herself say. Then she pushed away from the counter, away from Seth, and busied herself on the other side of the kitchen with the salad prep.

When the pizza arrived, Seth traipsed downstairs to fetch it and Levi helped. Summer set the table, and before January knew it, the four of them were sitting down to eat.

Levi peppered Seth with questions about his plane and being in the Air Force. Summer wanted to know if he'd ever flown anyone famous—"Not that I know of, but I don't ask that on the passenger intake form"—and January got to eat her meal and just enjoy the show.

Until they were almost done, and then Seth turned the questions around. "Hey," he asked Levi in that low, conspiratorial tone he used sometimes. "Anything you think I need to know about your aunt?"

Levi gave him a curious look. "I thought you were friends?"

Seth glanced across at January, a hard-to-read expression firmly in place. "We used to be, a long time ago. But I don't know your aunt that well *now*."

"You mean you're strangers?" Levi pulled a comical face. "Stranger danger at the table!"

"Levi, don't be dumb," Summer scoffed, rolling her eyes.

"What? Mom says we shouldn't trust strangers."

"He's not a *stranger*—you know him. He just doesn't know us *that well*." She was using that bossy thirteen-year-old voice to peak effect, and January winced.

"Hey," she said under breath. "That's enough."

Levi glared at Summer. Summer snarled right back and, under her breath, whispered something January missed because she was caught up on the truth that she and Seth *were* strangers now. Did he really want to get to know her again? And did she have room in her life for a friendship that would be more complicated than any other she'd ever had?

It took her a moment to realize that Levi had gone silent. Then he was pushing himself away from the table, and she only caught a glimpse of a hurt look on his face before he was gone. Summer gave her an accusing look, like January should have anticipated this somehow, even though it was Summer herself who had pushed his tender buttons after he'd had a rough day. She jumped up from the table to chase after her brother. January exhaled heavily. Now they were both mad and she was the only person they could take it out on.

"Excuse me," she said to Seth. "I'll be right back."

Upstairs, she found Levi curled up on his bed, Summer sitting at his feet trying to cheer him up, bossiness forgotten, as was her way.

"Hey," January said softly. "What's wrong?"

"Nothing," Levi snarled, in his hurt little boy way.

Oh, January wanted to sooth all those rough edges, but it wasn't easy.

Summer, though, could read her brother's mind. "He feels silly for saying stranger danger about Seth. And then I made it worse."

Then why did you make it worse? January wanted to ask, exasperatedly, but *that* would make *this* worse, and one thing at a time.

Summer chewed on her lower lip. "I apologized immediately."

But she still poked the bear. *Deep breaths, January.* "I don't think Seth cares at all. He probably thought it was a fair and funny thing to say."

Levi was unmoved by that promise.

"Tell you what. I'm going to go downstairs and make hot chocolate. In a few minutes, I'm going to tell Seth to let you know that dessert is ready. You take some time to yourself now, and then rejoin us."

Summer nodded. "Okay."

"Not okay," Levi mumbled.

January didn't know how to soothe that wounded part of him that needed to be belligerent right now.

August always knew. She'd take one look at her children's faces and get to the source of the issue in three questions or less. And then she always had the solution, be it a hug or a quiet talk or a run on the beach.

It was too late to call her sister, because it was already the middle of the night in Lebanon.

She was on her own with this. She retraced the evening. They'd talked to August as soon as they got home from school, then she'd put the casserole in the oven before they went shopping. When they got back, Levi had denied having homework, which January had challenged him on—leading to a freak-out and tears—and then Seth had arrived, followed immediately by their dinner exploding. Levi had seemed in good spirits through dinner, but maybe the stranger danger silliness had echoes of him feeling bad for saying the wrong thing about homework, too.

January knelt next to the bed and rested her head next to Levi's. His hair was getting long, she noticed as she gently stroked his back. A sign of how much time had passed since his mom had left.

"I sometimes worry that I've said something silly," she whispered to him. "And it's always worse in my head than it is for others. I promise you that Seth didn't think anything of that. And he won't care that you've taken a timeout for yourself now, either. He asks about you a lot, you know. In fact, he told me that he wanted you to know that you can talk to him about anything. Including what your mom is doing, if you want."

"No he didn't," Levi said softly.

"He really did."

That seemed to work, so she headed back downstairs to make hot chocolate as promised. She found Seth in the kitchen, washing up their plates.

"You don't have to do that," she protested.

"You were busy." He shrugged. "I put the leftover pizza in the fridge."

"Thanks."

She put the kettle on, then grabbed a tea towel to dry the plates. "I'm going to make hot chocolate. Levi's a little embarrassed at his outburst. I told him you wouldn't care."

He gave her an understanding look. "What outburst?" Those little lines around his eyes crinkled as he focused on her face. "Can I ask a question about the kids?"

"Sure."

"Their dad…is he not around?"

January shrugged, rolling her shoulders forward then dropping them with a sigh. "He's not cut out for full-time parenting. Never was. He's a bit chaotic. He moved to British Columbia five years ago. That's where he's from, and his family is out there. The kids will go visit him for two weeks after school lets out, but that's the extent of his ability to care from them."

They'd probably spend those two weeks at their grand-parents' farm, too, but that was probably too much infor-mation to share.

Seth nodded. "So you stepped into the role of guardian."

"I was happy to," she quickly added. "I've been a constant in their lives, so it made the most sense."

"Sure." He glanced around. "Have you always lived here with them?"

She blinked. Was it a surprise that he didn't know much about her life? When she knew more than she liked to admit about his? "No. I moved back in last year after I decided to sell my house and build a new place."

He absorbed that information as he rinsed out the sink. "How is it, being back under this roof?"

"It's…fine. Good. I mean, it's been August's house for years now. It's totally different upstairs, she's knocked down walls and moved rooms around." *You should see it,* she almost added, then changed her mind.

No, he shouldn't.

"Anyway, we're figuring it out. I am definitely looking

forward to school ending next month. It's very hard to be in the parent role around homework and school responsibilities when Aunt January has also always been Ms. Howe, the teacher." She gave him a rueful smile. "That's our biggest stumbling block. They think I'm on their teacher's side."

He leaned in a little. "I'm having flashbacks. I always thought you were on the teacher's side, too."

She groaned. "I wasn't."

"No, I know that now." He scrubbed his jaw. "When I went to RMC, I almost failed out that first year. I had to confess that I'd had the world's greatest tutor for two years, and needed that kind of academic support."

"Oh, Seth." She'd had no idea. "Did you get it?"

"I did. I had a really supportive professor who saw my potential, and she helped me get back on track. None of my peer mentors were as good as you, though." His cheeks darkened. "I owe you a much belated thank you for that."

She didn't know what to do with that information. It made her so happy, so bittersweetly relieved and honoured, and yet it felt like it was two decades too late. She wished she'd known that at the time. Wished they'd been able to get past their broken hearts to stay in touch.

More than anything else, the return of Seth to her life had made her realize just how much she'd mourned the loss of her high school best friend. She was able to put their intimate relationship in a box and almost forget it, but he had been her go-to person whenever she needed to talk.

She'd never managed to find another quite like him.

9

JANUARY TWISTED, ignoring the distant beeping. All she could focus on was his hot breath on her thigh, the way his shoulders pressed her legs apart, and that firm hold he had on her right breast, his thumb stroking back and forth as his lips got closer and closer—

Trill.

The beeping had stopped, and was now replaced by another noise, and it was even more distracting.

She rolled over and buried her face in the soft pillow, desperate for another few minutes with—

No. She shot upright in bed.

That noise was her second alarm. She was alone in her bed, and she'd hit snooze at least once. *Twice,* she realized after snatching the offending phone off the bedside table.

She ran downstairs, unlocked the door for Seth and his passengers, all of whom would be arriving any moment, and put on coffee. Then she darted back up to get dressed and bang on bedroom doors.

When she returned, her favourite pilot—*don't think of him like that, don't look at his shoulders, and* do not *think about his mouth*—was standing at the coffee station, two steaming mugs in front of him.

He glanced sideways. "Coffee?"

"Thanks." She nodded as she scooted behind the counter and turned on her computer.

A mug appeared next to her hand. "Two sugars and a bit of cream."

Exactly how she took it. She frowned, then glanced up.

"That's right, yeah?"

"Yeah."

"Good." He glanced at her computer with clear direction. "About that lunch I mentioned." *Check your calendar.* "How does Tuesday sound? I'm actually training a new pilot this weekend and she's going to be taking some of my flights next week as a test run. So I'll have Tuesday and Thursday free."

She grabbed the mug and took a fortifying inhale. "A new pilot?"

"Yeah."

"Wow."

"We'll see. I'm hoping it's wow. It's earlier than I planned—hiring people was year five or six on the business plan."

"Where are you in that?"

"Year four."

"Wow, again." She closed her eyes. She just needed a minute with her coffee.

She could hear Seth almost chuckling. Not quite laughing at her, but he was clearly amused. Well, joke was on him. She was still half-asleep and her brain was screaming at her to get back to that sex dream that was almost certainly about him. He wouldn't be laughing if he found that out, now would he? She was glad her subconscious hadn't shown her his face, looking up at her from between her thighs. The general vibe that it was probably Seth going down on her was distracting enough on its own. *You can't control your dreams.* She was hanging a lot on that defence.

"So…lunch." His voice was warm and low, and when she blinked her eyes open again, he was leaning against the counter, peering at her computer again. "Tuesday?"

"You're serious."

"Yeah."

"Why?" The honest question tumbled out of her.

"Because we have a lot to catch up on," he finally said. "And I want to know more about your new house."

She raised a skeptical eyebrow. Not that she wasn't interested—she was nosy as hell about all things Seth Kincaid—but she didn't need friendship charity from him.

"How about, I don't have anyone else to talk to about my amazing business plan?"

She laughed. "What about this new pilot you're hiring?"

"Not the same thing." He leaned in all the way as someone approached outside. "Nobody else says *wow* the way you do."

It was the sex dream warmth that was doing a number on her, not the way his voice caught as he said that.

Right?

They both straightened up and she clicked on her calendar. "Tuesday? Noon?"

He gave her a thumbs up, then moved out of the way so his passenger could check in.

———

Four days later, Seth liberated the vintage truck from the garage. "I promise I'm only driving her to Mac's for lunch."

"Do not take her on the highway," Josh warned. "She's not ready for the big time yet."

Seth decided not to tell January that detail about their ride. She was waiting outside the marina office when he pulled into the parking lot. He hopped out and joined her. She pointed at his plane. "Why does your plane say Fly North Aviation, and not Kincaid Air Ferry?"

Which was the name of the account from which he paid her invoices. She'd been paying attention. "I rebranded a couple of years ago. Kept the same business name, because that was a hassle to set up, but changed the website and logo. Look big, act big, and people think you're big."

"Huh."

"I know it's a bit obnoxious, but—"

"No. Not at all. Are you kidding? It's really clever." She turned toward the truck. "And what is this?"

"Josh's current project. I borrowed her."

"I could have driven."

"But then we wouldn't get to ride Betty."

"He named the truck?"

"He names all his vehicles."

"He's never shared that detail with me." She chuckled as she strolled around to the passenger side, then tried the door. "Uh… Betty doesn't want to let me in."

He jogged around to join her. "Sorry. She's a work in progress. Here, let me help you." His fingers slid over hers as he reached for the handle. When he couldn't jimmy it loose, he rested one hand on January's hip, moving her to the side more. Then he stepped up against the door and gave it a good hip check.

"There you go." He opened the door for her, resisting the urge to sweep his hand around her and "help" her into the truck. They weren't even at Mac's yet and he'd touched her two times too many.

It was probably time to name and shame his desire for her. As he stalked around the truck, he told himself he wouldn't look at her tits in that silky top—because she was back to a professional teacher outfit today, and he liked it a little too much—but then when he slid into the driver's seat, she was turned to the side, looking at him expectantly.

Cleavage very subtly right there. *Don't look down.*

He didn't. Gold star for adult behaviour.

"I forgot to tell you," she said as he buckled up. "I talked to our fuel supplier about adding a pump for aviation fuel, and they have a program that subsidizes the pump installation, so we're going ahead with it."

His brain skipped a few beats, then dropped into the right groove. "That's great."

She paused a beat, then exhaled. "It's hard to have confidence in revitalizing the marina sometimes, but we have to try new things. And August and I are both excited about tapping into the float plane market. Especially with the new brewery."

"Oh?"

"Josh hasn't told you?"

Seth searched his memory. "Not that I can remember?"

"Do you know Campbell Mills?"

"Don't think so."

"Army guy. Well, former army. He's started a couple of

businesses that primarily employ veterans. A moving company and a clothing line."

Seth knew the type. "Okay."

"He's bought the empty lot behind your brother's garage." She pointed in the direction of the road, aiming a little south. If the marina building wasn't in the way, he'd be able to see it. "They're building a microbrewery, and plan to be licensed and have a patio."

"That's exciting."

"Yeah." Her brows knitted together.

He should start the truck. But he wanted to know more about whatever just made her frown. "Is it not exciting?"

"No, it is. It's just…complicated. I want the harbour to be revitalized, of course I do."

From where his truck was parked, Seth couldn't see the derelict motel that sat just south of the marina, across from the future site of the microbrewery. He wondered if this Mills guy had a development plan for the motel, too, but didn't want to put worries in her head if they weren't already there. "What would your vision for the harbour be, if it were up to you?"

She shrugged. "I don't know. That's a good question."

"I remember coming here for parties with my parents."

She sucked in a quick breath. "That was a long time ago."

"Yeah."

He pointed the truck up the hill, away from the harbour and into town. And he let her little nervous inhale echo over and over in his head until they arrived at Mac's Diner.

So when he turned the truck off and the cab was silent again, he didn't open his door right away. They turned toward each other at the same time. "Would you rather I don't bring up—"

"This could be dangerous," she said.

He played it as light as he could, even though he knew what she meant. "Having lunch?"

That made her smile. "Revisiting the past."

"That doesn't need to be what we're doing."

"Good." She puffed out her cheeks and gave him a weak smile. "I'm not sure I have the bandwidth."

And if she didn't have space in her life to revisit the past, the unspoken addendum would also be true. She definitely didn't have room to explore the future.

Which left the present, and lunch. "Luckily, I'm only interested in the here and now. And sharing my fries, if you need them."

She relaxed visibly. "Sorry. I'm…edgy."

"You've had a lot happen in the last…what, two months? Your sister's departure, the kids adjusting to life with a very awesome aunt, the dock getting damaged, and then your high school boyfriend shows up and threatens to talk about long ago fun times."

She laughed. Her eyes crinkled, her gaze ducking briefly, but springing right back up to meet his. "One of those things is not quite as heavy as the others, despite my reaction."

"The straw that broke the camel's back, though, right?"

She nodded. "Another time…it would be different."

"Got it." He opened his door. "No pressure. No drama. Just hanging out."

Which sounded a lot like how their relationship started in high school, too, but he wasn't going to bring that up. He shouldn't even think it to himself.

As she joined him at the front of the truck, she lifted

her gaze to meet his. "That's the second time you've explicitly referred to the fact we once dated."

"As opposed to being *old friends*?"

"Mmm."

"Maybe I'm getting more comfortable here."

She smiled. "Good. Now buy me lunch and tell me more about your business plans."

"I could go on and on about that stuff for hours. It turns out I'm something of a business nerd?"

"I love it." She twirled around in a circle. "Keep going. Talk nerdy to me."

"I didn't realize how central spreadsheets would be to my ideal life, but they really do make me happy."

"Yes!" She pumped her fist in the air.

Because *this fucking small town*, that was also the moment that Will and Catie stepped out of the diner.

Will glanced at January, who was still laughing, then over to Seth, who silently commanded his brother to say absolutely nothing. His command was ineffective. "What are you guys doing here?"

January answered in the most literal way possible. "Grabbing lunch."

Seth grinned on the inside. No additional details offered.

And inside, there were other people who recognized them. Jake Foster, who was building January's new house, came over and reintroduced himself. He'd been in Owen's year at school, but he seemed to remember Seth. "It's been a long time, man. We just hear about you, and sometimes catch a glimpse of your plane."

"Nice to see you again. I hear you've hired one of my neighbours." They talked about Linda briefly, then Jake said he'd let them get to their meal.

But other people came over, and the conversation repeated a few times, sans the personal small world connection. The whole time, Seth was deeply aware of January carefully watching him handle all of them with as few words as possible.

When they were finally left alone with the menus, he took a long, steadying breath.

Then he refocused his attention where he wanted it to be anyway—on January—and blocked out that pulse of introverted alarm. "What else do you want to know about my spreadsheets?"

She laughed softly. "How about, how do you decide when it's time to hire someone?"

He didn't really know the answer there. He'd made the decision spontaneously, which was very unlike him. "It's always going to be scary. But if hiring out a job that someone else can do frees up more of your time to do something only *you* can do for your business, that's probably a good sign."

She fiddled with a sugar packet, and then the waitress came over to take their order.

Was she thinking about hiring part-time staff to help with the marina? She probably should—it was shocking that they ran it by themselves, even if it wasn't that busy. But that raised another question. How profitable—or not— was the marina? The more Seth saw of it, the more he was convinced it was *not*.

Why did they hang on to it if it was such an albatross?

Once they were alone again, he picked the conversation back up. "Is this a hypothetical, or do you want to hire someone for the season?"

"I mean, most of the time I am *not* busy." She held her hands out wide, then poked at the cell phone that sat next to her hand. "I can take a lunch break, I can run errands…I could probably play hooky for an entire afternoon and nobody would notice. So it's not like I *need* someone to make time for me. But on the other hand, I haven't dug into what else I could be doing for the business because I feel more like a caretaker while August is gone rather than a full partner."

"Are you? Full partners?"

She nodded. "I don't draw any money from the business usually. August does, when she's running it. But we both own the building. It was all we inherited from our dad. And it has a mortgage." She flinched on the last line.

Seth guessed it was debt the sisters hadn't known about when their father died.

"So while August's gone, are you working seven days a week?"

She nodded. "Some days it's only a couple of hours. And I can't afford to hire someone if we wind up being slow. Most of our tenants know to find me on the phone, anyway."

"Your 'Back in Ten Minutes' sign." Now he tapped the phone. "And why you carry August's cell with you?"

"Exactly."

"Is that what August did? Basically always on call?"

"Most of the time, yeah. In a pinch, I could cover the weekends, but…" She flushed, dark red spots appearing on her cheeks. "I have some resentment about the state my dad left the marina in, financially. I thought we should sell it. August wanted to hang on to it. So she rarely asks me to help. Which was deeply selfish on my part, I realize now."

"It's not selfish to want to protect your time," he pointed out. "Especially if you already work full-time. I just did that."

"It's not a hardship to help out," she protested. "August talked about maybe selling it when the kids are ready for university, and that was a bit of a wake-up call. Because I don't feel that same instinct the way I did when my dad died. Now I would want to preserve it, if we can."

He nodded, all out of questions. It wasn't a hardship, maybe, but it wasn't a thriving business plan either. And she wasn't selfish to not want to have to shore it up, but he wasn't going to get between sisters with an ocean between them. January was a grown-up who could fight her own battles and pick her own compromises.

"How about you? You took two days off this week from flying, so what are you doing with them instead?"

Figuring out his comfort limits around his hometown, apparently. "I've been meaning to run some analysis on the costs versus potential income of buying a new plane. I'm leasing one for the summer, but if I'm going to commit to hiring Teegan on, the investment might be wiser in a plane I own."

"Wow." She grabbed another sugar packet. "Wow, that's really…"

He grinned. "Wow?"

"Shut up, it *is*."

"I told you, I like hearing you say it. Don't stop on my account."

Their food arrived, saving them both from having to extricate themselves from where the conversation had turned.

"Your plate has more fries," she whispered.

To his eye, they looked about the same. "Feel free to even them out, then."

Her fingers darted across the table and snagged three

of his French fries. He grinned, stole one of hers back, and then they settled in to eat.

When they finally strolled out to the parking lot an hour later, he felt lighter than he had in a very long time.

"This was fun," January said once they were back in the truck. "When are you back again for an evening? We'd love to have you over for another dinner. We owe you one for the pizzas."

"I'm here all week," he heard himself saying.

That hadn't been the plan, but then he hadn't expected to laugh the whole way through lunch or actually enjoy planning a pre-wedding fundraising dance, either, which they'd ended up doing a fair bit of after filling their bellies.

"The kids have music lessons tonight, but how about tomorrow?"

"Sounds like a—" *Date.* Except it wasn't. That, too, would be dangerous. "Sounds like a plan. I'll probably be back around five, depending how the afternoon run goes."

She smiled at him, her eyes dancing. "I know. I'm the girl at the counter, remember?"

How could he forget?

After he dropped her off and returned the truck to the garage, he stood outside and looked across at the marina for a good long while.

Eventually, Josh came out to ask him what the hell he was doing.

Seth shoved his hands in his pockets. "I might need to stay here."

"Here? At my place again?"

He nodded.

"All right."

"For the summer."

Josh did a double-take. "Excuse me?"

Seth scratched his jaw. "Just from Thursday to Tuesday."

"That's most of the week. I love you, man, but we're not cuddling five nights in a row. Or any, for that matter."

"You can go stay at Will's."

Josh blinked hard. "*You* can go stay Will's."

"I need to be here." Across the road from the marina just made sense. If he was staying in town, he should be close to his plane.

"I *work* here."

"And I work across the road!"

"Since when?" Josh frowned. "Seriously, I thought you were just doing a few flights a week. Is this turning into something more permanent? Because then you really should just *move into Will's house*. Or, I don't know, *rent an apartment*."

He didn't need anything that permanent. "I have a house."

"A plane ride away."

"Yeah."

"So you want to kick me out of my place?"

"I don't know why you're being difficult about this. You can take your porn with you."

Josh flipped him the bird. "I don't know why you're being weird about—" He cut himself off. Stopped. Frowned again. "Wait, is this—"

"It's nothing."

A long pause stretched between them. Seth's heart hammered in his chest. This was a stupid idea, but he'd committed to it. It was fine. No biggie. A perfectly weird but reasonable request. "Will's house is nicer. Central air. Those new carpets."

Josh nodded sagely. "You know what? That's a great

point. He has the sports TV package and better water pressure. I'll just pack a bag and get out of your hair."

"Great. Thanks." Seth scrubbed his hand over his jaw. "And I need to borrow a vehicle."

"You're stealing my home and you want to drive Betty, too?"

He grinned, feeling wolfish and alive. "Yeah. Exactly."

10

JANUARY SPENT most of the following afternoon thinking about what to make Seth for dinner, and then immediately reminding herself that she was *not* making *Seth* dinner, but cooking for herself and the kids, and Seth was going to join them.

Spaghetti, because the kids loved it. But the really good version, with the roasted tomato sauce and slow-braised meatballs. And the good parm, because sure, the marina was a money pit and she was at the end of her rope a lot of the time, but good parm made a lot of things more manageable.

It was a gorgeous afternoon, sunny and warm, so she took the phone outside and read in the hammock while she waited for the plane to return. Once she spotted it, she told her pulse to settle the heck down, and went inside in case any of the returning passengers would need anything.

They didn't.

She watched as one by one they made their way to the parking lot and left, and then Seth was in the doorway, looking windswept and sun-warmed and hungry. She allowed herself a moment of pure pleasure at the sight of him, then locked it down to *hey, old friend*. Never again would she make the mistake of forgetting that his heart could only beat elsewhere, that Pine Harbour wasn't the place for him, and as it was very much the place for her, there was no bridging that divide.

He paused, too, looking at her for a beat before lifting his nose in the air. "Is that tomato sauce?"

"Spaghetti for dinner," she said briskly. "I hope that's all right."

"Amazing."

She shut down her computer, and was about to tell Seth to hang up the "Back in Ten" sign for the evening when someone approached down the path from the parking lot. Seth glanced over his shoulder, then opened the door for Isla.

She gave January a friendly wave, then handed Seth a large white cardboard box. "Dessert delivery."

January waited until Isla was gone, then raised one eyebrow at Seth. "Do you realize what rumour you've just started?"

"No." He returned her raised eyebrow look. "Do you want to be more specific?"

"Nope." She moved past him, flipped the lock and hung up the sign, then headed upstairs.

He followed. "Isla texted me, asking if it was true that I was staying in town this week, and did I want to come to their house for dinner. I declined because I already had plans."

"Mmm."

"Should I have not requested dessert for my hungry hosts, Summer and Levi?" He set the bakery box on the counter and gave her a playful grin when she turned to look at him. "That is how I explained dinner, by the way. That the kids invited me over. Artistic license."

"That's a good cover story."

He laughed. "Ouch. One might get the impression that you don't want to be associated with me. Are we sneaking around here?"

An excellent question. What were they doing?

Instead of answering it, she busied herself with pulling the baking dishes out of the oven. She'd used two Dutch ovens today, still traumatized from the exploding glass tray.

"January?"

"Nobody's going to gossip about us," she said, not really believing herself. "Especially not Isla. That was silly to bring up."

"Hey." He reached out and gently touched her hand, his touch lighting up her nerves with the warm contact. "It's nobody's business but ours if we're getting to know each other again."

"Agreed."

"But if people do talk—that's fine. Let them."

"That is my general policy." She checked the pasta water. It was boiling. "I should put the spaghetti in now."

"Are you worried about gossip?"

Wow, he really wasn't going to let it go. She stopped and turned to look at him fully. "No."

He gave her a cocky half grin. "Do you want to sneak in a cookie before dinner?"

That sounded perfect. "Yes, please."

He handed her one of Isla's famous chocolate chip cookies, and she took a restorative bite. If he didn't have a problem with half of his family already knowing they were hanging out, or whatever they were doing, that was fine by her. It was confusing as heck, but she could manage that. Boundaries, she kept repeating to herself, even as they got kind of fuzzy.

Because right now, standing toe to toe in her kitchen, eating cookies in a very comfortable silence, it was hard to tell where the lines should be drawn. Was the frisson of nerves she felt every time they touched accidentally all one-sided? Could friends hug, or kiss, or share other intimacies?

What would it be like to kiss him after all these years? What would his skin taste like?

January froze, the last bite of her cookie pausing at her mouth as a weird new thought flashed through her mind. When did she forget what Seth tasted like?

She'd compared every man she ever dated to the crystal clear memory of him. Her imperfectly sweet and predictably selfish high school boyfriend, who couldn't allow himself to love her because that would mean tying himself to this town.

And yet few had ever tasted half as good. Nobody had ever made her feel nearly as safe as his seventeen-year-old arms had.

She had known him inside and out. Memorized the weight of his body and the singe of his tongue. Until he strode back into her life, and that memory evaporated, apparently.

"January?"

"Mmm?"

"You're…" His lips tugged up on one side. "Staring at me."

"You have some crumbs on your…" she reached out and brushed an imaginary bit of cookie off the corner of his mouth. The lie came far too easily. An excuse to touch him.

To build a new memory.

That frisson of excitement zapped through her again.

It was nobody's business what they were doing. It didn't make any sense from the outside, so she wasn't going to try to explain it. Not even to Seth. *Boundaries.* Under no circumstances could she allow herself to fall in love with this man. Fun friendship only.

But she could have a lot of fun in secret. And maybe on the other side of this summer, she'd stop comparing every man she ever kissed to a teenage memory.

———

SETH COULDN'T BREATHE. He didn't want to, either. January's soft touch at the corner of his mouth had stopped his heart, wham, and now it was like time had slowed as she thought about her next move.

He had some very good suggestions, but he couldn't risk breaking the—

"Is Seth here?"

Mood broken, immediately. January turned to her niece and nephew with a big smile on her face. "Mm-hmm. And he brought cookies."

"Oh!"

"Which are for after dinner."

"But Seth is eating one right now."

He held up the damning evidence. "I didn't know the rules, sorry. But dinner's going to be soon, apparently, so...my bad."

Levi giggled.

Seth searched for a change of subject. "Hey, I meant to

say this last week, but I really like how much this place has changed."

January grabbed the lifeline. "That's all August. She has an eye for design. Basically if she sees something she likes on HGTV, she figures out how to do it herself." She gestured to Levi. "Do you want to give Seth the tour?"

The sprawling apartment above the marina office had three split levels. The kitchen was nestled in the heart of the home, with the living room taking up the other half of this level. A simple sectional dominated the bright space, which had once been crammed full with two sofas and mismatched reclining chairs, and panelled in dark wood. A picture window overlooked the harbour, and that wasn't new—Seth recognized a crack in the outer glass. But it looked refreshed, somehow.

"This is where we play video games…" Levi said, gesturing to the TV on the wall.

"And do your homework," January called from the kitchen.

The kid rolled his eyes. "And that."

"I used to play video games in here with your aunt and your mom." Seth nodded to the PlayStation. "Nothing this fancy, though."

"My aunt used to play video games?"

"She sure did."

"You want to play with me now?"

"How about we finish the tour first?"

Levi flushed. "Oh, right. So yeah, this is the living room…" He led Seth down the hall and up the half-flight of stairs to the bedrooms behind the kitchen. Once upon a time they'd been January and August's rooms, but now they were for Levi and his sister, and had cool connected closets that hadn't existed back in the day.

The bathroom was fully remodelled, too, and it had a tiny skylight he didn't remember. "Your mom is pretty talented, isn't she?"

Levi nodded. "She loves those TV shows. Gets all sorts of ideas."

The final flight of stairs went up to the top floor, which teenage Seth and January had never been allowed to explore.

Levi paused there and yelled downstairs to his aunt, "Can I show him my mom's room and your room?"

January's lovely laugh drifted up to them. "Yes, of course. There's some laundry on the bed. Just ignore that."

Seth grinned at the candor.

Halfway up the stairs, Levi pointed to a window which Seth was very familiar with. "This is how we crawl out onto the roof."

Seth forced a curiously innocent look onto his face, trying not to think of all the times he had waited on the other side of that window. He would climb up the antenna tower and wait for January to crawl out and meet him—and once, when he'd come over while her parents had been out, but then they'd returned early, she'd shoved him out this window and wished him good luck in making his way down in the dark.

Best night of his young life.

Still one of his favourite memories of all time.

Do not get a chubby on this house tour, he thought to himself. "Do you go out there?"

Levi nodded, a pleased expression spreading across his face, and cranked the window open. Then he hoisted himself up and pushed himself through the window frame. "See? It's easy."

Memories assaulted Seth as he gazed out onto the flat

shingles. It had felt easy to teenage January, too. And now as an adult, he wondered how January had been able to crawl out there so many times without her parents knowing.

Or maybe they had known and just didn't care. Because it was, now in hindsight, very close to their bedroom.

Then Levi hopped down, closed the window, and finished the tour.

This top floor was clearly a mother's retreat from the world. In August's room, a big bed was set as far away from the door as possible, under another picture window overlooking the harbour, and another one of those walk-through closets had been constructed between the bed and a remodelled bathroom.

That bed was the one covered in laundry. Next door was a room that he instantly recognized as January's. Bedroom furniture had been added to August's office, probably, although January had made it her own space. Three-dimensional jewellery stands decorated the top of both her dresser and the desk under the small window, and a packed bookcase in the corner overflowed with paperbacks.

Plus the room smelled amazing, which probably wasn't something he was supposed to notice.

"My mom organized Aunt January's closet," Levi said, pulling those doors open. This room didn't have a walk-in closet, but August had clearly put a lot of custom effort into maximizing the small space for her sister.

All of it was beautiful, and clearly a work of love. He could see why January was proud of what August had done.

They finished in the living room, where Levi flowed

right back into his video game. Seth watched for a minute, then returned to the kitchen just in time to drain the spaghetti.

January called for Summer, who liked to be in charge of grating the parmesan cheese, and then they sat down together.

They talked about school—just a few weeks left until summer break—and how his flights had gone that day. The soul-searing tension Seth had felt in the kitchen had faded, mostly out of necessity: he couldn't be consumed by thoughts of January's fingertips on his skin and carry on a conversation at the same time.

But January, too, seemed to carefully steer him to safe topics. She gave him the update on the avfuel pump. "August noticed that the app you mentioned has advertising packages. Any thoughts on if that would be worthwhile for us? As a user of the app, do you notice the ads? It looks like there's enough traffic to justify it as an experiment. It would be great to advertise the new availability of avfuel in this area, for people coming in this direction."

And he was a sucker for a good business conversation. He ran down the pros and cons of paid advertising, in his experience, and some alternatives that would be free, but take more time, like spending time in the app forums. "Brand promotion is so much more than advertising, I've discovered. Never thought being a pilot would mean doing deep dives into marketing podcasts, but here we are."

"Any good ones you can recommend for a marina manager?"

He grinned. "I'll send you some links."

Levi cleared his throat, clearly wanting to shift the

topic. "Aunt January, Seth says that you used to play video games."

She laughed, a pleased chuckle that Seth wanted to hear more of. "Did he, now?"

"What games did you play?"

Her brows pulled together, like she was trying to recollect.

"Mortal Kombat," Seth prompted. "And all the Mario games."

"That's right. And then Sim City on the computer." She gave a happy sigh. "I'd forgotten how much I loved that game."

Levi beamed. "We can all play Mario after dinner."

First they had to finish eating, with Seth wanting seconds, and then he volunteered to help Summer do the dishes while Levi and January worked on some homework together.

But once the kitchen was clean and Levi had survived the math review, they gathered in the living room. Seth sprawled at one end of the sectional, January at the other, and the kids in between.

No chance to elbow her in good sport, or lose his mind over the soft press of her thigh against his.

For the best.

What are you doing, Kincaid?

He didn't have a good answer for that. He was playing video games, and laughing, and…

"Seth! Come on!" Levi howled.

And getting distracted. He refocused on the screen and promised himself he could explore those thoughts in detail once he was alone.

At eight-thirty, January pulled the guardian card and put an end to the fun. "It's almost bedtime here."

"Noooo," Levi protested.

"Yessss," January said, a smile firmly in place on her face, but Seth caught the tightness in her voice.

"Is that usually a bit of a struggle, or did I make it worse?" he asked as the kids chased each other upstairs, arguing about who should have the first shower.

"Nightly battle. And my patience is pretty low at the end of the day, which doesn't help. It's this drawn-out routine. They're not like toddlers or anything, so I can't complain, because they are self-sufficient."

He held up his hand. "Let me stop you there. You *are* allowed to complain. We all need pressure valves. Feel free to tell me all about it."

She laughed. "It just takes them so *long*. First they have showers, although some nights Summer pretends she wants to have a shower in the morning. Of course, she never wakes up early enough for that, so then there's a debate about the likelihood of that happening. I've reached the point in the day where I just want a cup of tea and a book and some *silence* for twenty minutes before I nod off, and instead it's a stream of up and down and whispered explanations. Can I have a back scratch? Can I listen to an audiobook? I need some water. I forgot this homework needed to go in my backpack. And then the other one will come out and say, I need some water too."

"That's exhausting."

"Mmm."

"How long until August comes home?"

She sighed. "Three and a half months. But actually, they're going to see their dad and grandparents in a month. And I will miss them terribly when they're gone."

"I bet you will." Seth's pulse thudded heavily in his neck. "How long will they be gone?"

She hesitated before answering. Took her time thinking about how much she wanted to tell him, maybe. But then her gaze lifted, meeting his, and he was right back in the kitchen, unable to breathe again. "Two weeks," she whispered. "First half of July."

11

Seth: I want to get Levi something. A surprise gift.
Something small. Any ideas?
Will: Levi Howe-Martin?
Seth: Yes.
Will: I have questions.
Seth: I'm only looking for gift ideas at this time.
Will: Where are you?
Seth: Nevermind.
Will: Come over to my place. I'm packing. I might
have something here that would work.

On the one hand, it felt like a pretty clear trap for Will to question him on a bunch of shit Will had no business asking about. On the other hand, the house of a nerdy school principal *was* probably a good place to find a token gift for an eleven-year-old boy. Also, Seth knew better than to ignore one of his brothers. When he did that, it inevitably hit the group chat. They were all pros at leveraging the group against each other.

Seth: On my way.

Betty cooperated on the drive across town, but that's where his luck ran out. Because Will's vehicle wasn't the only one in the drive—in a manner of speaking. There was a baby stroller on the walkway, which meant that Owen and/or Kerry was there with their daughter.

Nothing like dodging questions in front of an audience.

He took a deep breath and let himself in.

Owen was stretched out on the couch, a sleeping Lila on his chest. He waved and silently pointed upstairs.

Since Seth wasn't in a rush to be grilled by their brother, he took a seat instead.

"I just arrived," Owen said quietly. "She's fighting her naps big time right now. Didn't have one this afternoon, and Kerry needed a break from the teething and the fussing, so I tossed some burgers and buns in the stroller and thought she might pass out on the walk over. Fought it all the way here, and then conked out as soon as we came inside. You staying for dinner? I brought lots."

"I might." He really wanted to invite himself over to the marina again, but he was pretty sure the kids had evening activities today. He needed to learn their schedule. He nodded to the not-so-small baby. "She's growing fast."

Owen nodded. "She starts daycare next month."

"Whoa."

"Yeah. I think I told you that Kerry needed to go back part-time in the spring—the locum they'd hired to cover her patients got a full-time job elsewhere—so we've been managing between our shifts, but it's time. It's going to be a big change." Owen smoothed his big hand over Lila's sparse little curls. When she didn't stir, he carefully transitioned her to a portable playpen.

For a guy who didn't have kids, Will's house was perfectly set up for babies. Kincaid Inn, Seth mused.

"I'm going to fire up the grill," Owen said. "You want a beer?"

"Sure."

Seth followed him into the kitchen, accepted one of Will's beers, then pointed upstairs. "Does he have one?"

"Don't think so." Owen took the cap off another bottle and handed that over, too. "Drag him away from his collectibles in twenty minutes."

"Will do."

Upstairs, Seth found Will sorting through old electronics. "Beer," he grunted.

Will took it with a smirk. "Took you long enough to come upstairs."

"I was just saying hi to Owen first."

"Avoiding the elephant in the room?"

"Depends what you think that is." Seth wasn't going down easy.

"You and January."

He shrugged. "Nothing to talk about."

That was the truth. It was deeply private. And very, very fresh. He couldn't name it if he tried.

"You kicked Josh out of his apartment."

"It's a stretch to call that hovel an apartment."

"And you're having lunches together."

"One lunch." Because they hadn't had a chance to set another date.

Will shoved a few cords into a box labelled *School*, and stood up. "You really want to be that close to her all summer long?"

Yeah. Seth needed to be there—for reasons he couldn't spell out for himself, but he knew for a fact they weren't his brother's business. "Maybe I can help her with the kids, you know? That's why I want something for Levi."

Will frowned. "What's going on with the kids?"

"Nothing."

"But you want—"

"Are you asking me as their principal, or as a friend?"

An understanding look crossed Will's face, and he raised the beer, taking a long sip before he answered. "I'm asking as your brother," he finally said. "And then as January's friend. This is a small town. We all know August is away, and we all know that's hard on kids. You don't need to protect them."

But maybe he did. "He's a great kid. Both of them, Summer, too. Clever and funny. Levi's eager to help me with the plane whenever he can. I just want to show them —him, particularly—that I see him." He scratched the back of his neck. "I told January if he had any questions about being overseas, he could talk to me about that. It hasn't come up yet, though. I kind of want to..." He puffed out his cheeks. "I don't know."

"You're not doing this just to win over January."

Seth didn't even bother to try to hide that he was offended. "No, of course not. I like those kids. I'm happy to spend time with them as a friend of the family and that would be true even if—"

Will's eyebrows rose, curiosity blatant. "If...?"

"Shut up. Drink your beer and find me something Levi would love."

"Whatever it is you're doing, you don't have to do it alone."

"I'm literally just asking you for a toy or..." He cast his gaze around Will's office. "Ooh, Dungeons and Dragons. Do you have any extra dice sets?"

Will paused before answering, looking like he might want to try to change the subject back to January. But it wasn't happening. "Yeah," he finally added. "Let me grab some. Summer knows D&D, I think. We have a club at school, pretty sure she's participated." He pulled a box out of the closet, grabbed two small bags, and tossed them in Seth's direction. "I'm going to have to build an office in Catie's backyard. There's no way all of this stuff is ever going to fit into our house. My camping and climbing gear has already filled her garage."

"It's a good thing she loves you."

Will grinned broadly at that. "It sure is."

"Thanks for these. Owen's started grilling, by the way. Dinner in ten minutes."

"Be right down."

From downstairs, he heard a confused cry. "And Lila's up. I'll go grab her."

Will saluted him with his beer bottle, and Seth jogged back downstairs, happy to have mostly escaped in one piece.

Until dinner.

And tomorrow, and the next day. Until Will talked to Catie, and if she circled back to January…

Lila had pulled herself up, holding on to the edge of the playpen, her eyes wide and watery, her lip sticking out to great effect.

"Hey munchkin," he murmured as he scooped her up. "Want to go see your dad?"

She let out a shaky cry. She might not say *Dada* yet, but she knew the word.

"Yeah, let's go find him. He's outside." He pushed the slider door to the back deck open, and Owen turned as soon as he heard Lila's cry.

"Hey, baby girl. Come here." She reached for him, clinging tightly, glaring back at Seth like he was the monster who put her in the playpen in the first place.

He grinned. "You're safe now."

Owen chuckled, too. "Can you take over the grilling? I'm going to grab her sippy cup."

That was a weird déjà vu moment, jerking Seth back twenty years. To when Owen was a too-young dad, and Becca was the toddler on his hip, and Seth desperately didn't want to be in the same position.

He grabbed the long-handled spatula and flipped the burgers.

"Did you get what you came for?" Seth heard the question, or at least he heard Owen's voice, but he hadn't snapped to an answer before his brother added, "Seth?"

"Yeah."

"Everything okay?"

"Mmm." He flipped the burgers again, then turned off the BBQ. "These are done. Cheese?"

"On all of them."

Seth slapped the cheese on, then lowered the grill lid to help keep the heat in and melt it.

"So Will finally asked about January?"

"Fuck." Seth hung his head back and stared at the sky. "You really like everyone being up in your business like this?"

"You know, I don't really remember anyone rooting for me and Kerry this way. We managed to keep it truly on the down-low."

"Jesus, who is rooting for me and January?"

"Everyone."

"Well, that needs to stop."

"Why?"

Seth took a long pull off his beer. "Do I like January? Yes. Am I looking to spend time with her this summer—on pain of death, do not repeat this to anyone other than Kerry—yes. I'm not trying to keep my feelings about January *secret*, but some things should be private."

Owen didn't respond to that. Maybe he sensed there was more coming.

Seth opened the BBQ and pulled the burgers off onto a tray. "We cannot be together. Not in any kind of way someone might root for. I am not a fairy tale ending for her, you understand? There's too much water under that bridge."

"Like what?"

"January was pregnant."

Owen cleared his throat. "I'm sorry. Is she okay? I guess it was a surprise, but at your age, maybe not the worst news—"

"Not this summer." The words rasped up his throat like sandpaper. "In high school."

His brother didn't have anything to say, suddenly. The silence stretched between them, heavy. Loaded. Then finally, "What happened?"

"She— We— It wasn't what either of us wanted. She had an abortion."

"That's understandable."

Out of the corner of his eye, Seth saw Owen rock back on his heels. His own baby in his arms, so much like Becca was all those years ago.

Seth couldn't look at him properly. "It didn't feel that way at the time. To the outside world, I mean. But it was right for us."

"She was sure?"

Seth nodded.

"Then that's all that matters."

Seth exhaled roughly. "I know."

"Does it feel good to share it now?"

He laughed. "Yeah, actually."

"Then can I yell at you a little for not sharing then? Did you tell *anyone*?"

There hadn't been anyone else to tell. Seth shook his head. "Fuck off." But he was smiling, and the words came out soft. Appreciative.

"You're a dumbass. Carrying that shit around on your own for twenty years?"

"Becca was still in diapers. No way was I going to tell you I'd gotten myself in the same situation, and I was taking a different path."

"Then it wasn't the same situation, was it?" Owen shrugged. "I don't know. Maybe it's easy for me to say this now, but I think I would have understood. I *definitely* understand now. You know that, right?"

"Yeah. And I love Becca with all my heart, you know." Seth rolled his shoulders. "I never judged you for having her. She's amazing."

"Don't worry, I know it. But it was a tough path, too. It has to be a choice, or it would be misery for everyone. It *was* misery, at times, even though I wouldn't change a thing." Owen looked at him carefully. "Why are you telling me now?"

"I can't tell Will. He works with her. It's not my story to give to him. But I need him not to get any bright ideas about playing matchmaker. I'm just January's friend. And I will always be that friend for her, as much as she wants, but…"

"I get it." Owen clapped him on the shoulder, pulling

Seth's gaze around so they were eye to eye. "I'll shut him down. He means well, though."

"Intentions don't mean shit if they hurt her."

Owen frowned. "You're worried about *Will* hurting her? Not you?"

"Of course I'm worried about hurting her. But I'm not making any wild, romantic promises, and I'm pretty sure she's clear-eyed about me. I mean, she might not even be interested in anything other than a tentative friendship, for real, and I wouldn't blame her one bit. But if she did want to hang out more this summer…" Those two weeks when her niece and nephew would be gone, for example. "I wouldn't want to talk about it with anyone. Not because I don't love you guys, and appreciate your earnest support"—Owen smirked at that—"but because it will end at the end of the summer."

"You sure about that?"

He had to be. "She's building a house here."

"So?"

She was building a forever home, and Seth had planted a sign in the ground somewhere else. But it sounded stupid in his head, so he wasn't going to say it out loud. "I'm leaving at the end of the summer."

Owen didn't say anything else. He just opened the slider door and gestured for Seth to take the burgers inside.

But the clear censure in his brother's silence still stung. Owen's understanding only extended so far, and apparently not to mediocre excuses.

———

THE NEXT DINNER invitation happened the day after Seth's visit to Will's house. January sent Levi over to the garage to share the news they were making Dagwood sandwiches, with "all the fixings, whatever that means."

"I bet it means your aunt bought a bunch of different toppings."

"I don't like toppings on my sandwiches."

"Do you think your aunt does?"

"Probably. She likes fancy food."

Seth filed that tidbit away. "I would be happy to join you for dinner. I also like fancy food. Especially fancy sandwiches. Wait here with Josh, I want to grab something from upstairs."

Josh handed Levi a torque wrench. "You can help me tighten these lug nuts. Did you know that my brother kicked me out of my own apartment?"

"Yes." Levi giggled as Seth pushed his way through the back door, rolling his eyes.

When he returned, the kid was covered in grease and grinning from ear to ear. And his eyes still lit up even more when he caught sight of the D&D handbook Seth was holding. "What's that?"

"That's *mine*," Josh said, sighing.

Seth raised his eyebrows.

"And Levi is totally welcome to borrow it."

"Damn straight," Seth muttered. "Have you ever played D&D, kid?"

"No."

"It's been a long time for me, too, but my brothers and I used to play all the time, and I thought maybe we could play together sometime. You'll have to read this book to learn about it."

"Okay," Levi breathed.

"And you need special dice." Seth held out the two bags. "So these are for you and your sister. You can pick which colours you want, and give the other bag to her."

"Does she have to play with us?"

"It would be nice to include her. Plus a little birdie told me that she knows how."

"That's because she knows how to do everything, because she's older than me."

Seth thought about the way his two older brothers had tag-teamed on the January topic the day before. "I'm very familiar with how annoying that is, trust me."

At the marina, January was down on the dock, spraying down the fish cleaning stations. She was wearing cut-off jean shorts again, her feet shoved into rubber boots, and the first sight of her hit him square in the chest.

"Go on inside," he said to Levi. "I'm going to talk to your aunt."

The boy scampered away with his book and dice.

By the time he reached her, January was done with the hose, and handed it to him when he reached for it.

"Wind it up and put it away?" he asked.

"Please and thank you." She pointed to the bucket of fish offal at her feet. "I'll just dispose of this, and then be right with you."

He followed her. "Busy day today?"

He always flew out in the early morning, and returned in the mid-afternoon lull, before the boats returned at the end of the day. So he usually saw her at her down periods, which was nice—it allowed him to talk to her more—but he missed out on seeing her in action.

"It was non-stop all day, which made me happy. Mostly fishing, but we had a plane stop in for fuel." She beamed at him. "Thank you."

"Is that why I've been invited for Dagwood sandwiches?"

"Only the finest food for friends of Howe's Marina." She winked at him. "But seriously, yes. It is a thank you dinner. If sandwiches count as dinner."

"They definitely do. No thanks required, though. You did the work in making it happen quickly."

Her smile softened at his praise, shifting from outwardly grateful to inwardly pleased. It looked good on her. It reached her eyes, making them bright and intensely pretty.

Then she blinked, her golden-brown eyelashes brushing her cheeks, and looked down at the now-empty bucket. "Gotta wash this, and then we can scrub up for dinner."

He fell into step beside her. "I should tell you I gave Levi some twenty-sided dice and Josh's old D&D handbook."

"How did Josh take that?" She glanced sideways, her expression teasing.

"Not well."

She laughed. "Did Levi like them?"

"Yeah, he's pretty excited."

"That was a nice thing, then. And it wasn't like Josh had probably looked at that book in years."

"I had to dig it out of a box that he hadn't bothered to unpack after pulling it out of Owen's crawlspace."

"He's cranky."

"My brother?" Seth shrugged. "Yeah."

"Do you know what that's all about?"

He had some ideas. But after telling Owen that some things were private, could he share Josh's demons with January?

I'm pretty good with secrets.

She always had been.

He opened his mouth to tell her, and she shook her head. "No, wait, don't. That was nosy of me."

"You can be nosy about Kincaid business." The Kincaids were all nosy about her, after all. Not that he'd given them much.

That got him another smile, but she also busied herself washing out the bucket, and then she changed the subject to sandwiches.

———

DINNER AT JANUARY'S became a regular thing.

And then one night, while the kids were fighting upstairs about who would take the first shower, January gestured to the couch. "Do you want to stay? I don't know how long bedtime will take, but we could watch something once they're finally out?"

Once upon a time, putting on a movie would have been cover to fool around quietly.

But in the two weeks of him coming over every other day or so, she hadn't given him any signals that this was anything other than friends sharing food, because it was nicer to eat with another grown up—and two pretty entertaining kids—than to eat alone.

He had a small catalogue of moments that might have been the start of something, if circumstances were different. The cookie crumb swipe at the corner of his mouth. The bright and warm spark in her eyes. A long, lingering laugh that started to feel like a private joke just between the two of them when the kids weren't paying attention.

But she didn't touch him again, other than the most

platonic nudges that didn't feel platonic at all on his receiving end. She'd been clear about not wanting to revisit the past, too. Maybe her sense of self-preservation was stronger than his.

But she'd also said if things were different, and once the school year ended, things *would* be different. At least for two weeks. Could they find a way to reconnect then?

It wasn't like avoiding her had worked.

Twenty years should have cauterized the self-inflicted wound that was their break-up. He'd hurt himself, and her, and then stayed away out of a messy combination of regret and shame. He'd been right that it would be hard to see her again. But where he'd calculated incorrectly was on how his feelings would land. Instead of reopening that wound, seeing her again had put it in a new perspective.

It was still there. And fuck if it didn't seem small now, a deep but narrow slice into his skin that he could have treated much differently in hindsight. Because all that was left was a scar that did nothing more than tell a story.

And the most disconcerting part of the last two months had been realizing just how much he still *liked* January. Hell, their connection had renewed the second he walked through the marina office door. It had just taken him a few weeks to admit it.

Now he couldn't get enough of her. He kept filing away little tidbits of information, like the fact she took her math students on geocaching field trips and her favourite TV show was *Ted Lasso*. He'd started watching it the night it came up in conversation, and he was into season two.

Did he want to ask her if she wanted to watch a couple of episodes with him?

Fuck, yes.

Did he think he could sit next to her on a couch, alone,

while the kids were elsewhere, and not think about tugging her closer?

Probably not.

He would want to tangle his fingers in her hair and kiss all those wild wispy strands. Ghost his mouth over her temple, her cheek, her neck, the whole time whispering for her to keep watching.

God damn it. "I should go. Early morning tomorrow."

"Right." Her nod was understanding, but he didn't miss the pulse of disappointment first. *Fuck.* Maybe he should have accepted the invitation.

But he really did have an early morning. And if they were going to spend time alone together, he wanted them to truly be alone—and he wanted to be able to give her his full attention for as long as she wanted it.

When he was alone, though, he didn't go straight to sleep. He took himself in hand and stroked himself slowly, fantasizing about quiet laughs and soft skin. Secret touches under a blanket. Panting. Slim fingers replacing his. And then a tumble of limbs, her mouth on his, as he repositioned them so she was straddling him. Wet, slick secret spots. The tight, hot squeeze of her pussy around his cock.

He couldn't have her again. But he couldn't stop thinking about her, either. And it wasn't just lusty desire, although he had that by the boatload for her. The way he wanted a long, lingering hug. Just to hold her in his arms and breathe in the scent of her hair.

There wasn't anything filthy about that fantasy.

It still kept him hard, anyway. He gripped himself more firmly. When was the last time he'd jerked off to a detailed fantasy of a specific woman? Too long. Especially a fantasy as tempting as January in her kitchen. Flushed, flustered, and a little giggly. A little handsy, maybe, if he peeled his shirt off for her.

Her fingers on his chest. Trailing down his abdomen. Stopping at his belt, then her eyes, her gorgeous fucking eyes, lifting to meet his gaze with an unspoken question. Could she?

Damn straight she could.

She could peel back the layers and take him in hand. He'd lean in, bracketing her against the counter, so the space between them was real tight. Close enough so he could hear her breath catching, feel her tremble as she found a rhythm that got him going. That made him wet at the tip and throb extra big in her hand.

Her sweet, soft little hand. *"If you keep doing that, babe, I'm gonna make a mess."*

"I want to see you come."

"Just like that, then. Harder, yeah. Oh, God. January, oh...fuck..."

Seth's whole body shook with the shock of his release, his come arcing into the air before he got his dick under control. He stroked himself again, gentler now, so fucking sensitive after that mindfuck of a slide from a fantasy to words he was pretty sure they had spoken to each other.

Damn it all to hell.

He balled up his t-shirt and used it to mop up the mess he'd made. It did shit fuck all for the tangle of feelings in his chest.

12

Seth's de facto move to Pine Harbour also meant he would be more available for Bro-mittee meetings, and regular hangouts with his brothers, too. So at the end of that week, on a Saturday evening when the only reason he wasn't at the marina for dinner was because Levi and Summer had a music recital, he texted the group chat.

Seth: Anyone free for breakfast tomorrow?
Adam: I come off shift at seven, could be there at seven thirty most likely
Owen: I'm in if I can bring the baby
Owen: Kerry's up a few times in the night with her right now, so I try to give her the mornings to sleep in
Seth: Baby is a requirement, actually…You're the add-on
Will: Count me in
Josh: Can we make it not so fucking early for once, if you don't have any charter customers?

Seth: Are you using the melatonin I gave you at Christmas?

Josh: Did it ever occur to you that some people do not naturally wake at the ass-crack of dawn?

Seth: No. Sleeping in is unnatural

Josh: You're unnatural

Adam: He has a point

Josh: You don't sleep at all for thirty-six hours in a row

Adam: Hey, I was on your side, dingus

Adam: Maybe you'd be less cranky if you got more sleep

Josh: On second thought, I'm not available tomorrow

Owen: Brunch at the garage, then BYOB

Josh: Hey, that's my place!

Seth: Squatter's party rights! But if you insist, fine…we'll eat at the diner. We can make it a civilized hour, though. Eight?

Josh: Nine

Adam: No way am I staying awake until nine after the shift we're having now

Adam: Take some of that melatonin and rack out, bud

Seth: Seven thirty it is

———

JANUARY WAS READING in the hammock early Sunday morning—because it was *Sunday morning* and anything other than the most urgent of work could wait a few hours —when August's phone vibrated beside her. The "Back in Ten" sign was up, but she hadn't heard anyone approach on the path from the parking lot. Frowning, she checked the text message.

Then she grinned.

Seth: Are we planning the stag and doe this afternoon?

She tapped his name and pressed the green call button.

"Hello?" It sounded like he was out somewhere, his voice set against a cacophony of noise.

"You texted the marina phone."

"It's the only number I have for you."

"We should fix that."

"I agree. If I'm going to consult on this planning—"

"Whoa, who says you get to *consult*?" She dug her fingertips into her bare knee, trying not to laugh. "You're either *on* the sub-committee or you're not, mister. No half measures."

A beat of silence was followed with a low laugh. "Josh approved my attendance at this planning session. You'll have to take it up with him."

"Josh is not in charge of allowing guests, though." She sighed tragically. "I don't see a way out of this, unfortunately."

"Is this planning session happening at the same time as dinner, by any chance?"

"Uh…"

"If Josh hadn't mentioned it, would it have been a *surprise* planning session?"

"Erm…" She stuck out her tongue, even though he couldn't see her. "I'm going through a tunnel, we might lose the call here…"

"I'll see you this afternoon," he growled in her ear, and she blushed from head to toe.

Then she copied his phone number from August's phone to her own.

January: This is my personal phone number, FYI
Seth: Did you steal my contact information from your place of business?
January: No comment
Seth: Noted. We'll come back to this later. Any requests for dessert?
January: It's going to be a hot one today, can you pick up popsicles?
Seth: Absolutely

She grinned to herself, enjoying the whole-body warm fuzzy that set of exchanges gave her, then hauled herself out of the hammock and headed back to the office. She texted the kids photos of waffles and pancakes, then reviewed the booking calendar to see if they had any new boats checking in this afternoon.

Only one, and it was a repeat customer.

She opened the secure video messaging app August was allowed to use on her computer in Beirut and sent a waving emoji.

August called her immediately. "Morning."

"Not for you."

Her sister laughed. "No, I'm halfway through my day already. It's too hot to be outside, so I was just catching up on some work."

January waved around the office space. "Same, although it's not that hot here *yet*. I was just outside in the hammock. So, you know, everything is going hunky dory here. Lots of reading time happening. Nothing to worry about."

August leaned into the camera. "Are the kids up yet?"

"Nope, they're sleeping in. I've sent them threatening photos of waffles, though, so breakfast is about to happen."

"You're a rock star." August sighed. "Call me back when the kids get up? I'll be in my room for the next two hours at least."

"Will do." January blew her a kiss. "Love you."

"Same, boo."

Upstairs, she knocked on doors, then cranked up some music. Summer roused first, then Levi, and to January's surprise, they both wanted to help with breakfast.

"I can *do it*," Levi snapped at Summer when his big sister got a bit bossy about the waffle iron.

"But you *aren't doing it*," she growled back.

"I'm waiting for the steam to stop." He crouched down, eyeball to iron, and counted to five very slowly. Deliberately slowly.

January's first instinct was to step in, to urge them to be kinder to each other. But she also knew they needled each other because they could, because it was safe, and this was an important part of learning boundaries and consequences.

So she lost herself in mentally replaying the funny conversation about popsicles and committee meetings. And before she knew it, waffles were on the table, both kids very proud of their efforts—and pleased with each other once again.

After breakfast, Summer wanted to work at the counter for a bit, so January stayed upstairs and folded clean laundry for the week. Levi went outside to play, and before she knew it, there was a knock at the door.

Seth was on the other side, holding a grocery bag and wearing an interesting half-smile that made her feel warm and soft, and want to sway into his tall, broad body.

Instead, she crossed her arms over her chest. "What time is it?"

"Not dinner time," he reassured her, holding up a grocery bag. "I'm early, but the popsicles need to go in the freezer and Josh only has a bar fridge. There's no room."

She led the way to the kitchen, not that he needed her to show him where they went. He was a regular now, helping with dinner and making himself at home.

But that was as far as their friendship had gone. He hadn't even had her phone number until that morning, and only because she'd brought it up and moved them in that direction. And she wasn't sure what she wanted within the bounds of knowing what she couldn't have— which was too much of anything.

So it was fine that they were just friends, more than fine, that was probably all it should be, but then he gave her those quiet looks when he thought she wasn't paying attention and the cocky half grins when he knew she was. And the line she kept drawing between those two things ran straight through *not just friends* and landed on *we're both grown-ups and life is short.*

Because somewhere in the last few weeks, her body had decided it was all in on Seth Kincaid. It very much felt like a first-time crush, all over again. Everything he did, from emailing her business podcast suggestions, to earnestly listening to Levi's recap of a YouTube video's recap of a game neither of them had ever played, to finding the first pint of fresh, local strawberries sold on the peninsula for a salad idea she'd mentioned once, all layered together to create those new memories she needed of him.

Nothing heavy. Nothing about the past, or the future. Just the present, like he'd read her mind. He'd taken stock of her life and all of her responsibilities, and just shown up as she needed him to.

How was she not supposed to fall head-over-tits in lust with that? She was a thirty-seven-year-old woman with a super functional libido. She wanted to peel Seth's clothes off and lick him like an ice cream cone.

Instead, she got a friendship and a box of popsicles, on request.

Maybe her feelings were one-sided.

She raked her gaze down the long stretch of Seth's body as he rearranged boxes in her freezer to make room. He was wearing a thin t-shirt today, and it clung to him like his skin was a little damp from the unexpectedly hot and humid day, the first of the summer. The worn cotton molded to the muscles in his back and shoulders, revealing more of his body than she'd seen before, even when he'd worn that wet suit.

In the dark, late at night, she sometimes thought of him peeling that suit off his upper body, unzipping it so it rode low on his hips.

Now she'd have a more detailed topographical map of his torso from behind for—

He turned suddenly, then stopped, his gaze tangling with hers. Surprise flashed across his face, like he recognized the hunger in her eyes. Heat flamed up her neck at having been caught ogling him.

He didn't say anything.

She didn't move.

Then he cleared his throat and looked away, and that was enough embarrassment for her. She spun around, busying herself at the counter. She'd pulled out some rice earlier, set it next to a recipe card, and—

"January."

He didn't say her name that often. She closed her eyes, letting it roll over her. His voice was low and intense, and a wild hope surged inside her, like she'd maybe misread his glance away.

If she turned around, would her hope be rewarded, or dashed? Would she see in him a match for how she felt?

Needy. Ready. A little wild and out of control, and all from a few brief touches and imaginations run amok.

He stepped closer, his body pretty damn near her back, and his breath feathered hot against her neck. "I know this is—"

"Aunt January!" The door clattered open, and before the kids tumbled into the kitchen, Seth was across the room.

She busied herself in the cabinet. "Yep?"

"Whose dog is that?" Seth asked, his voice firm and not at all affected by what had just happened.

They didn't have a dog. She whirled around and found a mud-covered Levi holding a mud-covered puppy. Behind him, Summer threw her hands in the air. "I told him not to bring the dog inside."

"He's hurt!" Levi's wide eyes were full of panic.

"Okay…" January blew out her cheeks. "Summer, you go outside and wait. This dog's owner is probably going to be looking for it, and worried. If you see them, bring them up. Seth…" She turned to her guest, once again asking him for help—and asking him to set aside whatever moment they'd just had. "Sorry."

"Don't be. I live to be helpful." He gave her an easy grin, betraying none of the sizzling heat she'd just felt rolling off him.

Did she imagine it?

Focus, January. "Okay, let's see this little guy. Why do you think he's hurt?"

Levi nodded toward the back paws. "He was limping and whining."

"He seems okay right now…" January gave the dog a quick once over as best as she could through the mud, then gently touched his back legs. He didn't whine at all when she touched the first one, but the second one made him whimper. "All right. Shhh, buddy. It's okay."

Seth circled around Levi from the other side and they both crouched down together. Seth used his phone's flashlight to put a spotlight on the paw, and they both said "Ah ha" at the same time.

"Levi, he has a splinter. Let's get him into the sink, carefully, and I'll get some tweezers."

By the time she returned to the kitchen, Seth had the puppy in the sink and was gently washing its foot and making Levi giggle.

Crisis averted.

January carefully removed the splinter, then they finished washing the puppy because it seemed to make both the dog and Levi happy.

They'd just finished up when Summer came running up the stairs. "I've found the owner!"

Behind her was Josh, who'd apparently heard the commotion and jogged over from the garage to see what Summer was doing talking to a strange man—and then recognized Trent Aitken, a military buddy of Will and August's who lived an hour away.

January more than recognized him. She'd dated him briefly. "Trent," she said as non-breathily as possible, trying to keep the surprise out of her voice. "This is your puppy?"

And what are you doing in Pine Harbour?

He flashed her a familiar grin. "Hey, January."

Beside her, Seth tensed—and didn't relax even when Trent's gaze dropped to the sink, where Levi was towelling off a wriggling and eager little body who clearly wanted to jump to Trent *right now.*

"Hey, Nugget," he crooned. "What did we talk about? No getting away from Maggie."

"Who's Maggie?" Josh asked.

"You know Maggie," Trent answered. "Campbell's little sister."

Seth cleared his throat. "Well, I for one don't know who either of those people are, or you, for that matter. I'm Seth, by the way. Josh's brother."

Trent sized him up, then glanced to January. Taking stock of why Seth was in her kitchen, maybe. Then he introduced himself. "I was just across the road with a couple of friends, Campbell Mills and his sister. We're bringing a craft brewery to Pine Harbour."

January's eyes went wide. "You're one of his partners in that project?"

"Sure am."

Seth glanced back and forth between them. She willed him not to ask how they knew each other, and he either didn't want to know, or he picked up on her vibe, because he simply nodded. "We'll see you around more, then?"

"Definitely."

Josh also clearly picked up on the vibe in the room, because he urged Levi to hand over Nugget. Once the puppy was back in her owner's arms, Trent winked at January, told her he'd see her soon, and left.

Josh took one look at Seth and herded Summer and Levi out the door, too, muttering something about wanting to see their favourite boats in the harbour.

Which left January and Seth alone, again, in what was suddenly a very quiet kitchen.

She swallowed hard, her pulse still racing. *Calm down.* "Do you want a drink?"

"No."

"Do you want—"

"Who is that guy to you?"

She took a deep breath. *None of your business* was right there on the tip of her tongue, a valid answer.

But a part of her wanted Seth to know she'd had a healthy dating life over the years. "A friend of my sister's. And someone I dated a few times."

"Is he going to be at the stag and doe?"

"I mean, anyone could buy a ticket..."

He groaned and pivoted, bracketing her against the counter, his arms braced on the cupboard behind her. His body pressed right against hers.

Her breath caught in her throat and she brought her hands up between them, but instead of pushing him away, her fingers curled into the front of his super soft, barely-there t-shirt.

"You aren't bringing a date to the wedding, are you?" He pinned her with a sharp, searing gaze. "Or the stag and doe? That guy, or anyone else?"

"I..."

"Don't bring a date." He breathed it like a command, but it was an ask, and a hard one at that. It revealed more than he'd wanted to show her, she realized. He'd been trying so hard to keep his desire locked up.

"You don't want me to bring a—" She flexed her fingers, imagining she was digging claws into him. Laying some kind of claim. But she couldn't do that. "And why not?"

"We only have this summer. We only have here, and now. Let's protect this time as ours. Let's not let anyone else intrude on that."

It was a massive leap forward from where they'd stood earlier that day. "I didn't realize we had agreed that we had anything at all."

"We haven't talked about it yet. But we should. We can, right now, if you want."

"The kids will be back." Every inch of her body was on fire. "Unless Josh can read your mind?"

"I'm pretty sure my face gave me away, but…" He dragged in a breath. "This isn't the right time."

"There probably isn't a better time?"

He chuckled, low and slow, then whispered her name. She shuddered and closed her eyes, as she always did.

The next thing she felt was the brush of his thumb against her jaw. "Look at me."

She blinked her eyes open, and he was right there.

"I can't stop thinking about you. When I'm gone, I just want to fly back to see you again. I know you don't have the bandwidth for much right now, but I'm not asking for a lot. What we've been doing is amazing. I just…" He swallowed hard, his gaze dropping to her mouth. "I need to kiss you."

She pushed up on her toes, her body fitting against his. He was warm and solid, his chest hard against hers, his neck held taut as she slid her hands around it, her fingers stroking up into his hair.

He brushed his lips against hers softly, once and then again. And again. As if this was their first kiss and he was reacquainting himself to her.

As if he didn't know what she would like next, and so he had to learn by doing.

Was her mouth so foreign to him after all this time?

"You're trembling," he murmured.

Damn it, she'd thought that was only on the inside. "Overthinking this. Ignore me."

"Can't do that." He groaned lightly as she kissed him back, eager to get him back on track. "Ah, you still make me want to go zero to sixty."

Her heart leapt. "Really? I thought…"

"I'm trying to be polite here."

"We're too old for that."

His mouth pushed against hers, then pulled, his lips finding the gaps between hers. Slotting them together perfectly. Firm, warm lips, then the wet slide of his tongue seeking entry. Demanding it, not waiting for her to respond, and then he was groaning, the sound so deep in his chest that she felt it against her own body. He shuddered, inhaling quickly, and she did the same thing, because he was about to pull her under and she was ready for it.

When his tongue stroked in again, there was no hesitation. He took what he wanted and gave what she needed, his kiss hard and thorough. Utterly destroying any doubt or lingering fear. This man wanted her, right here in her kitchen. His hunger was undeniable, and the pleasure he gave her? From a *kiss*?

It had never been like this. This wasn't a walk down

memory lane. This was discovery of something new. Something dangerous. An introduction to kissing a grown-up Seth Kincaid.

A stranger.

A dangerous, wild man.

13

———

SETH HADN'T MEANT to kiss her. Up until he said out loud that he wanted to kiss her, he'd thought he'd locked that feeling down, waiting for her to make the next move.

One minute he'd been washing a dog, the next he'd practically chased everyone out of the room with a jealous snarl and pressed her against the counter.

He still had her pinned, his beautiful captive, as he slowly and thoroughly poured everything he had into a kiss he'd dreamed of for far too long.

This was twenty years of regret, two and half months of pent-up but denied attraction, and days of barely repressed lust all colliding into an embrace he never wanted to end. And it needed to stop very soon. Too soon.

But her lips were so fucking soft.

Her fingers sure and clever as she pulled him down, holding him against her just as much as he was lifting her into his body. Together, they'd removed every bit of space between them, and the firm, sweet press of her curves against every aching plane of his body was so good it hurt to step back.

He didn't even step far. Just a half step, enough to feel the loss of her, then the crash back together as he wrapped her in his arms again.

"We need to stop," she whispered.

"Definitely." He licked the corner of her mouth. Her head fell back, and he dropped his mouth to her neck, where he could taste her fucking pulse, and stopping? No. Ha. That wasn't happening.

He curved his hands around her hips, down to her bottom, and lifted her onto the counter. Her legs slid open and he notched himself into the tight vee of her body.

But as he moved in for another ravenous kiss, his phone rang. Without looking at it, he grabbed it from his pocket and turned off the ringer, then swept his hands back up January's sides. She felt so damn good—

Ring.

"You better answer that." She kissed his temple as he glanced sideways at the offending piece of technology.

It was Teegan.

"It can wait."

A text appeared from her on the screen, too.

He groaned, stepped back, and tapped the answer button. "Hey."

"Sorry to bother you, but Linda's ferry crossing just got cancelled. Would you mind if I flew her down to Pine Harbour instead?"

"Oh shit. Yeah, no, that's fine. Will she need a ride somewhere when she gets here?"

"No, one of her crew mates will pick her up. I'll log the fuel usage as personal."

"Actually, the marina here has an avfuel pump now..." He glanced at January. "You could estimate, fill up when you land, and we'll call it even."

"You sure?"

"Absolutely. I'll meet you at the marina when you arrive."

He scrubbed his face as he hung up.

January hopped off the counter and moved over to the fridge, pulling out food. He trained his still-hungry gaze on the curve of her ass as she crouched to take vegetables out of the crisper drawer.

"That was Teegan," he offered. "The pilot I hired. Her wife is working here—she usually drives down for the week—but they're going to fly down instead. Ferry got cancelled."

January kept piling stuff on the counter for dinner. It looked like they were having a stir fry.

She nodded.

"She's also my neighbour. Up in Blind River. A friend..." He trailed off. "Do you want to meet her?"

"I probably will," she said evenly. "If she's going to buy fuel from me."

He shrugged, feeling too big for the space suddenly. "I don't know. You were quiet."

"I'm still reeling from that kiss." She touched her lips. And then she smiled. "You kissed me."

He moved in close, cupping her face in his hands. "I've wanted to do that for weeks."

"And now we have to make dinner and plan a stag and doe. And meet your neighbour?"

"Busy afternoon." He brushed her lips with his. "In case I don't get to kiss you again later, know that I will want to say goodnight properly."

"Was that it?" she murmured.

"Not yet." He sipped at her lips again, his head swimming from the sweetness of it. Then he stormed in, taking her mouth in a searing caress. She met him stroke for stroke, and when they broke apart, they were both out of breath. "That's what I want you to remember, later."

She nodded, her eyes bright. "Okay."

He blew out a breath. "Now…can I help with dinner?"

She nodded, and he let her put him to sous chef duties before pulling out his phone and texting his brother.

Seth: You can come back with the kids
Josh: On our way back
Seth: We're making dinner
Josh: That's nice
Seth: Don't be weird
Josh: I'm never weird
Seth: Please don't
Josh: I'll be completely chill
Seth: Thank you
Josh: On one condition
Seth: No
Josh: I'm not leaving the garage tonight until I get the full story
Seth: Enjoy sleeping in Betty, I guess
Josh: You stole my bed, jerkface, some good gossip is the least you can give me in return
Seth: January is never gossip
Seth: Do you understand me?
Josh: Sorry, that was across the line…on our way back

"What was that furious texting?" January slid him a knowing look. "Josh figure something out?"

"I wasn't subtle." He winced. "Sorry. If you wanted me to be, I mean. I'm not sorry for wanting to be alone with you."

She smiled. "I think it's okay."

"All right." He grinned, feeling ten feet tall. "So about this consulting role for the stag and doe…"

Her mouth quirked. "Have you ever planned a stag and doe before?"

"Never. I don't even think I've attended one." The fundraising pre-wedding dance was a uniquely Canadian tradition, he'd discovered when he was transferred to Colorado. And that was the only period in his life when he was social enough to attend something like that.

"So what is your important counsel going to be?"

"We've already covered the highlights."

Understanding dawned, making her eyes sparkle. "Whether or not I would have a date."

Never in his life had he felt so much like a caveman. His grin spread, his cheeks straining now.

She poked him. He caught her finger and spun her around—and that is when the kids came running up the stairs.

He let her go, regretfully, and whispered, "It was a clear and direct instruction. You are not to have a date."

She mouthed, *okay, got it*, and then rolled her eyes at him.

And over her shoulder, Josh gave him a Look.

———

AN HOUR LATER, Teegan and Linda arrived. Seth walked Linda up to the parking lot while Teegan refueled, then returned just in time to hear Teegan tell January she should come up to Blind River sometime.

He frowned at her.

She smiled back.

How was he that transparent when all she could have seen was maybe his hand in the small of January's back while they waited near the fuel pumps.

Maybe the person who tried to set you up with her friends for the better part of three years has an eagle eye when it comes to where your hand is, you dolt. And then there was the small factor of his usual utter disinterest in dating.

"I was wondering why Seth wanted to give up his cargo runs," Teegan said baldly as she opened the plane door. She let her gaze linger on January's face for a second. "It's nice to see him happy."

Was that what did it? Had he smiled too freely?

He grinned. Not that he could stop himself, damn it. "Get out of here with my plane."

"It's only a loaner."

"But with my name on the contract."

She winked at him. "Got it, boss."

January gave him a pleased look as Teegan took off. "She's nice."

He nodded. "In her way."

"She reminds me of you and your brothers."

"There's a lot in common there, for sure. She was a pilot in the Air Force, too. She flew helicopters, though, and got out a few years ahead of me. Never met while in the service and then we end up living six houses apart in a pretty small town."

"Do you have mutuals in common?"

"Yeah."

She went to open the door to the office, and he stopped her. "January…"

Instead of responding, she just tilted her face towards him, giving him her full attention.

"You make me happy," he said quietly. "That's what Teegan saw. She saw a happy man, and she barely recognized him."

She sucked in a breath.

He shoved his hands in his pockets. "Do with that what you will."

"You make me happy, too." She pulled the door open. "Now let's go talk wedding details."

———

Two hours later, Seth led his brother up the stairs to the apartment over the garage as Josh ignored Seth's clear preference to not talk about what had happened earlier.

"I shouldn't have called it gossip."

"That's right, you shouldn't have."

"But you didn't stop looking at her throughout dinner, so I feel like there's *something* there."

"She was talking."

"You looked at her while *I* was talking."

"I spent fifteen years sharing a room with you. I've looked at your face plenty." He turned at the top of the landing and caught his brother's cheeks in his hands. He blew him a kiss. "There, do you feel better?"

"Fuck off. But seriously, you and January?"

Seth opened the door, then sprawled on the couch. "A few ground rules before I share anything." He held up one finger. "First, there will be no matchmaking. I've already had this conversation with Owen, and I blew Will off."

"I'm the *third* brother to find out? You kicked me out of my *apartment*."

Seth gestured around. "We all agree it's a hovel, not an apartment, and before I leave I'm going to do some basic renovations for you."

Josh circled his middle finger in the air. "No matchmaking. Got it. I'm strictly a non-playing character in this scene. What's the next ground rule?"

"Don't talk to Will about this." Seth held up his hand. "No, listen. He's her boss. And her friend, I know that, but their relationship is their own, and I don't want to muddy that with the side effects of a summer fling."

Josh frowned. "A summer fling? Is that what you think you're about to start with her?"

"And the third condition. I'm not asking for relationship advice. She's fine with people knowing we're hanging out, but I do not need the input of the peanut gallery about how or why or what we are doing."

"So many rules."

"Take 'em or leave 'em."

Josh tossed himself in the recliner opposite. "I accept your terms."

"I'm fucking wound tight for her." Seth groaned. "And no, I don't know what is going to happen, but after you dragged the kids out today, we kissed. A lot. And it was..." He let out a long, slow exhale. "Really fucking good. Better than I'd imagined, and I imagined that a lot over the last few weeks."

His brother nodded, then opened his mouth, then closed it again.

Seth scruffed his hand over his jaw. "That's it? No ribbing?"

"I figure that would fall under peanut gallery shit,"

Josh said, his voice uncharacteristically gruff. "But since you requested it... I'm glad you shared. I hope you continue to stare at each other like nobody else is at the table all summer long."

Seth laughed. "Me, too."

14

THE NEXT AFTERNOON, January was gripping the steering wheel of her car like it was the front of Seth's t-shirt when Catie knocked on her window, making her jump.

She grabbed her water bottle and hopped out. "I didn't see you pull up."

"I walked."

"Ah." January tried to shake off the memory of the kisses, and focus instead on the busy construction site in front of her.

Her new home, or at least the outline of it in the ground. The forms were built for the foundation, and the concrete truck was approaching down the street. Across the street, Jake Foster waved a brief greeting before continuing a conversation with one of his crew.

"This is really happening." January couldn't quite believe it. "Thanks for the heads up, this is exciting to see."

"Of course." Catie squinted, holding up her hand to shade her eyes. "It's going to be beautiful. You know, it's good luck that they're pouring the foundation as planned today. That's a good omen for getting you into the house on schedule."

October first, she'd be given the keys to a front door that didn't yet exist. Two weeks after August should be home. Four weeks after Seth's final flight for the season. She'd be back in the classroom, though. She wouldn't be behind the desk at the marina that day.

She shook her head and forced a smile onto her face. "I can't wait."

"Everything okay?"

"Mmm." She nodded. "Yeah."

"How's August?" She gave Catie the latest update, which slid out almost automated now. It was a constant question. Every customer who came into the marina, everyone who recognized her at the grocery store, even her colleagues at school. Everyone wanted to know how her sister was doing overseas.

Few asked how January was doing. Nobody except Seth.

Catie nodded along. "And how about you?"

Okay, and Catie.

"I'm great. Pretty excited about the house."

Maybe few people bothered to ask her how she was doing because she would never really share. *With anyone except Seth.*

She needed to stop thinking about him. The way Catie was side-eying her, and the way Josh had read his brother like a book the day before, it would be a miracle if they got a chance to kiss again, or talk about what the heck they were doing, before the entire Kincaid family was fully briefed from all sides about the rekindled spark at the marina.

January was all flustered and couldn't focus.

Seth glowered at this guy like he'd touched his plane.

"Speaking of breaking ground on a construction project," January changed the subject. "Did you know that Trent Aitken is one of Campbell Mill's partners in the craft brewery?"

Catie frowned. "I did not."

January filled her in on the puppy story—minus the misplaced jealousy and subsequent kissing, because she wasn't ready to debrief on those yet—and the news Josh had given her later. "Apparently the building is going to be big enough that they're going to be able to lease parts of it to other businesses."

Catie turned her attention to the contractor across the road, now supervising the cement chute. "Is Jake doing the construction?"

"Apparently."

"No time like the present, then." Catie stepped onto the dusty street and waved at the contractor. "Let's go get the goss."

A call on August's phone from a new boat just arrived at the marina tore January away shortly after Catie started grilling Jake, who was going along with it good-naturedly.

She told him the foundation looked great, thanked him for his hard work, and headed back to the office.

Then she got busy with a sequence of customer service issues, and suddenly the kids were spilling in the door after school.

As Levi sprinted upstairs to get a snack, Summer lingered at the counter. "Are we going to call Mom soon?"

They always did. "Of course, sweetie." January gave her a close second look. "Is everything okay?"

Summer ducked her head. "I got my period today."

"Oh!" January jumped off her stool and gave her niece a big hug. "Wow, that's a big day. It happened at school?"

"At lunch time." She lifted her face, her cheeks pink. "Mom was right about keeping pads in my backpack."

"That was a great idea." January smoothed her hand over Summer's hair. Her chest ached that August wasn't here to give her a hug, too. Her sister had guessed that it would happen while she was gone, as many of Summer's friends had already started menstruating. "Do you need anything? We have hot water bottles or those rice bags I can heat up in the microwave."

"I'm okay. I'm not cramping." Summer said it shyly, then smiled. "I just want to talk to Mom."

"Of course you do. Go upstairs and call your mom on your computer, and send Levi down here to share his snack with me. I'll keep him occupied until you call him up."

Summer let out a big huffy breath, her eyes bright with unshed tears.

"Baby, this is a big day. Lots of big feelings. Whatever you need."

She got a big, tight hug for that, then Summer disappeared. Levi came running down a minute later, a bowl of grapes in one hand and a bag of Goldfish crackers in the other. "Summer made me stop playing my game!"

"You've been home for ninety seconds, how far into your game could you have gotten?" January pointed to the stool. "Come share your grapes with me and we can watch some hilarious cat videos on the computer."

———

TWO HOURS LATER, after Levi had a chance to talk to his mom, too, and homework was finished, January put chicken tortilla soup on the stove to warm up—Summer's favourite—then went back down to the office to check email one more time before Seth's plane was due to return with departing passengers.

She was surprised to see a familiar name on a booking request for a summer-long berth.

From: Campbell Mills
To: Howe's Marina
Subject: BOOKING REQUEST, July 1-August 31

The form details that followed in the email included his boat length and the amp requirement for his electrical hookup.

She double-checked the calendar, then replied that they had a berth available, and pasted in the details for paying via credit card or in advance in the office.

Ten minutes later, Trent Aitken's business partner strolled in the door.

"I was across the road and thought I'd pop over and finalize this in person," he said with a charming smile that had never really worked on her, but was nice to look at in a general way.

"Happy to help, then," she said with a smile. "Have you rented a berth from us in the past?"

"Nope. I know how it works, though, because a friend did last summer. That's what gave me the idea to buy a boat. And this way I can be close to the brewery as construction gets started."

"When do you break ground?" She grabbed a clipboard and a new customer details form for him.

"In a few weeks. We should be open by the fall. That's our goal, to be in production by September so we can hit the market before Christmas. And then we'll have kinks worked out before next summer's tourist season. Although we're hoping to start to build up a local clientele, too. Lean on those military connections."

Campbell was an ex-army guy, like Trent, and January knew them through her sister. Both of them were extroverts who loved to network and make friends, and since they were tight, she'd gotten to know Campbell a bit when she dated Trent.

She found them exhausting in anything but small doses. They were always working an angle, either pitching their business or simply trying to collect people in case they might one day be a useful connection. Which had a certain utility, but something about it grated at her.

On the surface, it might seem like they were similar to Seth—past military service, good-looking guys, close-knit family-first types—but in the two months she'd dated Trent, he'd never once cooked dinner with her. Never shared a quiet cup of coffee and made her feel deeply, intimately seen. And Campbell seemed similarly…busy.

There was an echo of something there that was just a hard line now for January. Which was probably unfair to Campbell and Trent, who were actually both pretty good guys by all reports. But she wasn't interested in dating either of them, so it didn't matter.

And she was thrilled to have another summer-long tenant.

Just as Campbell was handing over his credit card, she heard a familiar drone outside. He heard it, too, glancing over his shoulder. "How's the air ferry service going?"

January wasn't entirely sure, but she didn't want to let

her new tenant—and her soon-to-be business neighbour—know that. Seth often had a full plane. Sometimes he only had two passengers, and she worried about that, what with the price of fuel being what it was. She hoped it was a good move for him, because it was making a big difference to her summer in more ways than one. "This is the second summer for the flights," she finally answered. "People seem really happy to have the option instead of taking the ferry up north first."

He turned his attention back to her. "I noticed you aren't serving food this summer."

Ah, so this was a bit of friendly research, too. "August is on tour, so we pared down this year."

"And next year?"

"Is a decision for August to make in the fall."

"All right, I can take a hint. But you still have coffee in the morning, right?"

No, she wanted to snap. *That's my private time with Seth.* Except it wasn't. There were other tenants who came in and got a cup, after all.

But none of them were like Campbell. None of them wanted to work her like an angle.

None of them, she realized with a start, reminded her of her father. Whew, that was…a lot.

"Yep, coffee is on and the office is open from seven every morning."

The first passenger off the plane hustled past the window, heading for the parking lot. It would be nice if she could direct them to a brew pub across the road. She didn't think August wanted to reopen their wee kitchen anyway. And maybe if Campbell and Trent were really successful, they would buy the eyesore that was the motel and tear it down.

The brewery would only be a good thing for the harbour, and January's kneejerk reaction to the overly cocky men for her own personal reasons was misplaced.

"It's going to be great to have a new business down here," she admitted. "August will be able to get into that more than I can, but we hope the brewery is a raging success."

"Aww, thanks." He nodded at the window, where Seth was approaching. "There's your guy."

Her heart leapt into her throat.

How did he know?

But then he stepped back from the counter and waved. "I won't keep you, since you're so close to closing up. See you around, January."

Right. He meant, Seth was her last customer for the day.

She watched as Campbell stopped him just outside the door, introducing himself. And she pressed her lips together as Seth kept it super short, nodding and then moving right along.

But her amusement faded when he stepped inside. Seth looked exhausted. He paused at the door and pointed to the lock. She nodded, and he flipped it closed.

Then he glanced to the stairwell.

"They're playing video games, and the door is closed," she said quietly.

"Excellent." He came around the counter and caught her face in his hands, his fingers sliding back and into her hair. He exhaled briefly, then took her mouth in a bruising hello. The kiss was electric and all-consuming, and ended far too quickly. The way he followed it up with a slow caress of her bottom lip with his thumb did the funniest things to her inside. "I've been thinking about that all day."

She smiled, then turned her face to kiss his hand. "How were your flights?"

"Good. Long. How was your day?"

"Long. Good. Complicated." She lifted her face, wanting another kiss, and he gave it to her. His mouth was exactly what she needed. Warm, commanding, sensual. And quiet. She wanted to cling to him, but he *felt* bone-tired.

Which made it easier to tell him she needed to focus on the kids tonight. "About dinner…"

He yawned. "Do you mind if I beg off?"

"Not at all. I was going to say that I need to spend the evening with Summer."

"Everything okay?"

"Yep. She just needs my full attention tonight."

"I'm zonked. Is it embarrassing that I might go to bed at seven?"

"Not at all. I'm jealous, to be honest."

That made him laugh a little. She liked doing that. Liked the way his eyes crinkled just for her. "Want to get lunch tomorrow?"

"I would *love* that."

He stroked his fingers along her jaw, and looked like he might say something, then just nodded and stepped back to go to the door. As he opened it, he gave her a long, lingering look before he ducked his head and went outside.

"It's a date," she whispered to herself. She was pretty sure that's what he was going to say, and if she had a read on him, he held it back because he wasn't sure they were on the same page there.

But they were. If Seth wanted, they could spend the summer having quiet, easy dates with kisses that made her toes curl and her mind go to the dirtiest places.

And in a few weeks, she would have her evenings temporarily free.

She was game for a few dates at home, too.

15

BUT THE FOLLOWING DAY, there was no lunch date, because Levi woke up with a sore throat. On Wednesday, he was worse, burning up with a fever, and on Thursday, just as he was starting to feel better, January felt a burning tickle in her nose. Watering eyes.

And then Thursday night, she went to bed with the dreaded sore throat, too. When she woke up with protesting sinuses, January had to admit what she'd been denying for a day and a half.

She was sick.

Summer, at least so far, had avoided it—thank goodness for teens who were happy with keeping their distance and being wary—but it might just be a matter of time.

January knocked gently on her niece's bedroom door.

Summer opened it immediately. "What?"

Ten, nine, eight… "I'm sick," January croaked. "Can you put the coffee on downstairs? Seth can check his own passengers in—"

"I'll help," Summer said, her spine straightening. "We

need to get their license plate numbers and register them, and I know how to do that."

"Are you sure?" Even those three words hurt to get out. She leaned against the wall.

Summer gave her a look of alarm. "Can you go lie down or something? I know how to use the cash register. I can do this. At time and a half, right, because of the last-minute notice?" She winced at the look on January's face. "Just kidding."

"You're a good kid," January muttered. "Now go."

She didn't like pushing Summer into helping. She remembered all too well how much she resented being in the same situation herself twenty-four years earlier. It was some kind of miracle that August had come around to love the marina in the end. Both of them wanted Summer and Levi to have a better relationship with this place than they'd had in their teen years.

But for right now, this was the best solution, she had to admit. And as she heard Summer move around downstairs, confidently getting the coffee on, then unlocking the door, January smiled. The girl had this under control.

Had she forgotten anything?

She made it to the couch just before Seth arrived. "Where's your aunt?"

"Upstairs. She's not feeling well."

January closed her eyes in despair. She'd forgotten to coach the teen on lying tactfully.

"Can I go up and see her?"

No.

"Oh sure, yeah. She collapsed on the couch, I think. Very dramatic."

Seth chuckled.

January groaned to herself. She was sprawled on the

couch. Her hair was… She patted her head. Irredeemable. Nothing to be done for it. Her face was red and splotchy, and—

He was in the doorway. She could sense him, and imagined he smelled very nice. They'd kissed a lot in the last week, could he have gotten sick, too? That would be terrible.

"Don't come any closer," she warned.

He slowed, then dropped to a crouch a few feet away. "Hey. You look rough."

"Gee, thanks."

"Can I get you anything? Orange juice? Coffee?"

She made a face.

"How about some tea?"

"I don't think we have any." She craned her neck to look at the kitchen, then whimpered as her muscles protested.

Seth glanced at his watch. "Okay, hang tight. I'll be right back."

"Wait, what?" She waved her hand feebly. "I'll be fine. Don't…" Don't do anything, she wanted to say. Except now she maybe wanted some tea. "Where are you going?"

"I have tea at the garage."

She closed her eyes, too weak to argue, and she listened to his footsteps on the stairs. Time slowed while he was gone, then her pulse raced when she heard him return. She felt him check in on her, and she left her eyes closed.

The stillness in the living room as he looked at her, as she pretended to sleep, was enough to make her cry on any other day. It was too much, the feelings he brought out in her. But today there were no tears, because she was too sore, too tired, to bear the weight of those complicated thoughts.

The next thing she knew, Seth was kneeling next to her.

She really had drifted off.

"Shhh," he whispered. "Stay asleep. But there's tea here, and there are more tea bags on the counter. I also brought over Josh's emergency preparedness kit, which has a wide array of over-the-counter medicines in them, and eighty percent of them haven't expired yet."

"Thank you." She winced. It hurt to even say those two words, but they were the most important words. Worth the pain.

Seth didn't need to help her. But he seemed to really want to, and that meant a lot.

"I'll be back in nine hours or so. Do your best not to leave this couch until I return."

She mumbled something unintelligible, and drifted off again.

When she woke up, the tea was lukewarm, but it went down like butter on her sore throat, and she dragged herself into the kitchen to make more.

Summer was sitting at the table. "I used your phone to report myself absent at school today. I figured instead of closing the marina office, I could keep an eye on it instead." Her little brow furrowed. "And you know, you might need someone to make tea while Seth is gone."

"Oh honey." That was too much responsibility for a thirteen-year-old to take on. January wanted to wrap her in her arms, but she didn't want to get her niece sick if she hadn't already picked up the bug. "That is very sweet. But the office can definitely stay closed now that Seth's flight has taken off."

"Seth told me to call Will—"

"Mr. Kincaid," January interjected.

Summer rolled her eyes. "Right. Or Josh 'in an emergency, if necessary,' which was funny."

"We don't need to bother either of them. We can just close the office."

"But I don't think it's bothering them. They like to help us." Summer said it like she was explaining something very simple to a small child. "So you can go up to bed. You don't need to stay on the couch. Unless you want to?"

She did not want to stay on the couch and put up with a caring but know-it-all thirteen-year-old attitude if her bed was a real option. "Where's my phone?"

Summer handed it over. "I didn't read any text messages. Swear to God."

That made January want to laugh, except laughing would hurt. Like she left any evidence of anything on her phone. She wasn't born yesterday.

January: Hey, I've come down with something. Summer wants to keep the office open today, so can you keep an eye on our parking lot? Call me— or 911—if you see anyone creepy?
Josh: Seth already filled me in, and I came over and stole a cup of coffee from you, so consider it a fair trade

She set the phone down and gave Summer a thumb's up. Then she checked in on Levi, and crawled upstairs, back to her bed, and blessed unconsciousness.

———

Seth's voice woke her from a long afternoon nap. He was in the hallway just downstairs, talking about Dungeons & Dragons, and as she slowly dragged herself out of the sleep haze, it was the weirdest sense of déjà vu.

And she was suddenly concerned about how many of her teenage conversations her parents had been able to hear from this same position, although since they were both long passed now, it hardly mattered.

But still, D&D wasn't the primary thing she and Seth had talked about back in the day…

Math.

There had been a lot of math.

And some teasing discussion about rewards for finishing math homework, like blow jobs and Seth getting to lick her until she—

Up.

Out of bed. She was in no shape to get worked up like that. Those kinds of thoughts were only for healthy people who could kiss their favourite pilot in secret.

She pushed her bedroom door all the way open, and the creak caught Seth's attention. His head popped around the corner and he gave her a grin. "Hello, there."

She returned the smile, although hers felt weak in comparison. "Summer took care of me all day."

"I bet she did." He held up his hand to stop her when she went to take the first step. "I can come up, if you want to lie back down?" He paused a micro beat. "If I can come up, that is?"

She was already flushed head to toe because of the fever, but if she could blush, she would. She nodded, and climbed back into the bed.

He followed her in, leaving the door open, and sat on the edge, dropping his hand to give her calf a squeeze.

"Really not how I thought I'd get you in my room," she whispered.

He bit his lip, laughing, and nodded. Then he sighed and moved closer, sitting next to her hip now. "It's hard to see you like this. What do you need?"

She shook her head. "Nothing." *Just you.* Nope, that was too much.

"Did you take any medicine?"

She nodded.

"Is it time for more?"

Probably. "It's in the bathroom in August's room."

The mattress shifted as he got up, then he was back with a glass of water and some pills.

She pushed herself up to sit. "You're good at this. Being a nurse."

He looked surprise. "Really?"

She nodded as another wave of fatigue rolled over her. *So tired.* Her eyelids fluttered shut, even as she was sitting upright in bed.

"I'm glad to hear it," he murmured as his fingers brushed over her forehead. "I don't have a lot of practice."

"The tea was a good touch this morning."

"My mom used to make it for us." His voice was soft, the grief worn smooth by decades.

She remembered when it was fresh, though. She reached out and caught his forearm with her hand. Gave him a weak squeeze, trying to tell him without using her throat that she remembered.

He covered her hand with his, just for a second.

Then he moved away.

Right. They weren't dwelling on the past. Casual friendship, here and now. Kissing and fun times. They were her rules, and they were good rules, because now she was sick, and that was going to be a mess to come out from under once she was better, on top of everything else.

Twelve weeks until August got home.

But the countdown January was clinging to was also roughly the same countdown to when Seth's contract with the marina ended.

"Are you up to eating something? Summer said you have chicken tortilla soup in the freezer and it's *perfect*?"

She tried to smile at the way he mimicked Summer's praise. "You don't need…"

"Hey." He leaned in and caught her chin.

She blinked her eyes open.

"I don't need to." He brushed another damp strand of hair off her face. "I want to. Do you know how long I've been eating dinner for one? This is a nice change of pace. I'm always game for sharing dinner with the Howes. And I like helping with the kids. You go back to sleep."

———

HER FEVER BROKE at ten that night, and after she had a shower, she went downstairs, suddenly famished.

Seth and Levi were sitting on the couch, watching a baseball game.

"Seth said I could stay up a little," Levi protested, cutting off any comment she was going to make about him being up past his bedtime.

She leaned against the archway. "It's okay. Are the Jays winning?"

Seth made a face. "No." Then he smiled at her. "You look better."

"I feel a bit more human."

"Want some soup?" He got up, handing the TV

changer to Levi, then pointed for her to go into the kitchen.

She sat at the table and let him reheat a bowl of the chicken and tomato soup, then crumbled some tortilla chips on top. Summer was right—it was perfect, and even more so because someone other than she had prepared it.

Seth went back to watch the game with Levi, then when it was over she sent her nephew upstairs. "You can read for a bit, but lights out soon," she warned.

"But I'm not tired."

"But it's still bedtime," she countered. "Read for a bit and you'll discover the tired, I promise."

Levi slid a glance at Seth, like he might test her by trying to get the other adult involved, but he thought better of it and stomped upstairs.

She took a deep breath and went back to collect her bowl from the kitchen table. Seth followed. "Do you need anything else before I go?"

She shook her head. "I feel heaps better, thank you. I'll probably be up for a while, since I slept all day, but that's not the worst problem to have."

"I could stay?" He held up his hands. "No funny business, I know you're still sick. Just to talk? If your throat can handle it?"

She gave him a half-smile. "I'd like that."

She went upstairs to check on Summer, and give her the same read-for-a-bit suggestion as she'd given Levi, then told them she'd be back up in thirty minutes for lights out.

Back downstairs, Seth had made her a cup of hot water and lemon juice, with honey. Was this seduction at thirty-seven? No funny business and a never-ending supply of soothing beverages? When she was better, she would remember this, and reward him for it.

"Thank you," she whispered as she settled on the couch, in the corner, with her legs curled to one side. He sprawled near her feet, leaning on the back of the sectional so he was looking at her fully.

"You get that kind of complaining at bedtime every night?"

"That was nothing. That was the one-and-done version. And they're such good kids, they really are, and they miss their mom, but…" She trailed off and breathed in some of the hot lemon steam. "Growing up, August and I were on our own for bedtime. Which isn't better! And I've lived alone for almost sixteen years. I will say, they're better roommates than I had in university. But at my core, I'm a quiet, no-nonsense, straight-laced teacher. I like to clearly state an expectation and have it met. That isn't compatible with full-time child raising. They have limits. They have feelings."

"You're doing a great job." He shook his head. "I don't know how I would do it. I've babysat Charlie a few times, and now I love to take Lila for walks here and there, and then I'm very ready to hand them back to their parents. What you're doing here is a big ask. It would be for anyone."

"It's different with Summer and Levi, though." She wasn't sure how to say this part, although she didn't need to hide it from Seth—or justify her choices, at any point. "I moved back here because August was pregnant."

His exhale was audible. Maybe he hadn't done the math on how old Summer was, and how old August would have been when she was born. But he got it now. "Was that weird for you?"

She shook her head. "No. It was exciting. She was excited. That helps." She smiled faintly. "I thought it would be different for her. And it was for a while, but it turns out that being twenty and married isn't any more secure than being seventeen and…"

And knowing that your on-again, off-again boyfriend had signed a fourteen-year commitment to the Air Force. Twenty years later, she could still feel the panic at seeing those two lines on the pregnancy test. She'd known immediately she couldn't carry the pregnancy to term. She wasn't ready to be a parent. But that didn't make what happened next hurt any less.

Seth squeezed her ankle, then swore under his breath and moved around so he was sitting right next to her. "Can I give you a hug?"

She nodded, and he took her mug and set it on a shelf above her, then wrapped her in his arms.

He'd held her for weeks back then, too. Unable to say anything to make it better. Their prolonged goodbye was punctuated by secret research and a road trip to a hospital and then her recovery, instead of one final carefree summer together.

But that was then, and this was different. His embrace felt different, too. Less desperate. More stable, and she didn't think that was wishful thinking.

Most importantly, though, she was different, too. And she didn't regret any of the choices she'd made along the way. Not the abortion, and not the decision four years later to move home because her baby sister was going to be a mom.

"It worked out in the end. A teaching position opened up. I applied to other school boards, too, but this is where I got an offer first. And I've been Summer's bestie ever since, although that's wearing a bit thin as she's turned into a teenager."

Seth brushed his lips against her temple. "I regret not being here more when Becca was young."

She leaned her weight against him. "It's not like we have an Air Force base here."

"I can regret something that felt necessary at the time." He squeezed her again. "I don't want to miss any more time with my nieces and nephews."

"Is there more baby news I missed? Will and Catie—"

"No, not yet. I'm just saying, they're all settling down. And I want to be here more. In the summers, at least. That's why I've started flying out of here."

A clear, important addendum.

Uncle Seth was a seasonal feature at best.

She reached for her lemon water and took a long, soothing sip. Then since they'd gone into deep waters, she decided to keep going. "Why did you settle in Blind River?" *Why not Pine Harbour?*

"It made sense."

"Because of work? Or…was there someone there?" She made a face, hating how that sounded. They'd both lived their lives fully. That had been the whole point of going their separate ways. That they wouldn't be tied to Pine Harbour, that they could go wherever life took them. And partners were a part of a full life.

"Work, mostly." He paused a beat, stiffening. "Not for a person. Maybe because of the great outdoors. I don't know."

"We have world-class hiking right here," she whispered.

He kissed the side of her head. "I know."

The belly flip-flop didn't help her rational thought process.

"How about you? Did you stay just because of the kids, or…has there been anyone else important over the years?"

She didn't have any reason to feel bad about the relationships she had after he left town, but she also never imagined that she'd one day tell him about them while he held her against his body.

"I've dated. Some serious relationships, some not so serious. Nothing stuck. You?"

"Nothing serious, I guess, but a couple of long-ish friendship things."

That sounded like a Seth she'd once known. "That was the missing piece for me, actually. I dated a couple of really nice guys. Got engaged to one of them. But it never…"

If she'd thought he'd stiffened before, she'd been wrong. As soon as she said the e-word, Seth had frozen into granite.

So she trailed off and waited.

"I should have expected that," he finally said, his voice gruff. "But it took me by surprise."

"It was years ago."

"Is he still around?"

For a split second, January had a fantasy to indulge in. Seth going all possessive alpha male against her ex-fiancé, who in this fantasy still wanted her, even after she'd given back his ring and confessed she just didn't think they were that *close*, and she couldn't see herself actually *marrying* him.

"No," she finally admitted. "He moved a year later. Last I heard, he was married with kids."

Seth's hand tightened on her shoulder. "Sorry."

"Don't be, I'm not."

"No, I mean…" He grunted. "Sorry for the weird spark of jealousy there. That was out of line."

It was only out of line if he was a jerk about it, or…if he didn't want to lay claim to her.

And Seth wasn't a jerk.

So he was telling her that while he might have some jealous reactions—to Trent the other day, and now to the news she'd been engaged—he wasn't going to be that dream guy who made it all romantic.

She shrugged. "It was pretty mild jealousy, don't worry about it."

"Not inside my head, it wasn't."

She smiled. "Can I take that as a compliment?"

He laughed gently. "Sure."

"I don't regret anything about my life. Even right now, I know it looks like I'm a homeless girl tasked with babysitting my niece and nephew, but—"

"You're talking to the guy who is squatting above a garage right now."

She laughed out loud. "Okay."

"I'm glad you told me." He rested his head against hers. "I like knowing more about your life."

Because he'd spent a long time carefully avoiding everything. Including her.

It was a bittersweet reminder that he wasn't a forever kind of guy. She knew better than anyone that Seth Kincaid could be the sweetest, kindest friend, and still leave without looking back when the date that he'd marked on a calendar arrived.

Without a single look back, or any plans to ever speak to her again. And it would be so much worse this time, if she wasn't careful.

That thought kept her up long after he left, after she finally got the kids to turn out their lights and get all the drinks of water they needed and stay in bed, keep their eyes closed long enough to actually fall asleep.

January, though, had her eyes wide open. Literally and metaphorically.

Because Seth wasn't the same as he'd been twenty years ago. Now he was so much nicer, more mature, and had learned a kind of emotional awareness—for others, if not himself—that made him dangerous on a whole different level.

Young Seth had broken her heart—in a repairable way. A few cracks, easily mended over time. She rather liked the patch up job. It had made her strong and independent, and the high school heartache had prevented college drama. She'd learned to partition dating from the more important hard work of school, and then teaching.

Mature Seth had the power to smash her heart into dust, and he didn't even know it. She could fall in love with him so easily, despite knowing that at the end of the summer, he *would* walk away again in a heartbeat. To avoid hurting her, he would explain it away.

And he would believe it.

16

Summer insisted on working again on Saturday, gleefully counting how many hours she'd get paid for. January made a full pot of tea and used her freed-up time in the morning to dig into the marina's income and expenses once again. If they could afford to pay a thirteen-year-old to cover the counter in an emergency fashion, they had to have enough money to hire a part-time person of actual legal working age.

And if the business couldn't afford that, then the larger problems she had feared in the spring might actually be something to look at again. She had been ridiculous to think she could do it all herself, all summer long. Sure, August did it, but in a pinch January was there for backup.

The Kincaid brothers couldn't be her backup in the same way. They weren't family, no matter how close they got.

When Seth stopped in to check on her, on his way to the farmer's market with Owen and Kerry—"I'm either a third wheel or a babysitter," he said gruffly, but she could tell he was pleased to be included in the outing—she told him she was fine, but planned to nap in the afternoon, and the kids were excited to fend for themselves for dinner with sandwiches or ramen or both, so he didn't need to come back.

He frowned, but accepted the boundary.

And then she missed him all evening, like a silly ninny.

After the kids were asleep, she roamed around the quiet residence, her head swimming with thoughts about how hard it was to make the marina really prosperous, and how much of that was tangled up in the history of her father's choices—and her and August not wanting to be like him. Getting sick had pushed a pause button on her startling realization that she still had unfinished business with her father's legacy, but now that she was feeling better, it roared back.

On her way up to bed, she stopped at the window she used to climb out of to sit on the roof. Summer and Levi used it all the time now, but when was the last time she was out there? Probably the first time she showed them how to hoist themselves up, years ago now. And before that?

When she was a teenager.

She went back to the living room, grabbed a flashlight and a blanket, and then cracked the window open. It didn't have a screen, because teenage January had bent the frame popping it out one too many times.

She braced one foot on the far side of the stairwell, using that for leverage to boost herself up onto the ledge of the windowsill, then pushed herself forward and into the night air.

As a teen, this had been her favourite spot. It had a view of the south end of the harbour, with the old motel that had been shuttered for a decade right in front of her, the empty lot across the road from that where Trent and Campbell would build their craft brewery, and beyond that the forest that Old Whiskey Harbour Road disappeared into, curving away from the lake again.

Tonight, the motel loomed as a dark silhouette. She couldn't see the cracked concrete or the peeling paint.

Once upon a time, her parents had owned it. Then her father lost it in a bad business deal, and whoever took it over had run it into the ground a decade ago.

Staring at it every day had made her father a bitter man. He never liked to talk about it, yelling at August whenever she'd bring it up, and that negativity layered on top of January's complicated memories of Seth had driven her away from the marina for anything other than family dinners.

For years, she'd wanted nothing to do with this place.

But Augie had always loved it. She didn't get as upset as January did at the way the marina looked in the shadow of the motel.

"It doesn't reflect on us," she would say.

But January had internalized that it did. When was the last time she had actually sat and looked at it? Last year, Bailey had tried to buy it, but the current owners, communicating through a trust, made it clear they weren't interested. That had been a spark of hope for the Howe sisters, and then it had been extinguished.

A creaking sound at the side of the house interrupted her thoughts. She recognized the sign that someone was climbing the old and probably rusty antenna tower. "Seth?"

His head appeared at the roofline. He was grinning at the sound of alarm in her voice. "What are you doing?"

"Having a sit." She waited until he climbed all the way

up and made his way over to her, then she confessed the rest. "Thinking about my dad. And the marina."

"Ah." He paused before he sat down. "Is this okay?"

She silently lifted the blanket she'd wrapped over her lap. He settled in beside her, sliding his arm around her shoulders.

"Do you want to talk about any of it?"

Her breath shuddered as she tried to decide if it would be easier to unload some of her feelings. The marina was safest. "I've decided I need help here. It was naive to think I could just work around the clock because it isn't that hard."

"I can—"

"No." She had to cut him off. Stop that at the pass. "I mean, I need to hire someone. Like you did. I thought I could handle it for the whole summer but I underestimated how much easier some of it is for August—she knows how to scuba dive, for example, she could have done that visual inspection that you did. And she had me for backup, which I didn't think she used that often, but even two days of me being out sick is enough of a problem that I need someone on the payroll to come in. Plus the more I think about it, I'm just not cut out for this. I shouldn't have volunteered to be the marina manager. I could have taken the kids, and kept teaching, and we should have hired someone here. Why didn't I think of that?"

He didn't answer. He didn't need to. She knew the reason. "Because my father drummed into us that the only reason the marina was profitable was because he worked himself to the bone. Except I don't think that's true. And I hate that I accepted it at face value."

"I'm sorry. That's a lot." He made a thinking sound.

"But it might also have been that a part of you wanted to have a turn at running this place? You loved it as a kid. You talked about being in charge some day."

She choked a strangled laugh. "Wow, did those dreams die hard. Because it turns out, managing all the personalities of the different regular tenants, and politely dealing with endless vendor issues…being *on* all the time with that many people, none of whom I can threaten with detention? It's not my strong suit."

Seth groaned in commiseration. "It's not my strong suit either."

"Oh!" She pressed her hand to her chest in relief. "I'm so happy to hear that because I have been watching you with your passengers and you seem so good with them. Nothing like the Seth I knew in high school. You're quite different now." She gave him a soft smile. "I mean that in a nice way."

He caught her gaze in the moonlight, holding it for a long moment. "I'm not that different. Not on the inside. Just a bit more self-aware and able to manage life."

Her breath caught in her throat, and she pushed down on those feelings. "I suppose that's true for all of us. We're all still our younger self, deep inside. For better or worse."

"What does your inner, younger self want to do with her life?"

"Teach." She hated how clear that was. "I miss my job, Seth. Maybe it won't be so bad at the end of the month when I'd usually have a summer break, anyway. But I miss everything about it. The routines, the kids, my classroom. The stable, regular pay cheque."

He laughed out loud, warm and full of humour. The opposite of her sharp little bark. "That's all good stuff. Of course you miss it."

She shook her head back, looking up at the night sky. "That was good to get off my chest. Normally I'd gripe to August, but I can't share any of this with her. The selfish stuff, I mean. I did talk to her about the marina today, and hiring someone."

"It's not selfish to realize you're on the wrong path. Or, you were on the right path and life knocked you off temporarily. It's not selfish at all to be grumpy about that." He shifted sideways, sliding his arm around her. "And I'm happy to be your sounding board for that if your sister can't be."

"I don't know what to say."

"Do you need to say anything at all?"

"Yes?"

"Is that a question?"

She laughed. "I don't know."

He gently worked his hand from her shoulder to her neck, squeezing her flesh as he rolled his thumb across spots she hadn't even realized were tender. An exhausted but pleased groan slipped out of her mouth.

"Does that feel good?"

"Mmm. Very."

"Sit in front of me."

They rearranged themselves and he put both his hands on top of her shoulders now, his warm palms immediately making her neck feel better. And then he started stroking his thumbs across her skin.

"Ohhh…"

His thighs flexed on either side of her. "That's a nice sound."

"Don't stop."

"I like those words, too."

She rolled her head back, turning to butter under his fingers. "Seth…"

He didn't need a teasing reply to that. She felt the press of his growing erection against the curve of her ass, and they both stilled.

"Ignore that," he murmured, working her muscles harder. "Tell me about the marina."

How could she ignore that he was turned on from giving her a neck rub? She was achingly aware of every inch of him. His legs bracketed hers, solid and long. His chest was a solid mass against her back, broad and strong. And on the bare skin of her neck, sometimes dipping under her shirt, his fingers worked magic.

She could even feel his breath, warm and steady against her hair, like he was pressing his face there.

A wave of arousal pulsed through her, a slow roll of need.

But Seth didn't push the envelope. He just kept stroking her, working the kinks out of her tight muscles.

It had been far too long since she'd been in someone's arms. That had to be a contributing factor to how good this felt. It couldn't *only* be that it was Seth, and this had been their spot, and she couldn't stop thinking about his kisses.

As if to prove to herself that this was optional, she dragged herself back to the subject of the marina, and what brought her up here in the first place, even if it wasn't what she really wanted to talk about anymore.

She cleared her throat. "Our finances here aren't as tight as I thought. I'm starting to realize that my dad terrified us into thinking if we spent money, we'd lose money. I think he made a lot of bad deals." She gestured at the motel. "Evidence of that is right in front of us."

"It's never sold, huh?"

"Yeah, I don't know why not." She sighed. "Those podcasts that you sent me were great, by the way. There are a lot of things that we could be doing that would bring in more than enough money to cover part-time help. There's a lot of good business practice outside the space of hustling and making deals, which is all we learned. And August is so good at *doing* the work here, but there's more to it than that."

"How involved do you want to be?"

"That depends on the day. Today? I'm full of ideas."

He chuckled, his whole body shaking.

She raised her arms over her head, winding them around his neck and stretching her whole body against his. "You didn't have a better Saturday night plan than keeping an eye out across the road for flashes of light?"

He chuckled. "My Saturday night plans blew me off earlier, remember?"

She flushed. "Oh. Right."

"You had stuff to think about." He stroked his hands down her sides, his fingers coming to rest on her belly. "Is this okay?"

"Mmm." She wanted to sink all the way into him.

"I just want to touch you. You get to set the rules."

Turning her head, she brushed her lips against his neck. "Just touch?"

He groaned. "For tonight." His throat worked under her lips as she feathered the lightest kisses there. "It's been a long time, but I still remember how you taste."

She sucked in a breath.

He lowered his voice even more. "I miss that taste."

"We can't..."

"I know. This wouldn't be anything other than a secret release. Just you and me. Like old times. Fooling around on the roof." He stroked his fingers under her t-shirt, along the waistband of her pants. "Let me feel you. Let me have a little bit of you."

And then his mouth dropped to her neck, open and urgent.

"Can you be quiet?"

"Seth—"

"Is that a no?" He smiled against her skin. "Do you need to be loud, January?"

Her breath hitched. She shook her head.

"Good." His breath was ragged, too. "That's good. Because I need to touch you. And I don't want anyone to know what we're doing up here. This is just for us."

She tilted her head back. He looked down at her, but it was her who initiated the kiss. His lips were soft and warm, his breath sweetly minty—like maybe he'd hoped to get a little lucky on the roof, and she couldn't blame him at all—and he let her explore his mouth with her tongue for a long, sexy beat before he growled and tightened his hands on her body.

Holding her tight against him, he gave back as good as she'd just given. They parried back and forth, but even as his taut body flexed around her, he tasted like restraint. Like he wanted so much more than this.

He tasted like desire, and oh, she wanted that. His desire *of her* was potent.

When his hand dipped under her waistband and slid over her trembling lower belly, she was already soft and swollen. His fingers ghosted over her sex, a light tease at first, then he traced the seam of her pussy with one fingertip and the teasing was done.

Her head fell back against his shoulder, her legs tumbling wide, and he hitched her against his body. His other arm banded across her chest, filling his palm with her tit—his thumb finding her nipple with unerring accuracy—and surrounding her with his warmth.

"Is this all for me?" He groaned with pleasure as he dipped into her wetness. "God, you feel amazing. Been thinking about this for weeks. Wondering if you'd let me make you feel good."

"Seth…"

"Want to come on my fingers, January?"

Fuck. She panted and twisted her face, pressing it into his neck as he slicked the evidence of her arousal up to her clit.

They both moaned quietly when her body throbbed in response.

"Like that? A slow circle?"

"Mm-hmm."

"Tell me what else you like."

She opened her mouth and licked the sweat off his neck. "I like the way you hiss when I do that," she whispered.

He squeezed her whole sex with his hand. "This is about you."

"Licking you *is* for me, I promise." His grip tightened, making her gasp. "Okay, okay. I…want your fingers inside me. Can you…?"

He shoved her shorts dangerously low on her hips, giving him more space to work with and baring more of her torso. Her flesh pebbled up in the night air, and at the exposure to his gaze. She looked up at him, and the fiercely hungry look on his face made her whole body quiver. Then she followed his gaze down her body to where his corded forearm flexed against the paler skin of her belly. His head was bent now, his breath brushing against her temple. They watched together as he stroked her tender flesh inside her shorts.

Every inch of January was turned on. Her breasts were heavy, her thighs were shaking, and between her legs, her whole sex pulsed in anticipation. He circled her entrance with one finger, then two. She ached in a way that couldn't be named, a throbbing desire that flooded through her in waves triggered by his slow, sure touches.

She breathed his name, and he stilled for a second, those two fingers nestled just inside the tight squeeze of her body, then he thrusted.

Her back arched, her body curving against the muscular confines of his arms.

"You're so beautiful," he rasped, rocking his hand so the heel of his palm rolled over her clit.

Her?

He was the beautiful one. The gorgeous man who wanted her enough to climb onto the roof and play her body like a virtuoso.

"Next time, I need you naked. I want to see how this tight pussy takes my fingers, January. I need you bare for me."

Next time. All of his words were hot, working on her in a very good, yes please kind of primal way, but those two words were the hottest of all.

This was going to be her secret pleasure all summer long.

He desired her that much. He wanted her so much he climbed a rickety antenna tower and shoved her shorts down so he could stroke between her legs.

All. Summer. Long.

"Next time," she whispered, her voice hitching, "I want to touch you, too."

He groaned. "Fuck yeah. Need your hands on me."

"Let me…" She tried to wiggle her hand between them, but that made him drop his tight hold on her chest—her nipple missed the slow rolling pinch he'd been doing—and he dragged her hand in front of her body.

"Not tonight," he growled. "Be a good girl and let me make you come."

"But—"

"You deserve a selfish little orgasm. Fucking ride my hand and take it."

"Seth!"

"Shhh," he warned. "Give me your mouth if you can't stay quiet."

She twisted in his arms desperately, grinding against his fingers now like her life depended on it. He swallowed her next cry, then added a third finger—and the perfect stretch—just as the tight spiral inside her snapped.

He breathed her name, over and over again, as she shattered in his arms, her climax exploding from deep inside her belly and rippling out through to her extremities.

She was still gasping when she sagged back against him. "Wow."

He grinned, she could feel it. *Like the way you say wow.*

But when he spoke, his words weren't cocky. They were rough and full of emotion.

"I never forgot how sweet you sound when you come." His whole chest heaved as he slid his fingers out of her pants, and brought them to his mouth. Then he groaned, a sound that would live in her heart forever. As if he really *had* missed her taste.

"We should…" She gestured inside.

He reluctantly moved out from behind her and shuffled toward the antenna tower.

"Seth," she whispered sharply.

He glanced back.

She rolled her eyes and pointed to the window. "You can come inside. I don't want you to break your neck."

He stopped and gave her a careful look. "Is that the only reason you're inviting me in?"

Her cheeks flamed. No. She wasn't done with him just yet. She shook her head, and he prowled back—and then all the way on top of her. "Then lead the way," he whispered roughly against her lips.

She kissed him hungrily before shoving against his chest. "You need to get off me first."

"Mmm." Another kiss. "All right."

They were both grinning like idiots when they got to the kitchen.

"I tried to be quiet," she whispered, breaking out into a nervous laugh.

"You did your absolute best." He gave her an incorrigible grin. "More successfully on the tiptoeing down here. Less successful up on the roof."

She pressed her lips together, her cheeks blazing.

"Probably didn't carry across the water when you cried out my name."

Oh, God. She turned around, looking for any kind of distraction. She landed on the freezer. "Do you want a popsicle?"

"Sure."

She pulled two out. "Cherry or orange?"

"Orange." He took it from her, his fingers brushing against hers slowly before he pulled away.

The icy treat was an appreciated distraction from her

overheated thoughts. But Seth watched as she slid the popsicle into her mouth, his burning gaze locked on her lips as she sucked at the tip.

"Is it staining my tongue?" she asked.

He nodded. "And your lips."

She grabbed a paper towel, and gave him one, too, because the house was warmer than outside, and finishing the popsicle without dripping was a race against time. The last few bites were frantic. She giggled as a few drops of cherry juice dripping onto her fingers, and went to lick them off.

Seth caught her hand, pulling her fingertips into his mouth, and all those heated thoughts returned with a vengeance. *Liar.* They had never gone anywhere. The popsicle had been a pause button, not a stop.

She let him lift her onto the counter and guide their mouths together. Now they both tasted like an orange-cherry punch. They tasted like each other.

If this was how her nights might end all summer long, it didn't matter how chaotic the days were. She was ready for more of this. So much more.

17

January offered to host the next girls' night, which would double as Catie's wedding planning confab, at the marina. She had a kernel of an idea, sparked by something Seth had said in an off-hand comment, then fuelled by their blush-inducing night on the roof, and how intimate and quiet that had been. She'd run the idea past August already and she wanted to see what her friends thought of it in action.

When she was a kid, there was a stretch of time when her parents regularly had dinner parties at night. Families would come over, and the kids would play inside while the parents had drinks and dinner on the deck. By the time she started hanging out with Seth again as teenagers, those parties were long over. But she had a faint memory of crawling out onto the roof with him and Josh when they were all little. To young January, the dinner party they spied on was the most glamorous thing she'd ever seen.

It was time for glamour to return to the marina.

With the help of Levi and Summer, she strung up new strands of white lights over the deck. They'd put some up last summer for Canada Day, but she added to them this year, as many lines of them as she could get her hands on.

Then she moved some of August's best decor highlights, like a vintage bar cart and a privacy screen, outside for the evening. Summer had August's eye for styling, and by the time her guests arrived, the deck looked completely different.

In the dark, under the glow of the lights, it was easy to ignore the eyesore of the motel. The quiet lap of the lake against the dock, the pretty silhouetted outline of the sailboats in their berths…at night, the marina was gorgeous.

For too long, they'd undervalued the one feature Howe's Marina had that no other business could boast of —being right on the lake.

During the day, the harbour was nice enough, but a bit busy with boaters. At night, though, something special happened. It felt deeply intimate. She flushed, remembering how Seth had stroked her on the roof, how she'd felt in his arms, like it was just the two of them in the world.

They could rent out the deck for events. Birthday parties, small weddings, anniversaries. Other companies could provide catering. She could monetize the space itself.

———

THE NEXT WEEK FLEW BY. After she got the hive mind seal of approval on her plan, January poured herself into building an Events page on the marina's website, and then hired Bailey for a month of marketing support.

Suddenly Howe's Marina After Dark was a thing. Four evening bookings, even at the modest introductory rental rate, paid for Bailey's time and effort. Part of the booking contract included permission to take photographs and use them promotionally.

August was thrilled.

And for the first time since she'd taken over, January finally felt capable in her temporary role as marina manager.

Her handle on being a calm, cool, and collected guardian was slipping a bit, though. Nerves were getting frayed all over the place. There was only one more week of school. The kids knew that in a week, they'd be flying out west by themselves, which they'd done before, but August always took them to the airport.

They were both acting out, being a bit horrible to each other.

Summer was being bossy to Levi, and Levi was deliberately misbehaving to irritate his sister.

When he did it before dinner, refusing to set the table properly just to make steam come out his sister's ears, January snapped. "Levi, stop it."

He either didn't hear her, or didn't care. Even as part of January's brain was trying to tell her *he isn't processing this clearly*, the rest of her went straight to primal reaction. She flushed white hot and slammed the cupboard door shut.

Both kids jumped.

The silence that followed felt awful. January was shaking. Then Levi took off running, and the next sound was his bedroom door slamming in exactly the same way.

"Fuck," she muttered under her breath.

Summer gave her a look of reproach. She deserved it.

She paced into the living room, counted to ten, then went upstairs and knocked gently on Levi's door.

"Go away."

"I want to apologize."

"I'm calling my mom!"

"It's the middle of the night for her, Levi." January sighed. "Can I please come in?"

There was a long pause. "Fine."

She opened the door and found him curled up on his bed. She sat on the floor so their faces would be level. "I'm sorry. That was scary. I shouldn't have lost my temper."

"It's okay."

"No, it isn't. I should have just walked away, and modelled that for Summer, too. There are always opportunities to de-escalate, and I missed them."

"You sound like my teacher."

She winced. "Sorry. Can I try again?"

He shrugged. "Sure."

"I should have stayed calm. Full stop. I didn't, and I'm sorry."

"That would have been better."

"I know."

"I shouldn't annoy Summer so much." He screwed up his face. "But she's so bossy."

"What would your mom do in that situation?"

He chewed on his lip. "Probably slam the cupboard and tell us to stop it."

January laughed weakly. "That makes me feel a little better."

He wrapped his arms around her neck, and she squeezed him back.

"We're halfway through this, kiddo. She'll be home soon."

———

THE NEXT DAY, Seth came over to the office in the morning to have a cup of coffee, and after the kids left for school, she gave him an extra-long hug.

"I like this—a lot—but what's this all about?"

She told him about the night before. "It just feels like there's so much going on, and my fuse is getting shorter and shorter."

He kissed the top of her head. "I want to say something, and it's going to come out wrong."

"Then maybe don't say it."

"I need to."

"I'd advise against it, probably."

"I know." He took her hands and kissed her knuckles. "And your counsel is wise and appreciated. But in this case, I'm going to go for it anyway."

"All right. I'm braced."

"You haven't had a day off in three months."

"I slept for two days straight—"

"You were *sick*. Possibly because you haven't had any days off."

"You're bossy."

He shrugged. "Maybe you need a little bossy in your life."

That did weird and nice things to her insides. Would a bossy Seth make her tea and enforce breaks? "You're making me take a day off?"

"I think…yeah." He squared his shoulders, like he was bracing for an argument. "You need someone to say it."

But she wasn't going to fight him on this. Now she was just curious where he was going. "And what would you suggest I do with a day off?"

A smile curved up his face. "I want to take you on an adventure. How would you like to go flying?"

Yes. Her heart leapt, and she forced herself to play it cool. "I have a lot to do."

He grinned and glanced around the quiet office. "Yeah?"

She looked down the computer. Zero emails had come in over the last hour. Wednesdays were quiet days. Nothing was stopping her from putting up the "Back in Ten" sign with an "actually closed for the afternoon" Post-it addendum. "Nothing that can't wait until tomorrow," she admitted. "We'd have to be back by the time the kids are done with school."

"Of course." He glanced at his watch. "That gives us time for lunch and a swim, too. Pack your cutest bikini, and I'll get a picnic together."

She ran upstairs and changed into dark blue swim shorts and a white string bikini top that made her tits look amazing, but had the unfortunate tendency to go slightly transparent when wet.

Her cheeks flushed with excitement as she pulled on a tank top and shorts as well. Loose clothes that could be easily removed.

When she returned downstairs, Seth was still gone, so she set an out-of-office reply on her email, then called Catie.

"Hello," her friend said.

"Hello."

Catie waited a beat. "Did you need something?"

"Do you know about me and Seth?"

"Yesss… Sort of. I'm not sure."

"Which is it? Wait, don't answer that." It was the kind of code that said, Catie and Will had talked about them, and maybe Will had shared some secrets, because that's how it was with your life partner, but Catie didn't want to pry. And January appreciated the heck out of that. "So Seth and I are... I don't know what we're doing, but it's fun. And he wants to take me flying today? So I'm going to be out of cell phone range for a few hours. Which means you're next on the emergency contact list for the school."

"Okay."

"That's it? No questions?"

"I have so many questions, but they're really best dealt with over a bottle of wine and chocolate torte."

"That sounds good."

"Go have fun."

"Thank you." She hung up, then did a little happy dance before going down to the docks. There weren't many people on their boats today, but those who were around, she did a quick touch base with. None of them needed fuel, and one guy said he had a full jerry can in case anyone did need help while she was gone.

"Have a great afternoon off," another tenant said. "You deserve it."

Of course she did. She'd been silly to work herself to the bone. *Because it hadn't felt* that *hard. Because it hadn't been* all *that August did.*

So silly.

And that was going to change starting today.

As she approached the office again to lock up, Seth came around the corner carrying a backpack. "Ready?"

Without hesitation, she held out her hand, and he slid his fingers through hers, then squeezed.

He gave her a quick safety briefing, then helped her into the plane. From the outside, it looked small, but inside it was surprisingly spacious. There were two bench seats in the back—the middle one folding down so passengers could get to the back if needed—and two bucket seats up front.

"Where should I sit?"

"Right next to me." He pointed out her seatbelt, then handed her a headset to wear, then he hopped out again. When he climbed back in, the plane was floating away from the dock, and in a matter of moments, he had the plane started up.

January was captivated by the takeoff. By the confident way Seth moved the plane through the harbour, and the delightfully distracting flex of his forearms as he moved the controls. But most of all, she loved the surreal lift into the air.

"Freedom," she whispered.

"Isn't it something?" Seth glanced sideways at her. "You're on a hot mic."

"To anyone else?"

He chuckled. "No, just me."

She smiled. "Hello, you. This is fun. Thank you for dragging me away."

"Any time."

"Where are we going?"

His expression took on a secretive glint. "Do you know that Lake Huron has more than thirty thousand islands?"

"I do," she said slowly.

"Do you know of any that have geocaches on them?"

She gasped. "What did you find?"

He just smiled. "It's a short flight. Look down."

Although she'd never seen the shoreline from this height, she was familiar with this stretch of the peninsula. They'd just passed the provincial park north of town, and up ahead was a large island, a protected nature reserve, that she had led students on field trip visits to before.

She asked if that's where they were going.

He shook his head. "No. But close."

Excitement bubbled up inside her. "I've never done off-shore geocaching."

"I've never done it, period. But ever since Summer mentioned it as an example of your Sneaky Math Lessons for your students, it's been on my mind."

This was almost as good as the transparent bikini top plan.

She held her breath as he turned the plane, starting to circle the cluster of small islands that crawled up the coast. He told her what he was looking for, but she didn't retain any of it. It was magical how he had a quiet command of the aircraft, and still managed to captivate her, too.

This was what Seth left Pine Harbour for, all those years ago. To learn how to fly, and then use those skills to do something meaningful with his life. And now he was sharing that with her, and she would treasure this day forever—however it turned out.

Suddenly the plane was descending, Seth saying something about an aiming point and a last visual reference, as if he were giving her a flight lesson, and then the water caught them, and they were skimming forward, gliding and finally slowing.

Ahead of them was a…rock. And then Seth navigated around the rock, and they were looking at a small island that looked like a bite had been taken out of it, a tiny cove on the lake side, shallow and protected by that behemoth rock they'd just gone around. It was near the top of the chain of islands, and on this side, there was nothing behind them but the rolling surface of Lake Huron.

An inland sea, with Michigan on the other side of it—way too far away to be seen.

They were all alone, protected from the peninsula by this curved island.

When he got closer to shore, he gave her a wicked grin. "Don't be alarmed, but I'm going to jump out of this plane now."

She laughed. "I trust you."

He climbed out, quite safely, and then with a quiet splash, she felt the plane being towed around and tugged onto a pebble shore.

Then Seth reappeared in the door. "All tied up. Ready?"

She practically jumped him as soon as she was free of the plane.

He caught her face in his hands, kissing her long and slow as she clung to his broad shoulders, savouring the heavy strength of his body beneath her fingers.

She was breathless when he let her go.

"Ready to narrow in on the search?"

"Absolutely."

He grabbed the backpack and the GPS unit while she surveyed the cove's shoreline for the best navigation route.

Then she double-checked the coordinates, and pointed. "Over there."

He smiled as she led the way. His pleased, knowing look told her he knew *exactly* where they were going.

But he didn't give any clues, and when she got to where she thought they were going, she stopped.

Frowned.

And then turned around forty-five degrees.

"Wait, is it on the rock?"

She tilted her head to the side, then looked at Seth. He gave her an innocent look.

"It's on the rock," she breathed.

Well, it's a good thing she'd worn a bikini, as instructed. She peeled off her shorts and tank top, left them on the shore with the GPS unit, and stepped into the water, expecting it to be bracingly cold like it was in Pine Harbour.

But the cove wasn't freezing. The shallow water must be warmed by the sun quickly enough in the morning, and maybe not moved around as much as the rest of the lake, because it was very wadable.

"You coming?" She tossed over her shoulder, and took off as fast as she could for the rocky island ahead of her.

It was walkable the whole distance, maybe a hundred feet or so of a soft sandbar, and by the time she was halfway there, Seth was beside her.

He'd peeled off his shirt, too, leaving him in board shorts that rode low on his hips, and she had plans to fully explore every inch of him as soon as she found whatever surprise was ahead of them.

"You're cute when you're driven," he said.

She laughed.

Then she splashed him.

He growled and charged, catching her around the hips and lifting her out of the water.

"Put me down," she protested softly, not meaning it at all.

"But I know how to safely climb this rock island." Like that was the only reason he was carrying her, and not because they both wanted to touch each other non-stop.

She shivered as he kissed her, a quick pull at her mouth that told her he meant business, then squealed when he hoisted her over his shoulder like a sack of potatoes.

He clapped his hand on her butt, making her thighs tremble in anticipation, then stalked the last ten feet along the sandbar before setting her down. From this angle, which she hadn't seen as the plane floated in, there were natural steps up one side.

"Careful, they're slippery," he cautioned.

She could see how when it was really choppy, the waves would crest over this part of the island, but at the moment it was calm and relatively dry—until she reached the flat plateau at the top of the stairs, and then she realized this was not a round-on-top rock at all, but a shallow basin.

A natural pool, fed by the lake.

Her breath caught in her throat, and she even more carefully slid down the other side of the rock. It was a reasonably safe angle, and only a few feet to the water.

Like the shallow sandy cove behind them, this pool of water had been warmed by the sun.

"How did you find this place?" she asked as Seth joined her.

"Heard about it on a pilot forum. There's a bigger rock just like this in Lake Superior, called Bathtub Island, and someone mentioned this one on a thread about that place. That was a couple of years ago, and the water levels were higher, so it was mostly submerged. Basically, it's a little pool that makes an appearance every fifteen or twenty years, for a couple of years."

She sank into the water and moved across to the other side. From here she could look out at the lake. It was much deeper than the cove, and its dark water looked immediately colder.

Then she turned around.

Her breath seized in her throat at the sight of Seth lounging against the rock backdrop. People liked to tease that the Kincaid brothers looked like Canadian

Hemsworths, but right now he looked more Greek god than an Australian movie star. His brows were heavy and dark over a hooded gaze that promised he wanted *her* for lunch, not whatever he packed in that backpack. And his hair was damp, tousled this way and that, looking darker than usual because of the water. Droplets trailed down his thick chest, too, making it hard to look away from him.

Not that she was trying. "I should be looking for a geocache," she said, her voice catching.

"We've got a few hours." He shoved his hair back, his heavy shoulders flexing with the motion. Then he fixed his serious gaze on her again. "Come here."

She waded back to him, everything around them fading away. When she stopped in front of him, he slid into the water and picked her up. Heat radiated off his body. He walked her over to a rock ledge and set her down, then wedged himself between her thighs and kissed her like they had more than a few hours.

He kissed her like they had all day, all night, and maybe forever.

Then he dragged his mouth to her jaw, then her neck. "Lean back," he said huskily.

She walked her hands behind her. He slid his gaze over her body, lingering on the white triangles covering her breasts—she really liked the way his gaze heated up even more, and his hands tightened on her thighs—before slowly trailing his attention down to her swim trunks.

He tugged at her waistband, baring more of her hip. His fingers trailed lazily over her belly, making her quiver. "You're sexy."

She twisted her head to the side, smiling and blushing.

"Hey, don't hide."

But it was getting harder and harder to look at him and not want too much, reveal too much.

She turned up the heat instead, matching the possessive inferno in his eyes with a sultry sizzle. Rolling her shoulders forward, she shimmied against him. "Isn't it your turn? Let's trade positions and I'll make you feel good."

"We don't take turns." He tugged the shorts down even further, revealing the curls on her mound. "Is this okay?"

"Nobody's around…" she panted as he slid them off her completely. "Sure, why not?"

"So casual," he teased.

She was anything but. That wouldn't stop her from trying to guard her heart, though. "Oh? What would you rather?"

"Just keep looking at me." He bent over and kissed the top of her thigh, then moved in closer. Her belly. Then the trimmed triangle of hair above her pussy, where he paused to breathe in.

Heat swarmed through her as she watched his muscular back rise and fall on that slow inhale. But it was nothing compared to the singed-by-the-sun feeling when he lifted his head briefly, as if to check that she was still watching. His gaze locked on her face and he pressed her thighs wide open, then dragged his hands to where she throbbed for him.

"Don't stop watching," he murmured, his voice dripping with a heady, intimate promise. "I want to see your pretty eyes glued on me every time I look up."

———

JANUARY SUCKED in a breath as Seth stroked his thumbs up the outside of her sex.

He knew he was dragging this out, teasing both of them, but *God damn*, she was fucking sexy. He liked the shape of her so much. The way her hips curved to meet her thighs, the round fullness of her bottom. Little spots of softness all over. The insides of her arms, the backs of her knees. And long, strong muscles, too. Every bit of her was perfection, utterly captivating—and that was before she spread her legs and let him have a good, hungry look.

And having the chance to spread her open and feast on her in the daylight?

He wasn't rushing.

Once he got his tongue inside her and felt her clit pulse between his lips—there would be a reckoning, he knew that. There would have to be. But that was tomorrow's problem. Today she had let him whisk her away to this secret place, and he was going to make the most of it.

Keeping his eyes on her face, watching her reaction, he stroked her outer lips, then closer to her slippery entrance. His cock pulsed, eager to be inside her, but that wasn't going to happen today.

It might not even happen until they were alone for two weeks.

He wasn't going to rush things with January. She was too important. And as much as he wanted to be buried hip-deep in her tightness, he wanted her to have this period of anticipation more.

Plus he was enjoying the hell out of slowly rounding the bases.

He dipped his head and licked her, a slow, broad swipe up the centre of her sex to tell her that he meant business.

This would be a main event. She was going to come on his face, but first he was going to make a meal out of her.

The first glance up to make sure she was paying attention found her biting her lower lip. He pressed his cock against the hard rock in front of him, needing a distraction from how fucking hot *that* look was.

Then he eased back, teasing her lips with the tip of his tongue, making her squirm. He waited until her hips rocked up, greedy girl, then gave her another slow, full swipe. Tease, then please. And every so often, check to see how she looked as she watched. She went from curious to aroused to desperate, and he liked all of those faces a *lot*.

When she started to really bloom for him, her flesh all swollen and sticky and perfect, he settled in and kissed her pussy like it was her perfect, precious mouth. He explored every inch of her, always returning to her clit just as she started to get frantic for it.

And when she reached for his head to hold him in place, he settled in and didn't move. He latched onto her throbbing nub, savouring the way she flexed as he pulled it into his mouth, and he suckled in a steady, *fuck yeah get my face messy* kind of way.

It worked. Her orgasm ripped out of nowhere. Suddenly she quivered around him, her thighs shaking, and then she cried out and dug her fingers into his hair. Her legs tensed up, her heels digging into his back, and he felt a strong pulse against his tongue, followed by a convulsing flutter.

He kept licking her as she moaned softly, until she squirmed and squeezed her thighs to get him to stop. "Your tongue…the…award."

He peeled her legs away and lifted his head. "What did you say?"

She laughed and covered her face. "Nothing."

"No, seriously, I couldn't hear anything. Your legs were pressed a little tightly against my ears." He grinned as he hoisted himself up onto the ledge and sprawled beside her.

"I said, *your tongue gets the MVP award.*"

"And then you blushed."

She nodded, her eyes bright. "I don't say things like that."

"I remember." He brushed a strand of hair off her flushed cheeks. "You thought them, though."

"Well, yeah. You're…" She pushed at his chest and groaned. "You've always been sexy. You bring it out in me."

"I'm sexy?"

"Shut up, you know you are."

He cupped the back of her head and rolled her onto her back. "I know that I like you."

She kissed him back, all tongue and soft lips. "I like you, too. So much."

He caught her hand and brought it to the front of his shorts. "Want to show me?"

"I don't have to ignore this today?" She traced her fingers up the heavy ridge of his cock, then notched her fingertips into his waistband. And then waited for his answer.

He groaned, struggling for words already. So he grinned instead.

"Remember…on the roof?" She slid her fingers back and forth. "I wanted to touch you then…"

"That was then, this is now, my cock is all yours," he ground out.

She giggled, delighted, then pushed her hand under

his waistband and wrapped her fingers around his length.

At the first, sweet caress, his whole body heaved toward her, his balls pulling tight. Ready to spill for her before she even got started.

He mumbled her name and she found his lips, kissing him softly as she stroked him in the tight confines of his board shorts.

"Take these off," she whispered.

A siren call.

He needed to be a gentleman, because this hadn't been the plan. He'd wanted to seduce her, not turn into a lusty teenager again at the first opportunity.

"I don't have anything," he managed to get out as she shoved his shorts down and climbed on top of him.

"We won't fuck," she whispered. "I just want to feel you against me. You said it's all mine, right?"

He couldn't say no to that. He braced himself on one hand and reached for her with the other.

She trembled as she fit them together, his cock fitting perfectly against the lush slit that was her well-licked pussy. Her swollen lips moulded to the hard shape of him, and when she rocked, bringing her clit up to the sensitive spot just below the head, he saw stars.

Yes, he was all hers.

"Keep doing that and I'll come really fucking fast," he groaned.

"Good," she whispered, and swivelled her hips again.

He tipped his head back. She leaned in, her breasts brushing his chest. "Look at me," she moaned.

Repeating his command back.

He rolled his head, locking his lusty, raw gaze on her beautiful face. And he didn't look away, not even for a second, as she rode him faster and faster until she cried out, coming again. Feeling her pulse right against him, having her arousal slick him from balls to tip, was all he needed to follow. His shaft pulsed in long, heavy thrusts, covering his belly with his own sticky mess to match hers.

As she carefully slid off him, he caught her face in his hand and pulled her in for a soft, lingering kiss. They both broke away panting.

"That was…dirty." She gave him a slow blink, her golden eyelashes dusting her cheeks in that unsure way she had, that she only showed him because to everyone else she was confident and capable without exception.

The irony was, she was deeply sexy. She should be proud of a lot of things—her career, the way she supported her family, her ability to pivot in the face of adversity, her funny sense of humour—but the fact that he knew she had grown into having a very filthy side, too, a secret sensuality that was bold and fearless and utterly tempting…she had nothing to be unsure about on that score.

"That was the hottest thing I've ever done," he told her, and it was the truth.

Her eyes sparkled. "Same."

"Looking forward to topping it very soon."

She laughed and brushed his mouth with hers. "But not before we find the geocache."

Oh, right. The whole reason he'd brought her out here.

Liar. You brought her here for seduction purposes.

One could have two simultaneous and complimentary goals at the same time.

He snagged her swimsuit bottoms. "Better get dressed."

Would he ever tire of that pleased blush on her cheeks? Would he ever get enough of reminding her that they had just done very naughty things, and he'd liked it very, very much?

Probably not.

Don't think about how short the summer is going to feel.

He pushed up and shoved to the edge of the ledge, then dropped into the natural pool. Time to rinse the sex off his body and help the woman find—

"Oh!" She gasped. "It's right here."

Not that she needed his help.

He turned around just in time to see her grab the ammo can he had stashed in a rock nook.

When she had it out in the open, she read the stickers on top of the metal box, then stopped and looked up at him.

"Sponsored by Kincaid Air Ferry."

"I had some stickers laying around."

"And the geocache sticker?"

"You can order those on the internet." He shrugged. "Easy peasy."

But the pleased look in her eye said that she didn't think it was that *easy peasy* to plant a geocache surprise on a rock island. She was happy with his surprise, and that did funny things to his chest. It shouldn't. He'd planned this so she would be delighted.

And yet, he was still affected in a way he hadn't anticipated.

Inside the box were a few paracord friendship bracelets he'd had a local kid in Blind River make for him for a trade show. They'd been sitting in his house for four years, and this was as good a use as any for them.

"I think the deal is you're supposed to take one, then sign the log book, right?"

She nodded. She gripped the bracelet tight in her left

hand as she opened the pristine notebook he'd added, and quickly scrawled her name, the date, and then after a beat, a note he couldn't read.

The first person to fill it out.

"What did you say?"

She winked. "You'll have to come back to find out."

Then she clipped the cover back on and slid it back into place before crawling over to him with the bracelet.

He took it from her and clipped it around her wrist. She watched him the whole time, then he kissed her again before looking at his watch. "Time for lunch."

They walked back on the sandbar hand in hand. Seth retrieved the backpack and they spread out a blanket on a grassy spot where they could look at the rock island they'd visited.

He'd been a fool. More than once.

January snagged a grape from the bowl in front of him, then slid it into his mouth. "What are you thinking about?"

He finished the bite, then rolled his head, stretching his neck. "How foolish I was to forget."

"Oh." She leaned over and kissed his shoulder. "How much fun I am, you mean?"

He wrapped his arm around her. "How good you feel beneath me." Except maybe it wasn't that he'd forgotten so much as buried the memory deep, where it couldn't hurt him.

"Don't get all sentimental on me," she whispered. Like the weight of that might be too much.

He smoothed his hand up her shoulder and onto her hair. She'd twisted it up into a thick bun, but that had started to fall out while they'd been getting each other off, and now he tugged on it, wanting to see her waves fall out all over her shoulders.

She let him, and then he turned and buried his face in the curls. "Don't worry," he murmured. "I know what you need."

18

ON THE KIDS' last day of school, Seth was flying up north, but he made good time on the return flight and his passengers disembarked back in Pine Harbour just a few minutes after the kids got home.

When he strolled into the office, Levi was enthusiastically explaining to his mom on video chat that he had run screaming from the school on dismissal. "It was awesome," the kid said with a big, toothy grin. "Oh, Seth's here. I have to go. We're planning our first D&D game."

"What am I, chopped liver?" August asked.

January fought back a laugh as she waved to Seth. The friendship bracelet he'd given her was on her wrist, and it filled him with a possessive pride. He winked at her, a promise he'd come back downstairs after Levi had shown him whatever it was he'd carefully bookmarked in the handbook.

"I told Mr. Kincaid about our game," Levi said as they tromped upstairs.

Now it was Seth's turn to fight back a laugh. He loved how the kids earnestly respected Will's role as Mr. Kincaid, their school principal, even though he was also the brother of the guy who had started hanging around all the time.

"And what did Mr. Kincaid say?"

Levi stopped at the landing. "You don't need to call him that. He's your brother."

"I'm aware, but it's sort of fun."

That got a giggle. "He said he would want to play, too."

That had been Seth's plan all along, but he was happy to give Levi the credit for pulling together a group of players. "Who else should we invite?"

Levi grabbed the handbook off the coffee table and flopped on the couch. "Maybe your other brothers?"

"Absolutely."

"And my friend Anhad?"

"For sure."

Levi hesitated.

Seth waited.

"And my sister," Levi mumbled.

"I think she'd like that."

"She said we can work on our characters on the plane ride."

Seth's chest squeezed at the little wobble in Levi's voice. "You nervous about the trip?"

"Oh, no." Levi straightened up, trying to look very mature. It mostly worked. "Maybe a little about the airport."

"What's it like flying by yourself?"

Levi told him how January would get a security pass too, so she could take them to the gate, and then they'd be handed off to a flight attendant. "And they give us snacks on the plane because we're not old enough to have credit cards."

Seth grinned. "That's a sweet perk. Who will pick you up at the airport on the other side?"

"My dad and my grandpa."

"So fun."

"Yeah. They have alpacas."

They didn't end up talking about D&D much that afternoon, but Seth got a great visual tour of Levi's grandparents' farm in British Columbia, and then Summer came out of her room and asked Levi if he wanted to play video games, so Seth left them to that while he went in search of January.

She was helping someone fuel up their boat, so he grabbed the hose and pulled it over to the fish gutting stations. Might as well help her with the end of the day tasks.

As he sprayed down the wooden tables and the deck space beneath them, he watched her help customers. She was hitting her stride, and he needed to remember to tell her how confident she looked, how well she was representing Howe's Marina right now.

He couldn't *only* grab her with both hands and pull her into the storage room like he wanted to, tell her how fucking sexy she was in those jean cut-offs, her tan, strong legs shoved into rubber boots.

That was important *as well*. But he needed to make sure she knew he saw all of her. The hidden vulnerabilities, the confident boldness, the sweet kindness…and he liked all of it.

"You're very good at your job here," he growled as *she* tugged him behind the counter—not quite the storage room, but close—once they were inside the office and alone.

"Thank you."

"I think you should know that."

"Okay." She slid her hands under the hem of his shirt, making his brain short-circuit.

"How was your day?"

"Great. Picked out all the tile for my house." They usually didn't talk about the house she was building. Her dream house, for the fall, after his contract with the marina ended.

But before he could ask about that—*tell me more, tell me everything*—she breezed past it. "And I bought condoms. For tomorrow night, if you're free."

Free? He'd be counting the minutes until she returned.

It had been a week since their afternoon in the private cove, and they hadn't done more than kiss since.

Tomorrow she was leaving before dawn to take the kids to the airport in Toronto.

Her hand skated up his tensed-up abs, and he shuddered.

"Miss you," she said under her breath. Meaning, she missed their physical connection.

That made two of them. He missed more of her than just that, but his body was what she needed from him.

He groaned and hauled her close, needing every inch of her pressed against every inch of him—including the ones he was rapidly gaining. She kissed him back, her lips soft and warm and perfect.

And then there were footsteps on the stairs.

She twisted to the computer just as he turned to inspect something on the wall very carefully, and that was it.

That was all they had until tomorrow night.

———

THE NEXT DAY January left the marina in the capable hands of Bailey Patel. She hadn't had any applicants to her part-time job posting yet, and Bailey volunteered to cover the day while January took the kids to the city.

They arrived at the airport three hours before departure. That gave them lots of time to get through security and find a quiet place to video call August before going to the gate. Then January loaded them up with treats from the shops, hugged them both enough times they demanded she stop, and heard all about the D&D game they were going to play with Seth when they got home.

"It's going to take us all day," Levi said, his eyes wide with wonder.

"It *can* take all day," Summer corrected.

"That's what I said."

"No, you said—"

January cut them off. "No bickering on the plane, right?"

"Right," they said in perfect chorus.

And she knew they wouldn't. They saved that for when they knew someone they trusted could be in charge of the boundaries. That used to be their mom. Now it was temporarily January—and for the next two weeks, it would be their father and grandparents, and January would have a chance to exhale.

That didn't make it any easier to actually watch them walk past the boarding gate attendant, though. With a quick wave back, Summer ushered her brother through the doors, and they were gone.

She took a quick, sharp inhale, then messaged August.

January: They're on the plane

August: Thank you for seeing them safely there

January: Of course
August: Now go enjoy two weeks alone with Seth
January: I'm going to get so much done around the marina
August: Shut up, you're getting laid…repeatedly

January grinned. She was pretty sure that yeah, that was the primary plan. The stag and doe was next weekend, but other than that, she planned to hole up every night with her pilot and turn off her brain.

No thinking, only sex vibes.

That confidence got her all the way back to Pine Harbour, a straight shot three-hour drive, and all the way into Seth's arms. He was waiting for her on the dock.

"I sent Bailey home," he murmured against her mouth.

"More of your bossy nature coming out," she whispered before kissing him so hard it almost bruised her lips, and oh, how she'd craved that.

If only she could shut out the rest of the world. If nothing existed but Seth's lips against hers, then this would be perfect and all she would ever need. His kisses turned her on in a way that she didn't think she had ever experienced before, not once upon a time with an earlier version of this man who now turned her inside out.

This was less nostalgic than she'd thought—or worried—it would be. This was very urgently of the present. If she hadn't intimately known Seth of the past, if she met him today, she would already be in love with him. And when he kissed her like he, too, needed her mouth more than air itself, she felt like maybe he might fall in love with her too—if they were different people.

If, if, if.

They didn't have hypotheticals. They had two weeks to

be selfish together, and then it was back to being a full-time aunt.

She didn't realize she was shaking until he eased back from the kiss and took her keys from her. "Hey," he murmured. "It's okay."

Of course it was. She frowned, confused, and he touched her cheek.

His fingertips were wet.

Oh. Well, that was less hot than she planned this return to be.

He stood there, letting her press her cheek into his palm. "It's okay to miss them."

She shook her head and tried to nod at the same time. "We all needed a break." *I needed some time alone with you,* she tried to add, but it didn't come out.

"It's okay to want them out of your hair *and* to miss them at the same time."

She hiccupped, real tears threatening now, not just the few that had leaked out. "Yeah. I do miss them."

"I know."

She wound her fingers into the front of his shirt. "Seth?"

"Mmm?"

"Do you want to sleep over?"

"I had zero plans on leaving." He pulled her close, trapping her hand between their bodies. "We've got all night."

"You really sent Bailey home?"

She felt him grin against her forehead. "Figured I could field any questions that came up in the last fifteen minutes, and you might be sad when you got here."

He'd wanted that to be as private as possible for her.

She glanced around. They were alone on the steps

outside the office, but there were people on the boats in the marina. Were any of them paying attention to how she threw herself at him? She surprised herself a little by not caring at all. But she did wonder if any of them need help.

Reading her mind again, he held up August's cell phone, which had been left in Bailey's care. "We've got this. Let's put up the sign and go upstairs."

She let him make that call. She was too wrung out to protest, and she didn't even want to. "Thank you," she whispered as he guided her to the couch in her too-quiet home.

He sprawled in the corner of the sectional and tucked her in front of him. "Tell me how it went."

"They were arguing right up until they got on the plane."

He chuckled softly. "You know they stopped as soon as they were out of your sight, right?"

She sighed. "Yes. I already told myself that."

He squeezed her shoulders, then rolled his thumbs gently up her neck. "Does it help to have someone else say it out loud?"

"Mmm."

"Does it help to have someone offer you orgasms?"

She laughed, startled. "Yes, that helps."

His hands slid down her arms, raising goosebumps as his palms trailed over her bare skin. She twisted to look at him, and his fingers curled into the front of her shirt. Then his hands were holding her still, firm against her belly, and everything faded away again, just like when she'd kissed him, but this time it wasn't desperate.

All she could see were the dark flecks in his eyes.

She just didn't want to think anymore. She only wanted to touch, and feel.

"It's okay," he whispered against her skin. "This doesn't have to be anything more than what it is. If you need to use me as an escape then let me be that escape for you."

She shook her head. She was long past that. They needed to stop pretending this didn't mean something important. "I want you. Not as an escape. But because you're kind and sexy and funny."

"I'm funny?"

"You've always been funny," she murmured, turning all the way around to straddle him.

He sipped at her lips. "Does that mean I haven't always been kind and sexy?"

She smiled against his mouth. "You were sexy and kind back in the day, too. But now? There's no comparison. You're the real deal, Seth. And I want you so much it hurts."

He stilled beneath her, his thighs flexed, his chest broad and solid. Then he exhaled and surged. "You can have me," he promised as he ground their bodies together. "All night long."

The thick ridge of his erection worked against her clit, underlining his words and reminding her how good they felt together naked.

Legs shaking, she climbed off him and held out her hand. He laced his fingers through hers.

Neither of them spoke as she led him upstairs. He started to undress her at the side of the bed as she pulled a box of condoms out of the bedside table.

"I like the way you communicate your interest in my dick loud and clear," Seth said with a chuckle as he swept his hands down her sides, tugging her tight against him.

"Not just your *dick*," she said playfully.

He brushed his mouth over her neck, making her shiver. "Oh?"

"I'm deeply invested in your mouth, too."

He squeezed her ass.

"And your hands." Her breath hitched as he worked his thigh between hers, making her ride his leg. "Your whole body is very, very nice. Very…capable."

"I aim to please." He tumbled her onto her back.

"What about you?" She tugged at his belt as he loomed over her. "What do you need?"

He peeled off his shirt, then stared down at her with a searing look, his chest heaving. "I just need you."

Without saying another word, she hooked her thumbs into her panties and wriggled them down her hips. He pressed her legs apart and dropped his head, like a man in a desert at the first sight of water. He dragged his tongue through her folds, tasting her, then flipped her over, sinking his teeth into the curve of her ass before tilting her hips up and finding her slit again.

Her cheeks burned and her heart pounded as she arched her back. She pressed her face into the soft blanket and heard his words pounding in her ears. *I just need you.*

That look of craving on his face would get her to do absolutely anything. Ass in the air, legs spread shamelessly, sex shoved back against his hungry mouth—literally anything.

He traced the length of her clit with his tongue. She felt it, careful and slow, like he was mapping every inch of her. He'd gone down on her before, but never from this angle, and it felt…deliberate. Like he didn't want to miss anything.

And the way his breath thundered in the silence when he reared up behind her?

That was a drug she'd never get enough of.

After all this time, she made this sexy god of a man that turned on? January of three months earlier would never have believed it.

His fingers stroked lazily between her thighs now as he worked behind her to get rid of his own clothes.

Then he was back, one hand on her ass, the other circling her entrance. "I want to fuck you like this, January."

She rocked back. "Yes, please."

He grunted. "Not the first time, though."

"It's okay," she breathed.

He flipped her over.

He had a condom in his hand, which she caught a flash of before he fell on top of her. "It's not for me," he growled. "I sink into your pussy for the first time after all these years? I want to see the look on your face as you take me. Every last inch. Every little reaction. I need it all."

Oh. Her eyes flared wide and she nodded.

He caught her chin and held her still as he kissed her. Long, slow, and agonizingly perfect.

Then he hitched her leg up, hooking it over his hip, and left her spread open beneath him as he rolled on the condom.

His cock looked massive in his hand, and it felt just as big when he tilted her hips up and fit them together.

Inch by inch, he pressed inside her, his gaze on her face the whole time. And she gave him exactly what he'd asked of her—every reaction, unfiltered. The wide-eyed surprise at the first stretch, the bite of her lip as he pushed past her G-spot, and the shuddering relief when he was fully seated inside her body.

He took up too much space there, both physically and

emotionally. It was tempting to close her eyes and writhe beneath, to shift this from whatever it was he wanted—a claiming again?—to something she could handle more easily. A good, simple fuck.

The best fuck ever, probably, and it had only just begun.

But they'd established a special kind of honest connection when he took her to that cove, and she wasn't going to hide from that now.

"You feel incredible," he rumbled, bracing his arms on either side of her body. "So fucking soft and tight."

She sucked in a pleased inhale, then curved her thighs up, wrapping her legs around his hips. "I took you. Every last inch."

His thumb stroked over her cheek. "My pretty girl."

Oh, that one might just break her heart. And still she held his gaze, letting him drink his fill of whatever he wanted to see in her eyes.

And finally he started moving, with a fluid grace that took her breath away all over again. Pressing into the mattress, caging her in, he shifted his weight onto his arms and rolled his hips. She clung to him as his erection strained inside her, then dragged out, leaving a hollow ache at her core. She cried out, then he plunged forward again, bringing that blessed too-big, just-right stretch back.

He groaned her name.

She dug her heels into the hard curve of his ass.

He thrust again, and this time she tightened her hold on him.

"You need me inside you?"

She couldn't speak, only had a nod in her, but he slowed his pulsing movements, shifted his weight again, and then stayed inside her, deep. Just enough movement to keep her gasping. His mouth hovered above hers, his eyes locked on her face.

"We're not rushing this," he growled.

Someone had thought a lot about this, she realized. He had *plans*. "Oh yeah?"

"I see you. All wound up, ready to go. You want to come? You can come, January. But I'm not following you just yet. I want to play for a while."

Her heart leapt at that. Of course sex with Seth would be fun play. She arched against him, her breasts rubbing his chest. He spread his legs wider, changing his stance, then caught her right breast in his left hand.

"Then play," she whispered.

He ducked his head and sucked her nipple into his mouth. She trembled, then convulsed when he pulled off in a wet, satisfied plop. Her nipple stood tight and proud, and he rolled it between his fingers. Then he grinned. "Fuck, you're sexy."

She laughed and rocked her hips.

He kissed her again, and when he went back to the rolling, rhythmic fucking, she didn't protest this time. She still felt hollow when he pulled out, but the intense pleasure when he thrust in again more than made up for it. It was two halves of the same thing. She couldn't have the rush without the withdrawal, and oh, she wanted that rush now.

Over and over again, he moved their bodies together. She could feel herself hovering close to an orgasm, but getting there might require her brain sinking into a dirtier, more detached space, and she didn't want that just yet.

He was playing with her, and she loved it. She wanted to be fully with him in this moment.

"What do you need now?" he asked as he slid his hand under her lower back.

"This feels good."

He nipped at her lower lip. "But I want it to feel more like on the edge of destroying you."

"How cruel," she gasped, laughing.

His gaze glittered as he grinned down at her. "Only if you want me to be."

"I don't know what I want," she breathed. "Just you. And this. Don't stop."

"Not stopping." He scooped her in his arm and rolled them effortlessly, barely pausing in his steady hip thrusts. "Bounce on top of me. Let me see you."

She arched her back, liking the way he filled his hands with her tits as soon as he could. He rolled and tugged on her nipples until her thighs shook, then dropped one hand to where her sex was stretched around his cock. He slicked his thumb with her arousal and pressed it to her clit.

Gasping, she fell forward, catching her hands on his shoulders. Now her breasts hung in front of his face.

"Feeling destroyed?"

She grinned at him. "More like reborn."

"Oh, I like that," he growled. "My sexy phoenix."

Another shiver wracked her body as he simultaneously latched onto a nipple and pumped his hips in the air, sending her soul flying.

When she found her balance again, he was deeper inside her than he'd been before, pressing against new and exciting nerve endings.

Playtime was over.

He sucked at her breasts, pulling whole mouthfuls of her flesh into his mouth, his eyelids hooding even as he watched her hover above.

Words broke apart in her mind, leaving only feelings. Whole, full, complicated feelings that welled up and threatened to burst a dam. Then other sensations rose, too, just as fierce: need, arousal, blissful release.

Seth groaned against her breast. His thumb rolled over her clit faster now, and she was going—was he with her? —any second now—breaking…

She clenched down, her head bowing, his mouth tearing away from her skin, finding her lips. Biting her mouth, gently, then thrusting his tongue inside—not gently. A final claim. They kissed as her orgasm imploded, squeezing him tight. She felt him groan, his cock pulsing deep, then his hips stuttered against her bottom.

Every bit of her shook as she slumped on top of him.

He stroked her back and gasped for air, his legs falling flat on the bed.

His skin was damp, the hair on his thighs sticking against the inside of her legs.

His heart thumped heavily against her ear.

"You bite now," she said in the staggering silence that followed.

He hummed happily. "You're irresistible. Especially your ass."

She grinned. "To be clear, I'm not complaining."

"I didn't think you were. The way you arched your back and pressed—"

"Okay."

"More than okay."

She nodded. Very much so.

He stretched. "I'm going to replay the highlights reel of this night for a very long time to come."

Same. She hoped her brain stuck to the dirty parts, and

didn't linger too long on how it felt to have him demand her full attention as he slowly entered her.

Then he patted her bum. "Hungry?"

Whatever she'd read into that moment was probably romantic fancy. And that wasn't what they were doing.

They were fucking, and now eating. And later, they'd fuck again. It was all she wanted.

19

———

THEY WERE SNUGGLED on the couch an hour later when her phone vibrated.

"It's a text message from Summer," she murmured, showing him the screen. A GIF from a horror movie.

Summer: What it's like flying with Levi
Summer: Just kidding, he was really good. We've
found Dad and Grandpa. Love you!
January: Love you, too. Did you message
your mom?
Summer: Yes
January: Good girl. Thank you. Have fun!
Summer: We will

Seth traced her thumb, where she was clutching the phone tightly. "You okay?"

"Yeah."

"You ready for bed?"

"Definitely."

He took her phone and chased her up the stairs. Then

he revealed he'd already brought a toiletries bag over so he could brush his teeth and wash his face, which pleased her to no end.

"What would you have done if I'd told you to go home?"

"Grabbed my stuff and gone home." He propped his hip against the sink and tugged on her hair. "And come back tomorrow, of course."

She pushed up on her toes and leaned in, kissing his minty fresh mouth.

He was just wearing his boxer briefs, and she'd pulled on her jean shorts and a t-shirt. Under them she was commando, though, so when she took them off, she glanced at Seth, then at the bed.

"Do you want to sleep naked, or…?"

"What do you want?"

No point in not being fully honest about this, either. "I get cold at night."

"Are you going to wear that adorable shirt with the wine glass on it?"

She laughed. "That one is in the laundry. How about…" She pulled out a hot pink one. "Nap Queen?"

"Love it." His gaze darkened. "No panties, though."

Sucking in a quick breath, she nodded, and let him tug her back to bed.

———

FOR ONCE, January didn't need an alarm to get up, and she wasn't a groggy mess, either. She woke with a quiet start at dawn, confused for a split second about what was different—and then remembered she wasn't alone in bed.

Next to her, Seth was warm and big. A slumbering

giant who had the most delicious scent. She breathed him in, then traced the shape of his face, her fingers lingering on the faint lines that bracketed his mouth.

He was gloriously handsome. Tan skin, soft stubble, mature features.

"Are you watching me sleep?" he mumbled. "Come here."

"I need to put coffee on," she whispered as he turned her around, then snaked his hand between her legs and cupped her whole sex.

"Mmkay."

"The marina office opens in thirty minutes and I need a shower."

He groaned and pressed his face into the crook of her neck. "I know. How many hours until we can return to this bed?"

"Want to sneak in a lunch break quickie?"

"Can't promise I'll be quick about anything, but yes." He sighed and slid his hands up her torso to her breasts. "You feel amazing in the morning."

"That is the nicest thing anyone has said to me today."

He bit her gently for being cheeky, and she twisted around to kiss him softly.

"What are your plans for the day?"

"Month end accounting, and then nothing. Or maybe nothing, and then month end accounting this afternoon."

"That sounds amazing." She kissed him again, because stopping was hard. "I like accounting."

"That's my sexy little math teacher."

"Sweet talk me like that and I'll let you share my shower time."

He hauled them both out of bed and sprinted ahead to start the hot water.

IN ORDER TO keep his hands off the woman who just wanted to do her day's work in peace—at least until lunchtime—Seth headed over to the garage. He collected a coffee and pastries order from Josh, who had just arrived, then hopped in Betty and headed up Main Street to *Bake Sale!*

Adam was there as well, in his firefighter uniform, flirting with his wife. "Morning," he said when Seth walked in.

"Morning. Slow work day?"

"We like those," Adam drawled. "It means nobody's in trouble. I'm doing a breakfast run for the house."

"Same. Well, just me and Josh."

Isla laughed. "The Kincaids, keeping me in business."

Adam leaned across the counter and kissed his wife. "Perk of being in the family."

"Mmm." She gave him a secret smile, then turned back to Seth. "What can we get you this morning?"

He placed his order, then chatted with Adam for a few until the firehouse's order was ready to go.

Just as Adam picked up his tray of coffee cups, the radio on his shoulder went off. Seth couldn't make it all out, but it sounded like a multiple vehicle collision on the highway.

"Never mind these coffees," Adam said, setting the tray down. "Give them to whoever comes in next."

Then he was out the door and in his truck.

"Damn," Seth said under his breath.

Isla's face tensed up, just for a moment, then she took a deep breath. Like Seth and Adam, she was ex-military—a former infantry officer—and compartmentalizing feelings were a part of the training.

"It's always hard to see him race into danger," she said softly.

"Yeah."

She gave him an almost smile. "Do you still see him as a towheaded kid wearing a Lego shirt?"

"Not as much as Will and Owen do." His phone vibrated in his pocket, and he pulled it out. "Speak of the devil. Owen, what's up?"

"Hey, are you around? Any chance you could fly Kerry down the lakeshore a bit?"

"Absolutely." He glanced at the coffees Isla had just made. "Does she have time for a coffee on the way?"

Owen relayed the details—the highway was closed, Kerry's partner Jenna was at a twin home birth fifteen minutes south, at a cottage on the water, and needed backup probably sooner than the highway would be reopened, and Old Whiskey Harbour Road was currently closed for bridge repairs.

The perils of living on a peninsula with only so many north-south roadways.

And yes, she had time for a coffee.

Seth slid his phone away, then nodded to the tray. "I'll take two of these as well."

"Everything okay?" Isla asked.

"It will be," he promised. "It sounds like some babies are going to be born today."

Her face bloomed into a soft smile. "That's happier news than a car accident."

He didn't tell her just how many cars were involved in the accident. Adam could share that detail later, once everyone was safe.

By the time he returned to the marina, his sister-in-law, Kerry, was getting out of her car. She slung a big duffel bag across her body, then crossed to where he parked and took the tray of coffees from him.

"I really appreciate this," she said. "I hope you weren't busy."

"I had plans to do accounting." *And January, at lunch, but that can be a dinner plan instead.* He gestured to the marina office. "Let's drop off these coffees and we'll get you in the air."

Inside, he gave Josh's coffee to January, as well as the other bonus latte. "Can you run this across to Josh, tell him I haven't kidnapped Betty, she's here in the parking lot, but I need to take Kerry on a short hop down the lake."

"Is everything okay?"

For the second time, he relayed the briefest version of the story, and she shooed them out the door.

At the plane, he did his safety check, then pulled out his maps and figured out where he was going while Kerry called her partner and got the latest update on the labouring mom.

When she ended the call, he opened the plane door for her and gestured for her to hop in.

"Thanks."

"I always wanted to work on an air ambulance," he said with a grin. "This might be as close as I ever get."

"Hey, maybe I'll hire you again."

He untied the plane from the dock, then followed her in. "Wild day, huh?"

"Yeah." She blew out her cheeks. "I was with Owen when they got the 911 call. Lila's at daycare today, and we were having a picnic breakfast in his office—dating with children means you pick the opportunities when you can get them. I had literally just said, 'twin births can be intense, I hope nothing complicates today,' and then the dispatch radioed about the accident."

"It's good to have another option. And if I weren't here, you could have taken a boat."

She gave him a relieved smile. "I appreciate the Kincaid Calm."

"Want to tell me about what you know of the labour so far? Does that kind of prep briefing work?"

"Sure." She ran through what she knew of the situation she was about to walk into as he got the plane up to speed, then pointed south and took off.

Then she stopped talking.

Seth never tired of that little beat of quiet amazement when he took someone into the air. Flying was a real marvel of human ingenuity. Especially in a small aircraft like his plane.

It was a short flight, and someone was waiting on the dock at their destination, waving him in.

"I'm a friend of the family's," the woman said as she helped Kerry out. "You're just in time."

"Text me if you need a pick up," Seth said to Kerry's rapidly retreating back.

She tossed a wave and an appreciative smile over her shoulder, then disappeared up a path into the woods.

He texted Owen a quick update.

SETH: Your wife has been delivered safely! Pun intended.

OWEN DIDN'T TEXT BACK RIGHT AWAY, so Seth started his plane again and headed home.

Home.

When was the last time he'd thought of Blind River as home, instead of Pine Harbour?

He frowned, and his brow was still tight with thought when he landed again. Instead of going straight to his berth, he went to the fuel pumps—just in case there was more delivery assistance required, although he didn't expect that.

When he tied up, he spied January talking to one of the boaters. She waved, then slowly made her way in Seth's direction. The boater followed, continuing their conversation.

And just before they reached Seth, a dog bounded into view.

Nugget had grown since the last time they'd seen her, but she was still recognizable, as was her owner.

"Hello, girl," Seth said, crouching down. It was that or flex his shoulders unnecessarily at January's ex—who apparently knew the man she was talking to as well. They greeted each other with a deep familiarity.

January made the introductions.

"Seth, you remember Trent Aitken. And this is Campbell Mills."

Ah, the business partner. Seth stood and extended his hand. "Of the brewery. Nice to meet you. Seth Kincaid."

"Of the airline." Campbell nodded at the plane. "I'm familiar. Do you ever do sightseeing charters?"

"I haven't yet, but could do." There wasn't a lot of demand for that out of Blind River. "You interested in seeing your property from above?"

"Sure, but no, I wasn't thinking for myself. We're looking to partner with local businesses to build full-day excursions that include a beer tasting at the brewery."

But I'm not a local business was at the tip of Seth's tongue. He swallowed the protest.

"January's thinking of leasing a boat for island tours," Campbell continued.

That was news to Seth. He shot her a look, which she ignored.

"And Trent is our point person for land excursions."

The other man started talking, but all Seth could think about was how close he was standing to January, their shoulders almost touching, and how Seth didn't know January was considering adding boat charters to the marina.

What happened to it being hard and the marina barely being profitable?

At their feet, Nugget yanked on her lead, and Trent told her to sit. "Sorry, we're still working on the training. But I will need to go soon." He brushed his hand over January's shoulder, and Seth saw red.

She's mine, he wanted to snap, but something held him back. Maybe it was the look on her face. Maybe it was the fact they hadn't talked about what they were to each other in a while.

It was definitely that he didn't want to hear her say he was just a friend.

So when his phone vibrated, he was grateful for the distraction.

Owen: Sorry, at a callout, thanks for doing that
Seth: The highway accident?
Owen: In a manner of speaking

He attached a photo.

Owen: Kerry isn't the only one delivering a baby today… this little one couldn't wait to arrive
Owen: Delivered her on the side of the road
Seth: Holy shit, man, that's cool
Owen: Yeah. But Lila's having a rough day at daycare. Any chance you could pick her up? If you can't, I can ask Catie. And Isla's off work at three?
Seth: I'm on it

He caught January's eye. "Sorry to interrupt. I need to fuel up and go. I have to pick up Lila from daycare."

"You have kids?" Trent asked.

"My niece."

January helped Seth with the fuel, and told him she'd charge him later.

That's right, he wanted to say out loud. *Because I'll be back here later, making her scream my name.*

He really needed to get a handle on these feelings. Trent hadn't done anything other than exist in a space Seth had abandoned twenty years ago. And January deserved more than some testosterone-fuelled chest thumping.

He thought about that as he took Lila for a long walk that afternoon. Owen and Kerry had a monster truck edition of a stroller, with big wheels perfect for a trail, so he headed out to Mac's and the snowmobile path behind it that was a nice, flat running and biking route in the summer.

By the time he'd done an eight kilometre out and back walk, she was fast asleep, so he got a late takeout lunch, then slowly headed over to Owen's place.

Just as he was walking up the drive, a dark SUV pulled in behind him.

Owen's oldest, Becca, rolled down the window and waved.

"This is a surprise," he said as she hopped out. "Where's Charlie?"

"With Hayden, at his parents' place."

Becca and her boyfriend—who now played professional hockey—had been teen parents. Despite Owen's understandable concerns of history repeating itself, the couple seemed to be maturing into a relationship very different from that of Becca's parents. "I didn't know you were in town."

She smiled shyly, which wasn't Becca's personality at all. "Well…we ended up coming up a few days early." Then she shoved her hand through her long, sleek hair, and Seth was blinded by the rock on her finger.

"Is that— Are you—?"

She dropped her hand, her eyes wide. "Don't tell Dad before I can tell him."

"He's at work." Seth rubbed his hand over his mouth. "Do you want me to see if he's at the station, or…?"

She glanced at her baby sister, still asleep in the stroller, and her face went soft. "Are you babysitting today? Maybe we can just hang out for a bit."

Seth opened the house and Becca carried Lila inside, all the way to the crib in her room.

When she returned, he filled her in on what her dad and Kerry were doing today.

"So he's probably busy," she said, spinning the ring on her finger.

Seth poked her fingertip with his own. "Hey."

"Mmm."

"He'll be happy for you."

"Mmm."

He chuckled. "Are you happy?"

Her gaze flew to his face. "Yes."

"Then that's all that matters to him. I promise."

"He's not always Hayden's biggest fan."

"That's because Hayden was an eighteen-year-old shit-head who got his daughter pregnant." Seth ignored the tug in his chest. "Something your dad deeply related to, in a too-many-feelings kind of way."

"I know."

"But you guys didn't rush into marriage. You waited, and Charlie's getting bigger now—" Seth cut himself off. "It's none of my business, but are you pregnant again?"

Becca's eyes went wide. "No."

"Okay."

"That's not why we're doing this."

"Good." He shrugged. "So why are you doing it?"

A soft smiled curled across her face. "Because he asked. And when he asked, my heart leapt. It was a total surprise, too. He'd just received news that he was going down to the AHL again for next season, and I thought he'd be bummed, but he was buzzing. Couldn't sleep that night, stayed up late watching old game tape. I thought he'd sleep in for sure the next day, but when I woke up, he was up with Charlie, and they were making breakfast. He..." She blushed. "He said a lot of really sweet things, about how with all the ups and downs of his career, Charlie and I are the constant, central thing he holds on to. And then he got down on one knee and I burst into tears. Charlie got mad at him that he made me cry. It was hilarious and sweet."

"That's an awesome proposal story."

"Yeah." Her grin was broader now, more confident. More Becca. "So then we decided to drive up and tell everyone now, before the stag and doe, so it's old news by the time Will and Catie get married."

"Have you thought about picking a date?"

"Probably next summer. It depends how the season goes, and if he…" She trailed off.

"What?"

She made a face, somewhere between happy and nervous. "There's a chance we might go to Europe. It's a different kind of game there."

"Wow."

"Yeah."

"I wouldn't lead with that." Seth thought about it. "No, it's fine. Your dad will be happy for you either way."

"I'm definitely saving that piece for later. But if we do move there, then maybe a wedding will happen…I don't know." She fluttered her hands in the air. "One thing at a time."

Seth's phone rang. "Speak of the devil. It's your dad." He answered it, holding a finger up to his lips. "Hey, man."

"How's Lila?"

"Passed out cold in her crib. I took her for a long walk."

Owen sighed in relief. "Great. Thanks for doing that. Her first few daycare days were fine. Of course today would be the day separation anxiety reared its head. I won't be off shift until seven. Are you okay with her until then?"

"Yeah, absolutely." He winked at Becca. "I bet I can find some help, too. Not that I need it."

Owen laughed. "Of course. Kerry and Jenna have another client who just went into labour. She's transporting to hospital, but they'll want to follow her there as soon as they are done with the twins."

"Is four babies born on one day a record for Pine Harbour?"

"Probably." Owen's radio crackled. "Gotta go. Text me updates."

He hung up, texted January that he wouldn't be around again until later, then gave Becca the update.

"Who did you just text?" she asked, ever the nosy niece.

The back of his neck heated up. "A woman."

"The woman at the marina?"

"Who told you?"

She rolled her eyes. "Who didn't?" She ticked off her fingers. "Josh told me the second you kicked him out of his apartment. Hilarious, by the way. So then I asked Will, who told me that Dad said we aren't allowed to play matchmaker. I followed up with Dad, because that's a weird thing to say—"

"I asked him to do that," Seth interjected.

She sighed. "Oh, sweet summer child. That just stirred up more interest. So now instead of actively trying to push you together, your brothers are just compiling a secret timeline behind your back like conspiracy theorists."

He laughed despite himself. "And you?"

"Oh, I want to play matchmaker still. Need any help?"

He rubbed the back of his neck. "Got any advice for feeling jealous when it's not my place?"

She flopped back on the couch. "Oh my *God*, let me tell you about dating a hockey player. You have to differentiate between weird little pricks of jealousy that are external, and sharp stabbing ones that are like, a real problem. Don't ignore your gut."

"My gut says I have no reason to be jealous." He thought of January stretched out beneath him as he entered her. Her eyes were wide, deep pools of emotion, stormier than the lake even on its worst day. And he felt a deep shame for even entertaining the notion. He shook his head. "No, it's just irrational stuff on my part, because we have this long-ago history."

"And in between, you both led independent lives."

"For a child, you're very insightful."

She swatted at him. "I'm almost twenty-one, you knob."

"Language."

She snorted.

"It's going to work out," he said.

"You talking to me, or you?"

"Both of us."

————

THE SUN WAS SETTING by the time he made it back to the marina. He went past the garage to grab a change of clothes for the next day.

January had put the closed sign up, but left the door unlocked for him.

He found her upstairs on the couch, and a familiar video game was on the TV screen.

"I bought Sim City this afternoon." She lifted her face to give him a slow, interested kiss. "Thought we could play a bit while the kids were gone."

"I love it." He sat down at her feet, then caught her ankle and held it firmly as he leaned over. His gaze on her face, he brushed his lips beside her anklebone.

"You aren't interested in playing right now?" she whispered.

"Oh yes, I am." He sucked at the soft flesh there.

Her controller dropped gently to the floor.

———

AN HOUR LATER, he picked it up again as she caught her breath.

She gave him an amused, appreciative smile as he handed it to her. "Show me your city."

"We haven't even talked about the drama of the day!"

"Babies were born. Babies were minded. And then I got to come home to you at the end of the day, which is everything I wanted." He swept a damp strand of hair off her cheek. "Oh! I have a secret."

Her lips curled up. "I'm good at keeping secrets."

"Becca is engaged."

January gasped. "Oh, that's wonderful!"

"Hayden proposed after getting up early one morning with Charlie—and then making breakfast."

She pressed her hand to her chest. "Swoon."

"She's telling her dad tonight, so it's not actually a secret for much longer."

"You found out this afternoon?"

"Yeah. He bought her a massive ring. Hard to miss. She came by, looking for Owen, and found me instead."

"Awww." She snuggled close. "I'm happy for her. Young love is so sweet."

He kissed the top of her head. *Would you want a ring?* It would be added to the long list of things he wanted to ask her and didn't feel like he could—at least not right now.

Because he was thinking about stuff like that more and

more, and she always turned the conversation away from that. *Young love is so sweet.*

Nothing was sweeter than a second chance with January, though. He would take this on whatever terms she wanted, however she wanted him.

"Want to see my city?"

"I sure do."

"I haven't gotten very far," she said, her cheeks pink. "But I've already put in a town hall, and that empty block next to it will be where the school goes eventually."

"I love it." He really did. More than he thought possible. Watching her find a new joy in an old, simple pleasure did something profound to him.

And if he focused on the game, and the taste of her lingering on his lips, then he didn't have to think about just how much he hadn't liked standing next to a guy she'd dated recently and *not* being introduced as the man she was currently sleeping with.

"This is Seth, my first, current, and best fuck. Nobody else will ever compare."

That was definitely asking too much.

"Seth?"

"Mmm?"

"Do you want to start a city?"

He tangled his hand in the curls at the base of her scalp. "You keep building."

She set the controller down and looked at him. "What is it? You seem distracted. And not nearly relaxed enough after that very energetic bout of *nice to see you* sex."

He'd asked a lot of her lately. And she'd been open with him at every turn. But he didn't need to lead with jealousy. That was his issue to manage. He took a deep breath. "Are you getting into the boat tour business?"

"What? No." She laughed gently. "Why?"

"Campbell said you were thinking of leasing a boat."

"Oh." She groaned. "Okay, first rule of thumb with those guys is to understand that they're always working an angle. Like…I like them well enough, they're going to be great business neighbours, but they vibe at a different level. It's exhausting. What happened earlier was, *Campbell* said I should consider leasing a boat for tours, and *I* nodded because it's none of his business that I would rather poke my eyes out than hire a whole crew. I was stressed at the insurance claim on a broken dock. I haven't even successfully hired a part-timer for the office. But if Augie wants to get into that next year, more power to her. I don't want to tell him an unequivocal no when I'm only running this place for the summer, and his plans don't really kick in until next year, you know?"

Seth winced. "That all makes sense."

She raised her eyebrows. "You thought I was sharing my business plans with him?"

How big a serving of humble pie could he shove in his mouth? "The thought occurred to me."

"That's a ridiculous thought." She said it gently, but it was true. He'd leapt to a weird conclusion based on what someone else said. She hadn't said anything at all.

"Sometimes, I'm a ridiculous man." He stroked his thumb up the side of her neck. Might as well share all of his complicated thoughts. "I also wanted Trent and Campbell to know you were mine."

Her lips parted as she sucked in a little jolt of air.

"It's okay, don't say anything. I know it's across the line. Just…that's what was on my mind—"

She cut him off with her mouth. A soft, lingering kiss. "Trent and I never had anything like this," she whispered.

"He's never seen my Nap Queen sleep shirt. I never… Any of this. This is all for us, and only us. This summer, I *am* yours. I promise."

"We haven't talked about being more public."

"Mmm." She brushed her lips against his again. "Because what we do is very, very private. Sinfully private."

That made him smile. "But the stag and doe is on the weekend."

"Mm-hmm."

"I'm going to want a dance."

"Only one?"

"Gonna hold you in my arms all night."

"People are going to talk."

He stroked her cheek, then took her mouth. Harder this time. "How do you feel about that?"

She shrugged. "Let them."

He agreed. Yes. *Let them,* he thought fiercely. *Let them all see how I feel.*

And then maybe she would, too. Because he couldn't tell her yet. Not if she didn't feel the same way.

20

Saturday morning started far too early for a woman who had been kept up every night, all week, by a ravenous man.

And the ravenous man was whistling.

"I'll pay you to go put the coffee on downstairs," she mumbled.

He just chuckled and tucked her back into bed.

When she dragged herself out of that cozy nest two alarms later, she found him in the office. He was on the phone with one of his brothers, talking about the designated drivers list for that night.

Kincaids were safety conscious when they threw a big party.

She kissed him good morning, poured herself a cup of coffee, then opened the marina for business.

There was a decent stream of people coming in for coffee this morning. At least half of them asked her if she'd switched brands, because it was "so good today."

Seth was endlessly amused by that, and she muttered

darkly that he might find himself accidentally employed as their Saturday morning receptionist if he kept it up.

He left once Josh opened the garage, then came back with snacks mid-morning. Left again in the early afternoon to collect all the prizes for the stag and doe fifty-fifty ticket sales—which often went to offset the cost of the wedding, but tonight, Will and Catie were donating the proceeds to a few local charities.

The cash bar proceeds were going to good causes, too.

It was a down home pre-wedding let-loose celebration that would also give back to the community, and ticket sales had been brisk.

Josh was mostly responsible for that, but January had sold quite a few at the marina office as well. She'd done her job as the co-organizer, even if she was mostly distracted these days.

And today in particular.

The countdown was on for their first quasi-public date. Was it a date, though? He'd asked her to dance with him. Not be his date.

She was overthinking it.

January: What should I wear tonight?
August: Are you overthinking it?
January: A thousand percent
August: Jeans and a tight t-shirt
August: And a thong
January: What? Why?
August: You look casual to the outside world, like
this is no big deal, but if his fingers sneak under
your waistband, he'll know you dressed up
for him
January: LOL dressed up

But she thought about how he liked to flip her onto all fours. Seth was absolutely an ass man.

January: That's genius

———

"What are you wearing tonight?"

Josh pushed the last two-four of beer into the back of his truck, then stopped and gave Seth a confused look. "Excuse me?"

"Like…jeans and a nice dress shirt?" Seth frowned. "I don't have a dress shirt here."

"That will make wearing one difficult."

"I can borrow one from Will."

"I think a t-shirt will be fine."

Most of his clothes were branded with either Kincaid Air Ferry or Fly North Aviation. Why didn't this question occur to him sooner?

"January has seen you naked, right?" Josh held up his hands. "I'm not asking for details, but I noticed that you haven't been sleeping at the garage much. I don't think you need to impress her with a collar at this point, you know?"

But he did need to impress her with something.

They were at Will's house, loading up supplies for the dance, which had accumulated in his garage over the last few weeks.

And just down the street was January's future house. He'd driven past it a few times.

Owen pulled up in his truck, distracting Seth from that niggling thought.

"Maybe you can help this guy," Josh called out.

"Shut up," Seth growled.

Owen raised his eyebrows.

Seth sighed. "I made the mistake of showing Josh that I care a little about looking good tonight." He paused. "For January."

Both of his brothers grinned.

Then Josh opened the driver's side door of his truck. "I'm taking this stuff to the Legion. I'll be back in a few."

Which left Seth and Owen standing on Will's driveway alone—and the topic of January hanging in the air.

His oldest brother saw right through him. "You're serious about her."

"Yeah."

"What about your fears from before, that because of your history…"

"I need to talk to her about that." He rocked his jaw back and forth. "It doesn't feel like the barrier it once did."

"Oh?"

"Spending this time together… It's been eye-opening. I mean, she makes me fucking happy. You know?"

Owen grinned. "I'm familiar, yeah."

"I had a passenger earlier this year who was griping to me about his wife, and I thought…pretty sure that ain't it, dude. That's not what I see you having with Kerry, and Adam with Isla. How Will loves Catie so damn much, because she makes him happy."

"Sure. Yeah." Owen blinked at him. "Are you saying that's how you feel about January?"

"Look, she's not there. So I don't want to put any pressure on her. We've just started exploring what this is going to be between us."

"But you're talking about her with the family."

He rubbed the back of his neck. "Yeah."

"Because the last time…"

"I didn't want meddling. I still don't." He straightened up and rolled his shoulders. "I don't *need* meddling. I want to woo her on my own terms. But tonight is a chance to also be with her in public, and show her that I can be a guy she'd be proud to stand next to."

"Of course you are."

Seth made a face. "Yeah."

"Come on."

"She doesn't want big feelings."

"Well, that's her call."

"Yeah, I know."

"So you thought you might dress up for her tonight?"

"I was just making conversation with Josh. Always a mistake."

Owen snorted. "What was his advice?"

"She's seen me naked, so it's a bit late to try and impress her with a collar."

"Oh, bullshit." Owen sighed and shook his head. "Whatever happened to him in California made him way too cynical. Let me promise you, when I put the effort in to look good for Kerry, it's always worth it."

"He ever talk to you about that? His blink-and-you'd-miss-it marriage?"

"Never."

"If the family wanted to meddle…"

Owen laughed. "Oh, no. If it's not good for you, then it's not good for him, either."

Well, that was fair.

"Come on, let's go inside and raid Will's closet. Maybe he left behind some clothes that might fit you."

———

SETH PICKED her up a quarter after seven. Half of the people who used the marina were going to the Legion for the dance anyway, but January still made sure she had August's cell phone when she heard his knock downstairs, then his heavy footsteps on the stairs.

"I'm in here," she called out, taking one last look at herself in the mirror in the living room.

He stepped into the hallway, and her heart leapt at the sight of him. He'd shaved his usual stubble away, and his hair was a little damp from a recent shower. He was wearing a dark blue dress shirt with the sleeves rolled up to his elbows over fitted jeans that molded to his thighs, and head to toe looked absolutely delicious.

She'd left her hair down for once, letting her waves do their wild thing in all directions, and taken extra care with her makeup—the only fancy touch in an otherwise dressed-down look.

From the heated expression in his eyes, he liked her faded Summerfolk t-shirt and the soft, touchable black jersey skirt that made her hips look good.

"You're all made up," he said in a rich purr as he pulled her into his arms. "Can I kiss you?"

"Yes, please." She smiled as he brought their mouths together. The excited heart flutter she felt when he arrived —every time he walked into a room—was soothed into a warm squish in her chest as soon as his tongue traced the seam of her lips.

His kisses turned her into a human lava lamp. It wasn't only his mouth against hers, it was also the strong band of his arms around her, the way his body shook a little at the first taste, and the guaranteed repeat kiss at the end, like one was never enough.

She felt the same way.

"Ready?"

"Mm-hmm."

They walked up the hill. Everyone in town walked to a stag and doe, unless they had mobility issues, because most people would be at least a little tipsy by the end of the night.

January was no exception. She hadn't been to a Saturday night event at the Legion in at least a year, and tonight's party would be a good one.

When they arrived, the DJ and bartenders were setting up. For all the fun joking about organizing the event, that was mostly for the charity auction items. The rest of the night would roll out in a predictable, self-managed fashion.

By the time the doors opened at eight, Will and Catie had arrived and were "helping" the bartender for the first round, having a chance to talk to everyone that way.

Seth and January split up to sell raffle and fifty-fifty tickets, and the next thing she knew, the room was full of people and it was after nine o'clock.

Seth had found her twice, bringing her a beer once and a quick kiss in the back hallway the second time, after she pulled him back there to make sure he was having a good time and not too annoyed by people grilling him. "I'm good," he'd whispered against her mouth. His bright eyes promised he wasn't fibbing either. So now that she was out of raffle tickets, it was her turn to find him.

It didn't take long. Her body homed in on his immediately, finding him in the crowd like he was tagged with a special paint only she could see. That same floopy heart soaring reaction happened when she locked her gaze on him, and she moved through the chattering, dancing people, eager for the warm calm that would settle on her when she landed at his side.

He was deep in conversation with Jake Foster, a beer bottle slung between two fingers, holding it casually as can be, but it looked empty. He paused for a beat when she joined them, then looped his arm over her shoulders.

Yes.

This.

Then he went back to his conversation. "I'm having some growing pains this year, but that's to be expected."

January frowned. What growing pains was he talking about? At the start of the summer he'd been nothing but sunshine and roses about his ten-year plan.

But since then...when was the last time they talked about his business? Their conversations lately had been centred on her. And them. Sex.

Especially in the last two weeks... Her stomach tensed up, fear slicing through her. Had she distracted him too much?

His business was so crucial to his identity. He'd sunk everything he had into it.

"How many years in are you?" Jake asked.

"Four and a half."

"That was a rough year for me, too. And you've shifted bases a bit, right? You're flying out of the harbour now?"

"Just for the summer, yeah. I hired another pilot to take some flights for me so I didn't need to go back and forth as much."

"Taking on staff and the cost of another plane is signifi-cant." Jake looked impressed, but January only heard *risk risk risk.*

By the end of the summer, Seth would take a hard look

at his books and realize that splitting his business between two locations was stretching himself too thin.

The warm, squishy feeling had a squashed spot right in the middle.

"I'm going to go find Isla and Bailey," she murmured.

Seth caught her wrist. "Hang on." He flicked a glance at Jake. "Can we continue this later? Or another time. I made this woman promise me a dance."

"Of course." Jake pointed to Seth's bottle. "You want another one, man?"

"Nah, I'm good." Seth kissed January's temple. "You ready?"

She glanced at the line dancing happening in the centre of the room, then tipped her face up at him. "You want to get in on *that*?"

He gave her a crooked smile. "Maybe the next song will be slower."

He held her gaze, making her heart beat faster. And then the song changed, and not just to any slow song, but one of her secret favourites from almost a decade earlier, "I Don't Dance" by Lee Brice—which she listened to on repeat the first time she went through a private *what if* phase about Seth being the one who got away.

"Folks, we've had a request for some slow-dancing tunes, so grab a friend and come on up to the dance floor," the DJ said.

"A request?"

His crooked smile turned wicked as he set his empty beer bottle on the nearest table. Then he spun her around in a circle before pulling her into his arms.

The worries sparked by the tail end of his conversation with Jake were chased away by the earnest way he held her gaze as he moved her around the dance floor. It was the simplest of steps, with only a few turns to get around other couples as needed, but he held her in his arms like they were meant to dance together, and as if they'd been doing this their whole lives—when really, they'd only shared a few dances together twenty years earlier, almost all of them with her unexpectedly soaking his ill-fitted dress shirt with her tears.

But tonight was replacing that memory with unfettered joy.

That song ended and slid into another slow song, "Unlove You" by Jennifer Nettles. Something about the lyrics needled January right in the feels, and she burrowed closer to Seth.

He wrapped his arms tighter around her, and the twirling dance slowed to a simple sway. His lips brushed against her forehead, making her head swim.

That song spiralled into a classic, "Remember When" by Alan Jackson, and then the slow set ended with "Younger Me" by Brothers Osborne, which was more upbeat, and Seth twirled her around and around until they were both sweaty and laughing at the end of the song.

"Drink?"

"Definitely."

As they stood in line at the bar, Seth braced himself behind her and tugged her into his body, wrapping his arms around her waist. There was a pause in the music now, as Will and Catie did more raffles and auction items —and heckled the crowd in a good-natured way—but Seth still swayed her back and forth as they shuffled forward.

When they got to the bar, she dug out a twenty and asked for a beer for herself. "What do you want?"

"Same." He kissed the side of her head. "Last one for me."

She blushed at the unspoken promise in the word. They weren't going to get blitzed because he had private plans for her when the dance was over.

So she nursed that next beer as they moved through the party, holding hands and chatting with people here and there, and when it was time for the last three songs of the night, and he pulled her back onto the dance floor, she was glad she was still clear-headed.

She didn't want to miss a moment of the night to come. Except the three songs came and went in a flash, with her barely noticing what they were, because all she could feel was the eager pounding of her heart, and the matching thump of Seth's when she rested her head against his chest.

They were more than a week into their alone time. The next few days were going to zoom by, and then she'd be picking the kids up at the airport.

Thirty minutes later, they were barely inside the door of the marina office when Seth pressed her against the window there. "I need you."

"You've got me."

"Here. Where I first saw you again. Where I first wanted you again…" His words brushed against her skin, hot and aroused.

She tipped her head back, giving in. The lights were off. They were all alone in the building, and when would they ever get this chance again?

He curved over her and sank his teeth lightly into her collarbone, his whole body alive. "I loved dancing with you tonight."

She moaned softly.

"And you know what dancing leads to…" He fisted her skirt, dragging it high on her hip, then palmed that thigh, skating his hand around to her ass—and groaning when he found her cheek bare. His fingers quested further, until his arm was wrapped all the way around her leg and he'd found the scrap of fabric barely covering the slick seam of her sex. "Oh, January."

"I need you, too," she breathed.

He buried his other hand under her skirt as well, stroking her from the front. The soft jersey fell around his arms, hiding how he was touching her. "Let me get you off, beautiful."

"I want you inside me."

"Soon. But I need to see you come apart for me first. I need to feel it. Taste it." He dropped to his knees and pressed his mouth to the inside of her thigh.

This was why she'd worn a skirt and not the jeans her sister suggested. Because she knew that at the first opportunity to be wanton with Seth, she would take it.

He yanked her underwear to the side and snaked his tongue between her lips, curling it around her clit. She slapped one hand back against the window and tangled her other fingers in his hair, holding him against her sex.

And between licks, in the quiet of her office, he told her how much he liked what he was doing. "You taste perfect. Slippery and sweet. Give me more of that goodness. Fuck yeah. God... Can you come for me like this?"

She babbled something in the affirmative, then he pressed deeper, covering her whole pussy in a wolfish kiss that finished with her clit tight between his lips, the tip of his tongue pulsing against it in an obscenely effective move.

Her hips pulled off the wall, her body following the too-good, so-good sensations his mouth was pulling from her. He gripped her hips more firmly and sucked and licked again, finding a new rhythm that made her moan again.

Shhh…

She couldn't, though, because the climax he demanded was right there. Heat swarmed her limbs and made her heart race as her focus narrowed to the firm hold he had on her and the soft pull of his lips. *Lick lick.*

Desire roiled, her flesh swelled, and he didn't stop, not for a second, until she crashed like a wave that was more undertow than rolling crest. It was a yank into oblivion that knocked her legs out from under her and left her gasping for breath—but Seth had her.

His hands skated up her sides, catching her gently around the ribs, and he pressed her back against the window.

Then he rose slowly, notching his thigh between her quivering legs. "That tasted like a good one."

She clung to his shoulders as he kissed her, rode out the aftershocks with her thighs clamped around his and her tongue deep in his mouth.

"The best," she panted when he dragged his mouth to the pulse fluttering at the base of her neck.

"Show me how good it was," he growled. "Show me with your soft little mouth."

She sank to her knees. He braced his hands on the window above her, and in the tight space between him and the wall, she unzipped his jeans and swallowed as much of his length as she could.

He groaned her name, a long, low prayer, then shoved his hand into her hair. "Oh, fuck. Yes…" He hissed it out. "That's my pretty girl. You're so good to me. Gonna make you come again upstairs. Gonna get deep inside you and make you scream. Nothing better, sweetheart. Your hot mouth, your sweet pussy…"

It was filthy, crude, and perfect. And when he finished, he joined her on the floor and tucked her against his side, holding her tight as he whispered equally perfect and much sweeter things that her heart wanted to believe meant more than they ever could.

21

THE DAYS STARTED SLIDING FASTER. The kids returned, Seth picked up more weekend charter flights, and suddenly, it was August. The Civic Holiday long weekend brought another burst of activity to the marina, and January's to-do list grew exponentially. They had four evening events that week, and she had a new part-time person to train alongside Summer, who had come back from B.C. infinitely more mature than when she left, and very interested in earnestly working in the office.

January had started the long six months commitment expecting to do it all herself, but to her surprise, a team had formed organically around her, and now with only six weeks to go until her sister returned, they had a pretty good system.

As much as she was ready for Augie to return—and the kids needed their mom back—she had a renewed energy for the hard work of running the marina. And the more she focused on work, the less she had to think about her time with Seth starting to wind down.

When a woman with big, bouncy blonde curls walked

in on the holiday Monday, stiffly holding a manila envelope, and introduced herself, January assumed it was about the job posting.

"My name is Shaye Berkowski. And I—"

"Are you here about the part-time position? I'm sorry, I've filled it. But I'm happy to take your resume and keep it on file."

"No." She swallowed hard, visibly nervous. Up close, she looked in her twenties, maybe a decade younger than January. "I, uh, am here to see the owners of this marina."

"I'm one of the owners."

"I thought you might be. I'd like to introduce myself. I will be…well, the thing is, I…own the motel next door."

"Oh!" January forced her face to smile, ignoring a weird tremor of anxiety that warned her things were about to get weird. That was silly. "Nice to meet you. Sorry, you caught me off-guard. We didn't…that is, the motel has been vacant for a very long time. I thought some investors were going to try and buy it."

"They did." The younger woman twisted her hands together. "I couldn't sell it. It's all I have of…" She made a face. "Sorry, this is harder than I thought."

"That's okay." January pointed to the coffee station. "Want a cup?"

Shaye shook her head. Then nodded.

And then she burst into tears. "I'm sorry," she whispered as January grabbed a box of tissues and hustled around the counter. "It's just that I've never been here before, and you look so nice, and I can't do this."

"Do what?" For a split-second, January worried that this woman was a Seth conquest from the past, but that didn't make any sense. Not that a crying stranger ever made sense, really. Life was just odd sometimes.

"Are you January? Or August?"

The anxiety roared back. This woman knew their names, but didn't know that August was overseas.

"I'm January," she said carefully.

"Is your sister here?"

"She won't be back for a while."

Five weeks and six days, precisely.

"Oh."

"Maybe just say it. Whatever it is. It can't be that bad, and then we can start to deal with it. Do you need money? Because we don't have any. As you might be able to tell, this marina is on a bit of a shoestring operation."

"No." Shaye straightened her shoulders and dragged in a ragged breath. "I don't need money. Not really."

Well, that made one of them. January was done offering suggestions to help the teary girl out. She waited, silently, a teacher trick she hadn't had to use in months.

"Fuck." The other woman made a face. "I really thought this would be okay. Look, I'm sorry, all right? In advance. I bet this isn't what you want to hear, but, uh…" She laughed. And swore again, this time under her breath, like a little cursing pep talk to herself. "I'm your half-sister. Surprise. I'm sorry, again."

The floor—no, the whole world—shifted beneath January's feet. "*My what?*"

"Your father…" her voice wavered. "He was my father, too. But I never knew him."

"I…" January wanted to throw up. Instinctively, she knew this was all probably right. So much of her childhood, and the gaslighting lies her father told both her mother and August over decades, clicked into place. "You own the motel?"

There was a clatter of footsteps on the stairs, because of course the kids would choose right now to come down.

January held her hand up to silence Shaye—her *half-sister*—and partially turned around, issuing a stern order without even seeing who was there. "Go back upstairs."

"Is everything all right?" Seth's warm voice tightened in concern.

She twisted the rest of the way around, frowning at her lover, who was standing behind the kids. "Where did you come from?"

"Levi was climbing the TV antenna tower, and I showed him—you know what, it doesn't matter. Hi." He glanced from her to Shaye and back again. "You need anything?"

"Were you just taking the kids…out?"

He nodded. "Sure, yep. We were going to see if you wanted to… But I'll take them over to the garage first, how about that?"

"Great." She gave him a tight smile. "Thanks."

He herded them out the door, and Shaye's gaze followed his big, broad shoulders until he was out of sight.

"Is that your family?"

Her heart clenched. "Yes."

"Your kids are—"

"I'm their aunt. They're my sister's children."

"Oh." A sharp, bright pain visibly snapped across Shaye's face.

January heard her words echo silently a moment later. The emphasis she would have heard. *I'm their aunt. They're my sister's children.*

This woman might be their aunt, too.

She dropped her gaze to the envelope. "Is that something you want me to see?"

Shaye handed it over. "It's documentation of the trust that was set up by your father, leaving me the motel. There was money left, as well, to cover the property taxes until I turn twenty-eight."

January glanced at the papers. The words swam in front of her face. "And when is that?"

"Excuse me?"

"Your birthday?" January looked up. "How old are you?"

"Oh. I'm twenty-six." Shaye explained that she'd been raised by her mother, and only learned about the motel when she turned eighteen. "There's only two more years of funds in the trust, so I need to decide what I'm going to do with the motel."

"Sell it." January shoved the papers back at the other woman, feeling like some kind of fool for having wasted so much of her own life pining after this stupid marina.

The legacy of her stupid father. What had he been thinking?

And to think, I'd just been feeling like I was hitting some kind of stride here.

"I don't want to do that," Shaye whispered. "I was hoping to talk to you and your sister."

"She's not here," January snapped. "She's in Lebanon. My sister is in the army reserves." Again she heard it. *My* sister. She stumbled, but she was steaming now, and the words kept coming. "She does that because this marina doesn't really pay all of her bills. I'm a teacher, and I had to take a leave of absence to work here while she went on a tour of duty overseas. If you have some kind of small-town idealized fantasy of what it would be like to open up a motel next door to the marina run by your long-lost sisters, I promise you it won't be that. It won't be *fun*."

"Oh."

Shaye said that a lot. *Oh.*

What had she been expecting? A welcome wagon committee?

"Can I leave you my card, then? And will you tell her…if you speak to her?"

January nodded. "Yes. you can. And I will."

Somehow.

Shaye left a thick, square, rounded corner calling card on top of the manila envelope, then hustled out the door.

In the quiet space she left behind, January replayed their brief conversation over and over in her head. Each time she heard it from a slightly different angle. She saw that woman—her *sister*—as if through someone else's eyes.

Did they look alike? Maybe their hair, thick and wavy-curly, although Shaye had done something with hers, maybe with curlers and product.

January did nothing. She twisted it into a bun nine times out of ten, and on the exception day, let it air dry as if she was a surfer girl.

Girl.

She was almost thirty-eight years old. *Shaye* was the girl.

Twenty-six.

January would have been twelve, and August nine, when their father had a secret love child. A sharp, gutting pain ripped through her as she remembered how unhappy her mother was in those last few years of her life.

This was unbelievable. And yet, as she slotted all this new context into what she remembered of her parents' marriage, it made a sick kind of sense.

She had another sister. *August* had another sister, and

had no idea. She glanced at the clock on the wall set to the local time in Lebanon. It was late in the evening there.

Should she tell her now? Or should she wait?

On the counter, her phone vibrated. Seth's name was on the screen, and she laughed despite herself, a hollow bark, when she saw the first message.

Seth: You're pretty when you're mad.
January: OMG
Seth: Did I read the situation wrong? Are you
not mad?
Seth: You're still pretty
January: I cannot distill this moment down into a
text, it's the most WTF thing that has ever
happened to me
Seth: What do you need?
January: Can the kids stay with Josh for a little
bit? I need…

She stared at the screen, the last message unsent.

January: I need a shoulder to cry on… and maybe
a man to rage at, full warning
Seth: I'll buckle up my chin strap and be
right over

He arrived four minutes later with two cold bottles of beer in his hands. She flipped the open/closed sign to closed, and sagged against the door.

"Thank you," she said after he twisted off one of the caps and handed the bottle over. She meant it for more than just the beer, but elaborating felt too hard.

It was all too hard, too much. January was *tired*. "I have

a half-sister." She gulped back a mouthful of beer. "That person. She's my…"

"Wow." Seth's tone was gentle. "She just walked in and told you that?"

"I think it's true. She owns the motel. Wants to make it a thing again. I guess that's why Bailey couldn't buy it last year?"

Seth didn't say anything. It wasn't a question he needed to answer, and he seemed to sense that.

"My brain is spinning a mile a minute. She's almost ten years younger than August. I would have been twelve when she was born. That was the summer the motel closed, remember? This whole time, I thought my dad got fleeced by bad business partners, because it seemed like it was so hard to live next to that reminder of his poor choices." She let out another cold laugh. "Wow, I had no idea how right I was."

"He *gave* it to her?"

"Signed the land over to her in trust, to make her mother go away. There were documents she showed me, and it had some stipulations about no contact."

"Holy shit."

"I thought that the motel's failure had turned my father into a bitter man. When it turns out, it failed because he was a lying, deceitful piece of shit. He was bitter and unkind, not enough for either family, and *that* is what destroyed the motel—and nearly destroyed the marina. If August hadn't been so intent on taking this place over, I think it would have burned out in his final years, too. I hate him, Seth." She looked up at him, feeling hollow. "And I hate that we have so much invested in something he built."

"You had no way of knowing."

"That doesn't make it any less gross."

"No. I know. I'm sorry." He sighed. "And this girl never knew him?"

She nodded. "She was raised by her mom."

"How long has she known?"

"About the motel? Since she was eighteen. But she didn't have any money to do anything with the motel, because she was a teenager. And who he was? Since he died." January choked back a wave of unexpected, profound despair. "I haven't told August yet."

"What can I do?"

"How long can the kids stay with Josh?"

"All day. They're fine."

She tipped the bottle back, draining it. "I need a shower."

"Okay."

"And company in that shower."

"I'm your man."

Another wave of grief. Oh, how she wished that was the case in more ways than just the here and now.

———

SETH KNEW he was being used, so January could forget the shock of what she'd just learned. He didn't care. He let her lean against him as the shower heated up, then peeled her clothes off her tight, tense body and eased them both into the steam.

She seemed done with talking for now, so he didn't ask any more questions, even though they rioted through his head.

When the time came, he'd encourage her to ask Dean Foster and Zander Minelli to do a background check on this supposed half-sister. Seth knew that the marina was hard to keep afloat, but from the outside, it looked like a profitable business. August and January had so much pride of ownership, and they poured everything into making their family's legacy look good.

Seth wouldn't discount the possibility of an attempted scam of some sort.

And if it was true, then why now? Just because they had a partial blood bond didn't mean this other woman would want the best for January.

Every protective instinct in his body wanted Seth to put himself between her and this potential threat. He wanted to step in and take over, but that wasn't his place.

His role here was to be a big, handsome man who could help her forget for an hour. That was it. That was all she wanted from him. A summer of fun, with no obligation or responsibility.

So when she reached for the shampoo, he held out his hand. "Let me."

He worked the cream into her hair, gently tugging and massaging until she sighed and relaxed against him. Then he repeated the same again with the conditioner, and her body wash. Her breasts, her thighs. A slow roll of his thumb over her nipples, then he squeezed a firm handful of her flesh. He could do this for hours.

Whatever she needed, however she needed it, until that haunted look on her face went away.

———

"WE NEED TO GET THE KIDS," January finally said in the silence.

They were lying naked on her bed. Seth was drawing

on her back, patiently waiting for her to say something. Anything. *We need to get the kids* was not the something he'd been waiting for. But it was all she could come up with right now. "And then I need to call my sister, but it's…" She glanced at the time. "Too late now, so that'll be late tonight, if I stay up. I can catch her before work. Or maybe I should do that first? But I don't know how long Josh—"

Seth smoothed his hand flat on her back. Pressing into her flesh, giving her a little bit of *hey, calm down* pressure. "Josh will be fine. He loves the kids. They're probably breaking one of his cars right now. Don't worry about them. Do you want me to stick around while you call your sister?"

For the third time today, January had a surreal realization with that word. She had to call the sister she's always known. Because now she had another sister, one she'd snapped at and sent away.

"It's so weird to think that I have *another* sister."

Her voice cracked and Seth squeezed her close. "Yeah, you do."

"I didn't know. I had a sister there and she grew up without us. And August is on the other side of the world. They can't meet for six weeks, at least."

"That time will fly."

Oh, she didn't really want to hear any logic right now. She made a frustrated sound and he smoothed his hand over her hair. "It's a lot."

She nodded. It was. "I really hate my father," she whispered. "I hate his shame, hate that he kept her from us. Kept *us* from her. And now what are we supposed to do?"

"There aren't any rules. It's okay if it takes time to develop a relationship there."

She thought of Augie, and of how close they were. How they could finish each other's sentences. Read each other's minds. And now there was another person who shared some of their same genes, but who was a complete stranger.

Develop a relationship?

Fuuuuccck.

———

SHE CAUGHT her sister just as August was about to go for a late-night swim.

"Sorry to ruin your evening," she muttered, then launched into the whole story without making too much eye contact.

When she finished, they sat together in stunned silence.

"What did you tell her?" August finally asked. "About us, and…I mean, what could you say?"

"I mostly just listened to her. I didn't give her any information." She winced. "I may have snapped at one point and told her to sell the motel. It's a trap she shouldn't want any part of. But I think she picked up on the vibe that I was just shocked."

August laughed weakly. "Oh, Janie."

"I know."

"Do you think we have any right to part of the motel?"

"Probably not. Dad did whatever he did a long time ago. We can hire lawyers but…"

"Yeah, no. We can't really afford that. And it's not like the motel is worth much in its current state."

January shuddered. "Really, that poor girl. She's been saddled with a shit ton of work."

"And I don't want to take the motel from her but… I

mean, maybe... I don't know." August stared bleakly into the camera.

January slumped down on the desk, resting her head on her hands. "This is surreal. Should I have waited to tell you?"

"No. Honestly, it's better that I have time to process it before I come home."

"Right."

"Will she be there? Has she moved to town?"

January was shocked to realize she didn't know. "I didn't ask her." She turned Shea's card over in her hands. "She left her contact details. Do you think I should email her? Or do you want to? Maybe do a big sister power move, show her that we aren't freaked out."

"We are totally freaked out." August groaned. "And what would I say in an email? *Nice to meet you*? Is it nice? *This is a shock.* That would be true. *We want to get to know you...*"

"*But we want to take it slowly,*" January finished.

August tapped on her computer. "Okay, that's a good start."

January glanced at the door through the window. She could see Seth and Josh playing with the kids on the dock. "The kids don't know, by the way. I'll leave that to you to think about how you want to tell them, if you do. But at some point, you know how this town is, they will figure it out or hear about it on the playground."

August tipped her head sideways, thinking. "Maybe we can tell her that. Tell her that we'd like to keep this quiet until I'm home. Until I've had a chance to explain to my children that their grandfather was an absolute bastard, on my own terms. And if she accepts that..."

"Then that might be a step in the right direction." January exhaled, feeling more stable now.

"I'm going to sleep on the email. There's no rush for me to reach out to her, right? Other than buying us some time."

"That's right."

"Okay." She nodded. "I'm gonna go power my way through some laps to try to burn off this energy."

January blew her sister a kiss, then ended the call.

Dinner that night was muted. Seth hung around until she kicked him out, with an apology that he waved off.

"The kids are in camp this week," she said softly at the door. "If you want to come over for lunch tomorrow?"

His worried gaze softened. "Lunch." He caught his lower lip between his teeth and gave her a partial grin. "My favourite meal of the day."

22

———————

ONCE AGAIN, life intruded on Seth and January's best-laid lunch plans. This time it was a broken window at his house in Blind River.

"Rain check," he promised before flying north midday.

Teegan met him at the dock. She'd just returned from her supply run up north, and the second plane he'd leased was tied up on the other side.

"Hey boss," she said.

"I'm not your boss," he muttered.

She frowned. "You literally are."

"You're doing me a favour."

"And you're paying me for it. What's with the grouchy attitude? Haven't seen that in months."

Because he hadn't been consumed with conflicted thoughts in the same period of time. He grunted and pointed to his truck, which she'd been driving for the summer—along with checking on his house and keeping his core year-round business afloat. "Let's go."

And then because he wasn't really an asshole, he said

thank you before climbing heavily into the passenger seat. "I know this isn't how you planned to spend today."

"It's fine. Better you come and patch it up, buy a new window, or whatever, than we try to figure it out over the phone. It doesn't look like a break-in attempt," she said. "Might have been kids playing around."

There was a small ball diamond behind their street. That could definitely be it.

"It probably wasn't what you had planned today, either." She gave him an expectant look.

"What?"

"That's a subtle way of asking how it's going with your friend at the marina."

He frowned. Then shook his head. "No, it's great."

"I can tell."

That made him smirk. "Smart ass."

"It's why I'm your number one employee."

He changed the subject. "How's Linda?"

"Good. Busy. She's working in Sudbury this week."

"Coming home at night?"

That got a secret smile that made him burn with an unfamiliar envy. "Yeah."

He scrubbed his hand over his mouth. "What made you move to Blind River?"

Teegan was from Ottawa originally. Linda had family in this area, though, and had always lived in Blind River. He'd never asked about the start of their relationship because until this summer, he hadn't cared one way or the other about how people fell in love.

It hadn't applied to him.

Now he was deeply worried about a woman half a lake away, and annoyed by the pull of his responsibilities here.

"I fell in love, and nothing else mattered half as much as that." She shrugged. "Plus the fishing is great."

"Do you ever miss your career?"

She took her time thinking about the answer. That was one of his favourite things about his neighbour. She was always careful. *And she still took the leap.* "Sometimes," she said. Then she looked sideways at him. "Not at all this year, though. You've kept me busy."

"You want to do it again next year?"

"Yeah." She narrowed her eyes. "What's your plan?"

His mouth was dry. He didn't have one, and there was a time-limit to how long he could squat in Josh's apartment. Although if January moved into town, he could stay at Will's more often.

He'll sell that house at some point.

Which meant Seth had to make a move before *some point.*

And in order to make a move, he had to have a plan. "I don't have one," he admitted. "But the summer is going by too fast."

"I remember that feeling."

"Did you guys do the long-distance thing?"

She pulled into his driveway. "Yeah. For a year."

"And you stayed together."

She shook her head. "We broke up twice. If I were to do it again, I'd have moved here sooner. As soon as I knew she was the one." She opened the door. "But I didn't own a business and a house, either."

He winced and followed her out of the truck.

———

THE REPAIR TOOK ALL AFTERNOON, and it was well after dinner by the time he got back to Pine Harbour. January wasn't at the marina, and the office was closed.

Seth: I'm back
January: We're at the park

He went in search of them, and found Summer playing soccer with Josh while Levi and January were reading on a blanket nearby.

He dropped down beside them. He couldn't press a kiss on her shoulder the way he wanted to, because the kids didn't know they were sleeping together, but he nudged her with his elbow.

When she gave him a tired smile, he wanted to ask about her day, but it probably involved Shaye, and the kids didn't know about her, either.

"Did you get the window repaired?"

He nodded. "I did." He glanced at Levi, who was deep in the D&D Handbook. "Talked to Teegan about working for me again next summer."

A tremor flickered at the corner of her right eye. "Oh?"

"Thought I should start planning ahead."

"Ah."

This wasn't going as he expected. "Want to go for a walk?"

She glanced at her watch. "We need to head back soon. Bedtime. Camp starts early. And you have flights tomorrow."

He knew that. But talking was important, too, and they couldn't do it freely in front of her nephew. "A quick stroll."

"Sure." She left her book with Levi, and pushed herself up.

"I know this isn't a great time to talk about us," he said under his breath. "And I promised you no drama at the start of the summer. This isn't— I'm just saying that I want to come back next summer. And I'll find a way to fly down…there are airfields…"

"You don't have to do that," she said softly.

"I want to."

"It's a lot to juggle."

"It's not juggling."

"I know your business is stretched thin."

"What?" He stopped. They were at the corner of the soccer field.

She turned around, ready to head back to her blanket. They'd barely gone eighty metres.

"January, what are you talking about?"

"You were telling Jake at the stag and doe."

He tried to remember the conversation from three weeks earlier. "Because he owns his own business. We were getting into the nuts and bolts of it. I'm not worried about my business, and it's not a problem that I'm spending more time here."

She licked her lips, her attention locked on Levi and her book. "Okay."

He caught her face and gently turned her head so she was looking at him. "I want to keep talking about this. I'm not going anywhere."

"But you are," she whispered. "In a month. You're going home. And I just want to enjoy the time we have left before you turn back into an occasional visitor, all right?"

No, it wasn't.

But then Summer sprinted over, thrilled she'd beaten Josh, and then it was time to leave.

He walked down the hill with them, then watched her disappear into the marina with her wards, leaving him vibrating with unexpected frustration.

After an hour of radio silence, he texted her.

Seth: Can I come over so we can continue our conversation?
January: Tomorrow night

———

"I'M SORRY ABOUT YESTERDAY," she started. The kids were asleep and they were on the couch. "I'm struggling this week. It's not you, it's me."

"I get it." And he did. He'd spent a lot of his flying time trying to remember if there were any clues that her father had been a philandering jerk. Her parents' marriage hadn't been happy in those last few years before her mother died. He remembered tension and snarled comments.

He would never be unkind to January. He would never, ever be unfaithful to her. But it felt cheap to just say that, when it was pretty clear he wasn't her father—and he didn't think she thought he was.

This wasn't about him.

So when she crawled into his lap, he let the conversation about the winter slip away.

If she needed a sweet distraction, that was a better way to spend the evening anyway.

———

THE NEXT DAY was their last chance for a quickie at noon. The last day Seth had off while the kids were in camp.

Later, he would realize he should have seen the cracks forming. He should have anticipated from the two and a half months of very clear messages from January about limited bandwidth and needing simple friendship that she didn't actually *want* him for more than just the summer.

But the truth was, he forgot. Or maybe he hadn't wanted to remember, because it was hard to hold himself back and it was so damn easy to love her.

So when it happened, it was a surprise. He strolled over to the marina and kissed her the same as always, and she responded with delightful ease.

He worked his way into her hot, curvy body and watched her come apart, and maybe he should have known then, when she closed her eyes and twisted her head away instead of giving him the stormy gaze he craved.

He'd been so focused on wanting to know her from the inside out that he had missed the armour she'd started to layer back on. He was on the inside already, and his vantage point was skewed now, because he could *feel* how much she wanted him.

Of course she wanted him. Right?

But when they were finished, and he tucked her in against him as the little spoon, and he asked her about her house—he'd driven by it that morning, and the siding was going on now, great progress—she didn't answer.

He frowned and kissed her shoulder. "January?"

"I'm sorry," she whispered.

"For what?"

Her breath hitched. "I'd rather if we don't talk about my house."

Something about the emphasis there was a red flag. *My house. Not yours. Back off.* Of course it *was* her house, but she'd never sounded brittle about it before. They hadn't talked about it much, but it was coming together nicely, and the fall was around the corner—

"Why?"

"You know why."

"I don't."

"Because you're leaving in a few weeks."

"I don't have to." It was the first time he'd said it out loud, and suddenly he was filled with a desperate panic. He should have said it sooner. "We didn't get back to that conversation. Let's talk about it now."

"No." She pushed away from him. "Please don't."

"Jan—"

"*No.*" Her voice cracked. "I can't do this. I can't…" She took a deep breath as she rolled up. "Hang on, I need to think."

"You're going through a lot right now."

"Please, just…" She was sitting on the side of the bed, her back to him, and her shoulders shook.

I need to think.

He felt like there was a thousand-pound weight on his chest.

In horrified silence, he watched as she got dressed without meeting his gaze. She disappeared into the washroom for a minute, then came back. Emotional armour he barely recognized now fully in place, and he was on the outside again.

A complicated understanding gripped his chest, shoving his true feelings lower, into the pit of his stomach where they would have to drown a little.

"How long have you been thinking we should stop

doing this?" His voice sounded like he'd just skidded out on gravel. Rough and rubbed raw.

"I don't know."

He pushed off her bed and pulled on his jeans. "You need a break?"

"Maybe."

That wasn't what he wanted at all, but he still heard himself agree to it. "Fine."

What are you doing, Kincaid???

"It's just that…this will get messy. You know?"

It was already chaos. The solution was not a break. Unless she had a different vantage point than he did. "Best to avoid that."

"You're mad."

"I'm…" He shoved his hands into his hair. "I need my shirt."

———

JANUARY WATCHED HELPLESSLY as Seth shoved his big body that had just been so good to her—before she fucked everything up—into clothes. He was vibrating with tension and it was all her fault.

He cast about for his phone, which she spotted on top of the dresser.

"Here." Her throat tightened up as he took it from her, his fingers brushing hers. "Seth—"

"No." He shook his head. "It's okay. Take some time."

"I don't know that I need *time*."

"You just don't want to talk to me about the house you're going to move into in two months."

"It's hard! I told you that at the start of the summer. This is hard."

"It felt pretty easy when I was inside you." He shook his head. But if he was going to say something after that, he thought better of it at the last second.

"It was easy," she admitted. "But now it feels hard again."

"I don't want it to be hard."

"I know."

"What happened today?"

"Nothing."

He searched her face.

After he left, his boots heavy on the stairs, she let herself have a good cry—all right, it was actually an ugly, gross cry—and then she went downstairs and took down the stupid sign that said she was at lunch.

And then she cried again at the counter, because what did she just do?

She hadn't meant for her raw doubt—in herself, in her faith about relationships—to be revealed in exactly that way.

How long have you been thinking we should stop doing this?

Probably since that morning in the spring when he paused behind her for a split-second, and her soul wanted to cleave in two because he was so close and yet so out of reach.

And then he'd floated into reach, and she'd grabbed on with both hands, even though she really couldn't handle having her heart broken again.

It wasn't that she thought they should *stop*. It was just that she wanted to freeze them, exactly as they had been, before the feelings got too big.

Now it was too late for that. Seth was mad at her, and for good reason. But she wasn't going to do a long-distance thing with him all winter. And she wasn't going to follow him to Blind River, not when she had a gorgeous house being built for her here, one she'd purposefully designed to be everything *she* wanted in a home.

Not to be shared with anyone else.

And Seth had noticed that.

She hadn't even realized that she was guarding it from him. That made her stomach twist in the worst way. Once upon a time, he'd been her best friend. How could she admit to seventeen-year-old January that she had Seth back in her life, but only to fuck, not to trust with her hopes and dreams for the future?

Her younger self would be very disappointed.

———

THE KIDS DIDN'T MISS him that night, because he didn't come over *every* night, but he was an *at least* every other night dinner guest now, so the next evening when she told Levi to set the table for only three people, he asked an innocently clarifying question. "What about Seth?"

January didn't look at her nephew. "He's probably busy."

"But he loves stuffed chicken."

Hot irritation prickled under her skin. Of course she'd made his favourite dinner. It was one of their regular dinner nights, and she'd started to cater to his tastes as much as she did the kids. The one person in this place who could take or leave a chicken breast? The foolish woman standing in front of the stove, wishing she had the fixings for a Caesar salad on the side. She glanced at the clock, but there wasn't enough time to drive across the peninsula to the grocery store in Lion's Head.

She could get takeout salad from Mac's Diner, though—

A knock at the door interrupted her desperate train of thought.

"Something smells good in here," Seth's deep voice rang out.

Levi gave an excited shout. "He's here!"

She busied herself with transferring the chicken to a platter, because the casserole dish was hot.

A casserole dish Seth had bought her because it wouldn't explode.

And then he was in the doorway. She could feel him, even though he didn't say anything.

Twenty-nine hours had passed since she freaked out and pushed him away. It felt like another twenty-year chasm had formed between them, and this time she couldn't blame the fact they were too young to know better. This time she knew better and did it anyway, because she was a coward.

"I brought a salad." He cleared his throat. "A friendship salad."

How could he have known?

Her chest squeezed in brutal protest. *Stop being so perfect,* she wanted to snap. But there was no reason to snap at him, it wasn't *Seth* she was angry at, it was her father. Who was Seth's complete opposite in every way, so why had she taken out her pain on him?

She turned around and found his gaze caught on her wrist. Self-consciously, she touched her fingertips to the friendship bracelet she still wore.

Memories of that day in the cove pummelled her like a cold wave.

He moved into the kitchen and set the bowl he'd

carried in on the counter. Then he carefully lifted his head, his gaze colliding with hers. "I won't apologize for inviting myself over."

She didn't say anything.

"Because it's important to separate out the different things we've been doing." He paused a beat. "Dinner is not, has not ever been, about wanting too much of you. Dinner is about our friendship. And if I have to choose between being your lover and being your friend, I will pick the friendship every time."

23

A WILD, desperate confusion took hold of January as Seth's words sank in. It wasn't the worst feeling in the world. It was better than empty sadness.

"But I pushed you away," she whispered back. "I hurt you."

He nodded. "Yeah, I didn't like that at all. But we only have slices of time together right now, and I don't have any practice at being a good…friend. Not like this. So I could have handled it differently, too."

This reminded her of the day he firmly whisked her away for the afternoon. Except less sexy and more bittersweet.

She'd had enough of bittersweet to last a lifetime, but she didn't have the bandwidth for confusingly sexy, either.

"I don't know what to say."

"Can I stay for dinner?"

"I mean, you did bring salad. And I really wanted a salad…"

He reached out and brushed his fingertips against hers. "First rule of friendship: we try not to say no to salad."

She nodded.

"And maybe the second rule of friendship can be, we don't deflect direct, fair questions with sarcastic answers."

Oh. She jerked her face up and found a gentle understanding looking down at her.

Another nod. "Please stay for dinner. We would all be happy to have your company."

It turned out, he had another reason for boldly showing up even after her meltdown. After much delay—and a fair amount of little boy anxiety—Levi felt ready to host a Dungeons & Dragons game, and he wanted to have it on Sunday.

"In two days?" January glanced at Seth. "Is that doable? What all do you need?"

"Will has all the gaming supplies. I'll take care of food. It's going to be great." He gave her a warm smile. "You can take the day to do whatever you want."

He left soon after dinner, and they didn't see him again until Sunday, when he arrived carrying a case of Mountain Dew on his shoulder. In his other hand were three overflowing grocery bags.

"Hello gaming buds," he announced as he pulled out two jumbo bags of Doritos. "I have lunch sorted out."

Levi looked like he was going to pass out from excitement. She'd heard about the Mountain Dew and Doritos unique combination a few times over the summer, but thought it was something people joked about on the internet.

Not something Seth was actually going to feed to her wards for a meal.

"Don't worry," he murmured. "We got hot dogs and s'mores supplies for a bonfire later."

She smiled faintly. Truthfully, it sounded like the best day ever.

And it was, for all of them. Levi's friend Anhad came over, and so did Josh and Will.

She got out of their hair, staying downstairs in the marina office for most of the day, and there wasn't a single peep from upstairs that needed Aunt January's attention. Only the occasional dull roar or cackle that made her smile.

Toward the end of the afternoon, she put up the "Back in Ten" sign, grabbed a basket, and headed over to the motel.

Shaye wasn't there. She hadn't come back around, although they had exchanged a few emails. She wasn't moving to Pine Harbour until the spring, and agreed to not tell anyone else about her connection to the harbour area until August returned.

January's mission today wasn't about her half-sister. It wasn't even about her complicated feelings about her dad.

Today, she was on the hunt for sun-warmed raspberries. She'd spent part of the afternoon digitizing old family photos, and came across one of her mother, August, and herself—both little—picking raspberries from a patch on the far side of the motel.

She'd spent so long mentally erasing the motel from the landscape in her mind that she never thought about what was beyond it. But now, as she walked down the quiet road, she took in this stretch of Old Whiskey Harbour Road. Across the street, the building for the brewery was coming along. And past it, beyond the marina, was a lush, green twisty forest drive right along the water's edge for a bit, then curving away.

She snapped a quick photo on her phone, then turned

into the cracked concrete stretch that used to be a parking lot. Now it was a weed lot. But where the weeds met the forest, she found raspberries. Lots of them. She filled her basket, then took a photo of that, too.

Time to make some new memories.

When she returned, she crept up the stairs, not wanting to disturb the game. And maybe a little bit she wanted to listen in, undetected. She slipped into the kitchen and set her berries down, then slowly ate a handful as she listened to Will and Seth talk about their military experiences overseas.

"When I joined the Air Force, video calls didn't exist yet," Seth said.

"What?" Levi sounded earnestly shocked. "How old are you? You look really good for someone who's ancient."

That made January laugh.

He *did* look good, though.

There was more murmuring, then she heard clear as a bell, "One day, you'll want to go on an adventure, and your mom will be your biggest cheerleader."

She pressed her hand to her heart. It had taken all summer, but Levi was finally talking about August being gone.

———

"One more s'more?"

"One more," January and Seth said at exactly the same time.

He gave her a soft grin that made her tummy flutter.

And once Levi had that final treat, Seth chased them inside, growling that *he* was going to enforce tooth brushing tonight so their aunt didn't need to.

Then he returned to the bonfire pit to collect the remaining marshmallows and graham crackers.

January took her time folding the blankets. Watching Seth, too. She wasn't going to lie about that to herself. She missed him. He was a beautiful distraction from the pressure of guardianship, the responsibility to shepherd these two kids through this summer of missing their mom—and making sure they didn't get any cavities in the process.

Catie had joined them for the bonfire, but she and Will, and Josh, had all left a half hour ago.

It was just the two of them on the beach now.

Seth tucked the food into the curve of his right arm, then ushered her in the direction of the marina with his left hand, ghosting it for the briefest of moments against the small of her back. "I'll stick around in case the sugar keeps them up."

"You don't have to."

"If it's a messy situation I have contributed to, then yes, I do." He opened the door for her. "After you."

She expected a fight about bedtime, as Seth suggested, but the kids surprised her.

When she went upstairs to check on them, there were yawns as they jockeyed for position at the sink, and when Seth said he was going to head out soon, the only protest was that he had promised them a moose story, apparently.

"Just one," he said sternly, but the good kind of stern. One that promised a solid reward for respecting his boundaries.

Seth's bossy side worked on the kids just as well as it did on her.

Levi climbed into his bed, and Seth sat at the foot, while Summer sprawled on the bean bag chair in the corner. January leaned in the doorway, because she didn't want to miss the story, either.

You just want a few more minutes of his voice. There was that, too.

"I want to tell you that zero moose were harmed in the making of this story," he deadpanned. "You need to know that off the bat, because there will be a point where you are seriously concerned that I harmed a moose, and you need to know that I didn't."

That was a pretty solid hook. And the story was just as entertaining. It started when he dropped off some hunters at a fly-in lodge on a lake, and almost ran into a moose.

"So a week later, I return to pick them up, and I swear to…" Seth glanced at January, his eyes dancing.

"You can say God," Levi said solemnly. "Aunt January says way worse. And she's a *teacher who should know better.*"

"I'm right here."

Summer poked her. "Shhh, Seth's almost done."

"I circle the lake, checking out the landing space, and that same moose plods into view. And the thing is…they can go fast when they want to. Which makes me think, they can go extra slow when it is in their interest, too. And this guy was like, look Mr. Pilot. You narrowly missed me once. Now I'm staking my claim on this lake. Land at your own risk."

"Did you?"

"Damn straight I did. And I gave him lots of space, too. You gotta respect nature."

"You didn't show that moose who was boss?"

Seth leaned over and rumpled his hair. "Ah, Levi. The moral of the story is, the moose *is* the boss of that lake. He showed *me* who's boss, and I learned a lesson. Always check your landing zone at least twice, and be prepared to adjust your plan at the last second."

"It would be pretty cool to fly up there." Levi's gleaming expression was not at all subtle. Almost like he knew the summer was almost over, and he might not get another chance to ask so subtly as part of the conversation.

January's neck heated up. If Seth—

But he didn't overstep. He shook his head instead. "When I was your age, I had to wait until my parents thought I was old enough to get into a plane. Your mom and aunt will let you know when you can do something like that, all right, bud?"

Levi groaned, but still snuggled into his blanket with a pleased smile on his face. "All right."

And then his eyelids fluttered shut.

January hustled Summer off to her bed next, and Seth went downstairs, his footsteps heavy and slow on the narrow stairs. She listened to see if he'd go all the way out, but it sounded like he stopped in the kitchen.

She sat on the stairs and quietly did some reading as she listened for the inevitable footsteps, the six-part charade to begin around delaying actually falling asleep.

It didn't come.

Five minutes of blissful quiet passed—and four pages of a beautiful book—when she realized they actually *had* fallen asleep, and in record time.

She poked her head into Levi's room to be sure, then pulled his door shut with a quiet click.

Downstairs, she found Seth sitting at the table.

Waiting.

"Thank you for today," she whispered, her voice catching in her throat. "We haven't had an easy night like tonight in a while. We all needed this."

He nodded.

She wanted to cross to him, to crawl into his lap and hug him with all her might.

"Was the moose story true?"

He laughed. "Yes."

Then he stood up.

Her chest tightened, bracing herself for him to say it was time to go.

Instead, he came around the table, slow as could be, and handed her his phone. "Some photos from today."

She swiped through them, smiling. "These are great. Can I send myself a copy?"

"Be my guest."

She scrolled through, selecting all of them. Then her thumb stopped moving when she got to the first photo of the game. Because the photo before it was of her.

Seth didn't take a lot of photos on his phone. Not every day. Not even every week.

Before today, the last photo he took was at the stag and doe, of her in animated conversation with Catie.

Her heart leapt into her throat, and she quickly tapped on the AirDrop icon to send the photos of the kids to her phone.

"Thank you," she said thickly as she shoved it back at him.

"Hey." He caught her wrist. Rubbed his thumb back and forth beneath her bracelet. Then he took the phone, but didn't let her go. "Look at me."

She lifted her face.

The corner of his mouth tugged up. "Hi."

"Hi." She swiped at her eyes with her free hand. "I really don't know what's wrong with me."

"Absolutely nothing."

"Then why is my face leaking?"

"Thirty years of gaslighting by your father, twenty years of thinking I was strictly a past tense emotion, maybe ten years of angsty feelings about co-owning the marina, a year of knowing you were going to be sole guardian to two teenagers who would much prefer you just be their aunt and not the boss of them, and…" He took a deep breath. "Two months of me not saying I love you when I should have."

She shuddered.

"I think friends can hug, right?" He let go of her arm and wrapped his arm around her waist, tugging her against him.

January sank into his chest. He stroked her hair and kissed her forehead, and she tried to form her mouth around so many important things to say.

We aren't just friends was one of them. *You love me???* was another, although that was the knee-jerk sarcasm defense he'd asked her not to use. Because of course he did. Now that he'd said it, of *course* he did, and she felt foolish for not knowing, but how could she know for sure?

And she did need to know for sure. For all of those other reasons he listed.

Which gave rise to the one thing she could say with ease, right away. "You see me," she whispered.

"Always," he murmured back.

"I'm so sorry."

"It could just have easily been me, sweetheart. We're both carrying some baggage. Yours just got heavier than you could carry this summer."

She slid her arms all the way around him and squeezed tight. There was an important question on her mind, and it might threaten to ruin a perfect day, but she was pretty sure she needed to ask it anyway. "Seth?"

"Mmm."

"Do you ever think about what if?"

She heard the way her voice cracked, and closed her eyes against the wave of emotion that rolled over her. Was she prepared for his answer?

He exhaled into her hair, and his arms gently tightened. "You mean what if we'd decided to have children?"

"Yeah."

He paused before answering. "No. You?"

Relief flooded her limbs, filling her with a sharp warmth. She hadn't realized just how much she needed that confirmation. She shook her head. "No. I sometimes think I should, but I don't."

"Same." He pressed his lips to her temple. "And I should also say, I don't help with the kids because of any *what if* thoughts," he whispered roughly. "I help because… they're a part of your family, and because they are funny human beings, and they make me happy. And a little bit because they remind me of Josh and Adam back in the day."

She leaned back so she could see his face.

"But I have been thinking about us more. Not about *what if*. But maybe about *what next*."

A tremor racked through her. "Oh, Seth."

"Shhh. You don't have to say anything. Not now. I know your plate is overflowing. Right now, I just want this. I want to be your friend. And separately, when you have space, your lover. Your confidant, if you're willing to share what burdens you. But when your sister gets back, and your life is more normal…when you have time to think about maybe wanting more, I'll be here. Thinking I want more, too."

Before she could say anything back, his lips found hers, and he kissed her as quietly as possible, the barest little sips at her mouth. He kept it up until she smiled against him, then he eased back. "Good night, January."

Oh, that was a lovely trick.

She pressed her fingertips to her mouth and smiled.

"I like seeing you like this. A little breathless and anticipating my next kiss." He tugged on her ponytail and lowered his mouth to hers again, pausing just before making contact. "I'll see you tomorrow."

This time, it was her kiss to initiate, and she did, pressing up on her toes. She ignored the way her heart raced, and focused on how nice his mouth felt. How warm and perfect and *right* it was to kiss him goodnight, and then watch him amble down the stairs.

Tomorrow couldn't come soon enough.

24

THE NEXT MORNING WAS A SHITSHOW. Levi woke January up, proud as a peacock that he had made the coffee already, and then he insisted on hanging out at the counter with her while Seth's customers arrived. She couldn't tell him to go away, and she didn't get a second alone with Seth.

She also wasn't sure what she'd say to him even if she could have had a few moments.

When his plane took off, she felt like she'd run a marathon and come in dead last.

So that afternoon, before he returned, she leapt at the opportunity to go and do something that would for sure make her feel better. And it meant leaving Summer in the office truly by herself for the first time.

"Josh is across the road if you need anything."

"I know."

"I'll only be gone for an hour or two."

"We'll be fine." Summer gestured to Levi, who'd brought a Lego set down to the office and was building it as he sipped at a cup of coffee.

"Call me if there are any questions."

"There won't be."

"And—"

"Go!" Summer rolled her eyes and Levi laughed.

January went.

Her first stop was *Bake Sale!* for a latte, then she drove to the house. Her house, which was looking more and more every day like the forever home she'd envisioned. The exterior was really coming along, although the driveway didn't exist yet. She parked on the road and carefully picked her way over the torn-up dirt to the front door—which was currently three feet above where she stood.

A porch was still to come as well.

The door swung open, and Jake sighed. "Guys! Where did the temporary step go?"

She laughed as they found her a ladder.

In the kitchen, plywood covered her cabinets, because the counters hadn't been delivered yet, but the shape of the room was now whole. Her breath caught in her chest. "Oh, I love it."

"Ready to see how your backsplash is going to look?" Jake stacked a few pieces of tile. "Pretty sharp."

"Better than I imagined."

"So this…" He gestured to a few paint colours up on the wall. "Here are your options for the main floor. I like to have homeowners make this decision in the space. What is your first instinct?"

That Seth should be here.

She covered her mouth and took a step back. "I'm not sure."

"I'll leave you with it for a few. There are swatches on the walls upstairs, too."

She nodded her thanks, then did a slow turn in the space.

Not once had she allowed herself to imagine sharing this home with Seth.

"Why is my face leaking?"

"Two months of me not saying I love you when I should have."

And then he'd kissed her.

She'd kissed him back.

The ball was now in her court. He'd shown her he wasn't going to run away, wouldn't even be pushed away, and he would adapt to what she needed from him.

But what did he *want?* His business was a plane ride or ferry trip away.

He'd moved a good chunk of it here.

Temporarily.

The Great Lakes weren't appropriate for winter take-offs on skis, she knew that much. He needed an airfield for that, or a small frozen lake or river.

She had done more research than a woman who *was not thinking about the future* should reasonably have done.

The kitchen spilled into a family room that looked into the backyard. More dirt.

Off the family room was a den with glass inset doors. She'd planned to use it as a library, but could it be his office?

Heart in her throat, she climbed the stairs to the bedrooms. The primary suite was at the front of the house, with a big arched window above where she'd imagined her bed. She noticed the paint swatches on the walls, but didn't *see* them really, because out the window she caught sight of Will pulling into his driveaway.

Moving more stuff from there to Catie's house.

The wedding was just two weeks away.

"Jake," she called out for the contractor.

He appeared from one of the smaller bedrooms. "Yep?"

"Can the paint decision wait until tomorrow? I need to get a second opinion."

"Sure. Are you going to bring someone by later?"

"I hope so."

"I'll be here until five."

She thought about Seth's schedule today. "Any chance I could sneak in later than that?"

He pulled a key from his pocket. "Don't tell anyone I'm letting you into a worksite unsupervised."

"We'll be careful. Thanks."

One way or another, she'd be glad to be alone tonight. If Seth wasn't interested, she'd bring a couple of popsicles and cry to herself about being a foolish romantic.

Then she flew out the front door and down the back-in-place temporary steps.

She pounded on Will's front door until he appeared. "Hey," he said, immediately heading back into the house.

Apparently unperturbed by the fact she looked flustered and consumed with thoughts of his brother.

"I need advice," she burst out.

That made him stop in his tracks. He turned around, his eyebrows curved. "About?"

"Seth."

"Finally." He reversed course and sat in the living room. "Do you know how hard it has been to keep my mouth shut?"

"Don't make me regret coming to you."

He held his hands up. "I would never. What's going on?"

"I need to swear you to secrecy. It's not really about Seth at first. It's about my dad."

"Absolutely."

She told him about Shaye, and August asking her for some time to process the news before they tell the kids, and then January's subsequent freak out. "And your brother has been really good through it all. Like…unbelievably understanding. Maybe it's because the summer is coming to an end? We're both starting to have to look at the fall and realize that our time together is limited, you know? He doesn't want to waste it fighting."

Will frowned.

She stopped talking.

"Keep going."

"No, what are you thinking?"

"It doesn't sound like he only wants to avoid fighting, although that's not the worst instinct. If he's being a fool who won't admit he loves you—"

"No, he said he loves me." Her voice sounded small even to her own ears.

Her fear had been that he'd walk away again, but it had been her that had done the pushing. And she'd told herself that it had been to avoid pain. Exactly the excuse she'd expected him to use.

He hadn't, though.

He'd stood his ground and told her they were friends. He'd touched her friendship bracelet, quietly telling her he'd noticed she hadn't taken it off, without saying it out loud.

He told her he loved her without a hint of asking for the same in return.

Will just looked at her. Maybe he could tell she was reeling on the inside.

When she groaned and tossed her head back, he prodded her along a little. "Then what's the problem?"

"I want to ask him to move in with me." She gestured down the street. "I was picking paint colours just now and I couldn't do it. I don't want to make every decision about that house all by myself when I could have a partner by my side."

"Okay…"

"But he's never moved home," she whispered. "Not even when he could, when he got out of the Air Force and had his choice of where to set up his business."

"That was years ago. Everything is different now."

"It's even *more* complicated now."

"It shouldn't be." Will dragged in a rough breath. "Look, he's my brother, and I will love him no matter what, but you deserve someone who puts you first. And if he came to me for advice, that's exactly what I'd tell him. Since he's being a stubborn mule and keeping everything to himself, then I hope he's arriving at the same realization on his own. Stick up for yourself. Tell him what you want."

She nodded. "Any chance you have paracord lying around?"

———

AN HOUR LATER, she watched Seth's plane gracefully circle the harbour, then land with ease. She waited with breathless anticipation for the passengers to disperse. But after the last one headed up to the parking lot, there was still no sign of him.

She asked Summer to watch the counter again and headed outside just in time to see him going the wrong way around the marina. Up the grassy back slope, heading straight for the garage.

"Seth!"

He didn't turn around.

"Hey!" She chased at him, not caring if anyone saw her making a scene.

He slowed down when he realized she was pursuing him, then stopped as she closed the gap.

"Where are you going?"

He pointed to the garage.

Well, she knew that.

"Why?"

He turned enough for her to see his profile. "It's been a long day."

"Want to talk about it?"

"Nope?"

"What happened to the guy who kissed me last night?"

"He's…" He turned around fully. "I'm still here. I'm just tired, that's all."

She frowned. His expression was unreadable. "Okay. But I missed you today, and I wanted to talk to you about something."

"What?"

She crossed her arms over her chest. "Nope. Not if you're being grouchy with me."

"You're the one running hot and cold." He shoved his hand into his hair. "You barely said two words to me this morning."

Because Levi had woken up early with her. Because her heart had still been in her throat from the night before. Because there had been a non-stop flow of people through the office, and she thought she might cry if she held his gaze for too long. "That was not intentional. I thought after last night, maybe you wanted to take things slowly."

He laughed. It was sharp and not at all funny.

She recoiled like she'd been slapped. "Or not. I don't know, okay? I'm still figuring this all out. It's terrifying."

"Yeah, for me, too. I don't like seeing you upset and not knowing how to make it better. I *hate* seeing you hurt and not knowing how to prevent it from happening in the first place. I wish I could stand between you and every awful reminder that your father wasn't the man you deserved. I don't want to take things slow. I'm *willing* to because that's what is required. Last night was *hard* for me. Did that occur to you, even for a second?"

No. She flushed with embarrassment.

He glanced at the antenna tower. They'd stopped at the same side of the building where he used to climb up to see her.

A long silence stretched between them.

"I used to think I left half my heart here."

"No." It was hard for her to swallow around a ball of regret that big. "Don't say that."

"Why not? Haven't we lied enough about what we mean to each other?"

A fat tear rolled down her cheek.

"It wasn't half my heart, January. It was the whole fucking thing. And if you aren't going to take care of it, I'd like to have it back. Twenty years is long enough to go without it in my chest."

"Don't put that on me," she whispered.

"For all this time, I never have. I've only had the sweetest, softest memories of you. But now? Now that we have a chance to move forward and be something together, and you don't want to? But you still want me, in a limited way.

Right? *Now* I get to be mad about that. Because I want more, so that makes all of this a bit challenging."

That wasn't even how she felt, but if he was going to let his emotions fly, then so was she. "You're the one who has the ten-year plan that cannot include me fully!" She threw her hands in the air. "You forget about that part, though. The part where you would only be here part of the year, like that's acceptable for a woman staring down the last few years of viable eggs."

"What?"

"Nothing."

"Wait, *what?*" He stormed towards her. His whole chest heaved as he stopped right in front of her. "You want babies?"

Fucking tears. She swiped at her face. Useless fingers. Didn't absorb shit. "I don't know. I'm confused. But I know one thing. If I'm going to fall in love, I don't want it to be long distance. I didn't want that before, I never have, and—"

He cut her off, his hands gripping her shoulders. "We'll figure it out."

"No."

"Yes."

"Your plan—"

"Is nothing compared to spending my life with you. You know the best part of my business plan? It's all mine. I created it. I get to shred it. And I fucking enjoyed building my business from the ground up. I was good at that. *So good at it, sweetheart.* I'll be good at it here, too. We'll figure it out."

"All because I said I wanted to have kids?" She shook her head. "No. What if we can't? What if it doesn't work out? What if—" This time, she cut herself off. "You need to choose me for me. Not for a potential future we could have together."

"I *do* choose you. Every fucking day. I moved in across the road from you! I haven't slept in my own bed in months."

"Because the summer is short. And we want to maximize this time together."

"Yes."

"And then the summer will *end*. You have four more weeks of charter flights. And then what?"

His mouth fell open, then snapped shut. Then opened again. "Why do you think I'm here?"

"To expand your business."

"Really?"

"And to spend more time with your brothers. That's what you said."

"I'm here for you."

"Not for me. For your family."

"You *are* my family. You are everything I have ever wanted. And because I needed to go off by myself on a wild adventure, because I was a dumb kid who thought he couldn't possibly fall in love at sixteen, I lost you for twenty years. But now? I'm not going anywhere. Ever. I'm here, and I'm in your face, telling you I love you. That isn't going to change, even if you aren't sure about *me*. Love doesn't have an on-off switch."

"Then why are you mad at me right now?"

"I'm not—" He stopped and swore. "Okay, it feels like I'm mad at you. But I'm not. I'm mad because I'm frustrated, and I don't know how to do this."

"I wanted to ask you to come to the house with me," she whispered.

He kissed her tear-streaked cheeks. "Fuck, I'm sorry."

"If it feels like I'm cold to you, I'm not." Her voice broke. "I'm just scared."

"What are you scared of?"

"Me not being enough for you." She gasped a little. That was more than she'd even thought to herself, in her saddest moments. But it was the truth.

"You are everything," he breathed. He wrapped his arms around her. "Leaving you behind was the hardest thing I've ever done. I cannot do it again. Can we lay that on the table now? Whatever has to happen in the short term is just work stuff. And I will sort through that in a way that has me back in Pine Harbour sooner than later, every time."

She clung to him, letting the truth of what he was saying sink in. He meant it.

"Seth…" She backed up, pulling him up against the house with her. She wanted to kiss him in a minute, in a pretty indecent way, and it would be better if they weren't out in the open for anyone to see.

He bracketed his arms on either side of her as she unfisted her fingers from his Kincaid Air Ferry t-shirt.

She smoothed her hands over his chest.

He waited.

Her heart pounded in her chest, her pulse heavy in her neck.

"I never want you to think that I don't care about your feelings," she started. "I'm sorry about this morning. And I know you're tired, I know it's been a long day. But I want to know what you think about the colour Beacon Gray."

"Excuse me?" He gave her a startled half-smile.

"It might make more sense in person." She squeezed her hand against his chest.

"January."

"Mmm?"

"What are the other options?"

She was having trouble breathing at the moment, so remembering paint colours was a real stretch. "Something blue…and there's a nice sage green too…"

"Important decision."

"Do you want to come and see them on the walls?"

"That depends."

She lifted her gaze from his solid chest to his achingly warm gaze. "On what?"

"Why you want my opinion."

She couldn't look away. "Because I love you," she whispered. "I don't want you to leave at the end of the summer. I want you to move in with me, and make a home with me, starting with the paint colour on the walls. I've been a fool, I realize, because maybe if I'd opened up more about the house earlier, then I'd have come to this realization sooner, and we could have—"

He cut her off with his mouth, then his tongue, then his whole body pressed against hers. He swallowed her sighs, and gave her his groans, and they twisted themselves together so tightly nobody would be able to tear them apart.

"I love you, too," he finally said, when she was out of breath, her chest heaving against his. "And you are not a fool."

"I am."

"Then you're my fool," he said so endearingly that it felt like praise. "And I don't know if I'd have wanted to have this meltdown any sooner, because I was really enjoying all the sexy demands you made of my body. That was a lot of fun."

"That doesn't stop now," she muttered.

"I hope it only gets worse." He kissed her again. "Can we go see the paint now?"

———

THE KIDS WERE THRILLED at the thought of feeding themselves ramen, so thrilled they didn't even care why January was taking a picnic dinner somewhere.

She shoved cheese, fruit, and possibly stale croissants into a lunch bag, then ran outside to meet Seth.

He'd had marginally better luck, finding beer and granola bars at Josh's apartment.

They took Betty because the truck had a bench seat and she wanted to sit next to him. She gripped his thigh the whole way up the hill and across town.

At the construction site that would one day soon be her —their—home, he parked on the street and she dug out the key Jake gave her.

He was quiet as she opened the door and let them in. Every step they took echoed through the empty space, even after they took their shoes off.

She thought her heartbeat might be loud enough to trip an echo, too.

"This is the front room," she finally said. "That's what it's actually called on the floorplan. A modern-day sitting room, I guess. Could be a dining room. I like the window for a Christmas tree."

He took her hand and laced their fingers together.

That gave her a bit of courage.

"The slider door here goes through to the kitchen, or we can go around down the main hall again."

He tugged her back into the foyer, past the stairs, and

into the space where the kitchen spilled into the family room.

She pointed to the painted sections on the drywall. "They look different in the late light." She tipped her head to the side. "This is where I realized I'd been letting fear hold me back."

"Right here?" It was the first thing he'd said since they arrived.

He wrapped his arms around her, cradling her from behind.

"Jake asked me what I thought of the paint, and my first thought was that I wished you were here to help me decide."

"I'm here now."

"And which one do you like best?"

He paused a good, long beat. "They're all great."

She laughed. "Seth!"

"I'm just honoured to be asked."

She twisted in his arms and poked his side. "Come on, help me decide."

"Which one do you like?"

She turned around again. "The blue feels very timeless. The grey…could be more modern? But maybe it'll be boring? And the sage is apparently the colour of the year."

"Maybe we need to hold stuff up against them."

"Like a swatch?"

"Mmm." He picked her up and crossed to the wall. "Or you."

He kissed her against all three paint samples, and they decided the blue was the winner.

"Is there more paint to pick out?" he asked as he traced the curve of her lower lip with his finger. "This is fun."

"Upstairs," she panted. "No! Wait."

She wrenched herself out of his arms and grabbed his hand. "Come here, I have something else to show you."

She pulled him across the family room to the den. "What do you think of this room?"

"It's nice." He flicked his gaze over the built-in bookcases. "A library?"

"Or an office." Her heart fluttered wildly in her chest, like it had come undone from the rest of her body. "It could be your office."

"It's hard to compare it to my current office…" He made a thinking sound.

She tried not to say anything else, didn't want to pressure him, but a nervous squeak came out anyway.

He turned and looked at her, really looked at her, then shook his head. "January, my current office is a laptop on a second-hand coffee table in Josh's hovel of an apartment. Before that it was that same laptop on a second-hand kitchen table in my house in Blind River. I've never *had* a proper office, and it's not because I didn't have the room there. This is something I never imagined for myself."

"Do you like the idea of…" Her words jammed in her throat.

"Yes," he said with a grave solemnness. "I like the idea very much."

Upstairs, she spread out a blanket and they laid out their makeshift picnic. He asked her about the house—when she would get possession, how he could help her with the finances, and what she had to move.

"I sold almost everything when I moved into the marina. I have my bedroom furniture, which might make a good guestroom set here, and some odds and ends. I planned to buy pieces over the winter, once I got a sense of what living here would feel like. How about you?"

"I have a big bed." He shrugged. "Nothing else of real value."

She leaned her head on his shoulder. "Will it be a challenge to move here?"

He was silent long enough that she feared the answer might be yes. "It would be a bigger challenge to try and continue on the path I'd previously set for myself. That would be impossible. This will be a good kind of challenge. And we'll make it work."

She sighed happily.

"Tell me something." He tugged a strand of her hair, loosely curling it around his finger. "Was college everything you thought it would be and more?"

"What?" She twisted to look at him more fully. "Why do you ask?"

"I think we've spent enough time talking about the bittersweet moments in the last twenty years."

"Oh." A lovely warmth flooded her chest. "You're right. It was…amazing. My dorm was covered in ivy, and my roommate was this rich girl from Toronto who had a cottage in Muskoka."

He groaned in horror.

"I know. I loved every minute of it."

That made him smile. "What else?"

"I pulled so many all-nighters. I took a bartending certificate, and worked at this place where we wore jean shorts cut *real* short and tank tops that we tied just under our boobs, and I pulled three hundred dollars a night in tips. I fell madly, foolishly in love with my English Lit TA, only to discover it was totally in vain because he was having an affair with one of the sociology faculty—big scandal, I dodged a bullet—and…" She sighed happily.

"Four years of the most juvenile shit. And then I went to teacher's college and grew up."

"Again." He brushed his thumb against the corner of her mouth. "You grew up, again. Because the girl I once knew was pretty mature to begin with. Maybe you needed a break from that. A chance to be youthful."

"I did." She smiled at him. "How about you? What were your peak moments in your career?"

"Getting to live and train with the American Air Force was great. Colorado is incredible. I'd love to take you there sometime. And…honestly, the relief I felt when I started to send money home to Owen. That filled me with a kind of pride that I needed."

"So I had four years of immaturity and you were a model citizen."

He laughed out loud. "What we both needed."

"Mm."

He played with her ear piercings. "When did you get these?"

"Ten years ago? After I'd been teaching for a while. I went to Nashville on a girls' trip with some friends from university. Two girls wanted to get tattoos. I wasn't interested in ink, but the same place did piercings."

"Very cool. You have a t-shirt from the Grand Ole Opry."

"I do!" She laughed. "Wow, observant."

"Your tits looked amazing in it. Seared right on my…" He tapped his forehead.

"Maybe I'll change into it when I get home. You want to come over later and reacquaint yourself with it?"

"It's been a long time since I've snuck into your bedroom late at night. Will you leave the window unlatched for me?"

She giggled. "You can come in the front door."

"Probably safer."

"Mm-hmm."

"But we can pretend…" He ghosted his mouth over hers again, then growled. "Okay, let's go."

"Yep."

They both paused, then she pulled him in for a kiss, that turned into him crawling on top of her.

"We could…" She panted as she pulled his shirt up. "Right here?"

He caught her face in his hands. "I want to take my time with you tonight. And there are two kids currently stuffing themselves with ramen who need some evil eye bedtime instruction."

She loved that he cared about that, too. "You're right."

"Plus the sooner they go to bed, the sooner I can crawl into your bed. Plywood floors are not meant for thirty-eight-year-old knees."

She started laughing, and didn't stop until they were packed up and quietly tiptoeing out of the half-finished house.

25

JANUARY BRIBED the kids to go to bed a bit early without complaint, then tidied the kitchen while she waited for Seth.

She didn't have to wait long.

His quiet footsteps up the stairs made her heart leap.

She met him in the hallway, and instead of leading him upstairs immediately—she'd give the kids a bit longer to sink into deep sleep—she pulled him into the living room.

"I have a present for you," she whispered.

The words were loud in the quiet space, and they shared a private smile.

This wasn't the first time he'd been over after the kids were asleep, but it felt different.

Tonight was important.

She turned on the TV, putting on a long YouTube baking show for background noise. Something they wouldn't need to worry about in two months.

Because we're moving in together. She almost couldn't quite believe it.

Levi's D&D supplies were stacked on one corner of the

coffee table, but his set of dice were spilled beside his papers, because she'd temporarily repurposed the small bag the dice were usually kept in.

She scooped it up and handed it to Seth, who sprawled on the couch after taking it.

"Open it," she urged when he just looked at her.

"Come here first."

She crawled into his arms. "Hi."

He exhaled happily. "This is better."

She was never going to run away from her feelings—or him—again. The fierce hold he had on her told her everything she needed to know about his priorities now.

After he tipped her face and captured her mouth with his, then he lifted the soft bag in the air between them. "These are dice."

She shook her head.

He tugged the drawstring open and dipped his long fingers inside. Hooked the gift, and drew it out.

The friendship bracelet he had made for her, that she'd found in the geocache box, was bright red paracord.

This one was a deep, rich blue. And instead of a clasp, which was pushing the good-luck-finds-at-Will's-house possibilities, she'd looked up how to make a sliding knot.

"If there's a choice between being your friend and being your lover, I choose both," she murmured, her voice shaking. "Always both. But I never want you to forget that I, too, value our friendship above all else."

He had shown her twenty years ago that he was the best keeper of her secrets. She would never again lose sight of that.

"Always both," he repeated, sending her heart soaring. "Where's the TV remote?"

She snagged it for him off the shallow shelf above the couch.

He peeled off his sweatshirt, leaving him in a very touchable worn t-shirt that clung to his muscles, and turned up the volume a few more beats. "Friends make out on this couch."

"Makes sense." She wriggled into his arms, and he pressed her into the back of the couch, the baking show fading to background noise immediately.

"Thought about this a lot." He fit their bodies together. "One night you invited me to stay for a movie…" He groaned as his hard length found her core. "I thought it would be too hard to sit next to you and not do my damnedest to get you into this position."

She barely remembered those early days now. They blurred into a wave of longing.

"I'm the luckiest man in the world because I get to do this…" He slid his hand under her shirt and sighed happily. "You feel good."

She stroked his body, too, and he kissed her. Hard at first, then soft. Languid pulls and eager pushes.

When she unbuttoned his fly, he sucked in a breath that was another smack of déjà vu.

They'd come a long way from being teenagers who messed around for a long time before they went all the way. At some point tonight, she would lead him up to her bedroom and take him into her body.

But right now, all she wanted was the feel of his straining cock—impossibly hard for something still so soft on the outside—trapped between their bodies, her hand shoved into his pants.

The perfect innocence of it all. The delightful fun.

She squeezed his shaft, then stroked him slowly as he

pushed his tongue deeper into her mouth and made her shake with need.

There was also something deeply fun about the quiet way he followed her upstairs a half hour later. Her whole body was on high alert, pumping with desire.

They showered together, then tumbled naked into January's bed.

Seth stretched her out and cupped her breasts, pressing her nipples up to his mouth. He sucked and licked her there until the heat swirling through her body settled distinctly between her legs.

He stroked her sex, and when her arousal spilled onto her thighs, he growled that he needed a taste before fucking her.

Instead of crawling down her body, he sprawled onto his back and tugged her on top of him. "Come here. Turn around."

He lazily swatted at her ass as she straddled him backwards. And his immediate, lusty praise was all the encouragement she needed to get closer.

"Yes, that's the pretty pussy I've wanted all week. Sit on my face. Back it up. Fuck yeah."

She rocked back with pleasure. "You're filthy, you know that?"

"Twenty years to make up for, sweetheart. Gimme that p—"

She pushed her hips the last inch to shut him up, then laughed and wrapped her hands around his cock. She had two decades to make up for as well. The only solution was multitasking.

At the first swipe of his tongue through her folds, his erection pulsed and a bead of pre-come appeared. She stroked him slowly, firmly, watching his body react to the pleasure of going down on her. Or up, in this case, because she was splayed on top of him.

The flick of his tongue against her clit jolted her forward. His hands clamped on her hips, dragging her back. *Mine*, his grip said.

Yours, she thought happily as she arched into his blissful licks. Then she lowered her mouth to the thick cock head she'd just smeared with the evidence of his arousal, and took it hungrily into her mouth.

———

Seth bucked his hips at the first contact of January's warm, wet tongue against his dick. He clamped her body tight against his and buried his face deeper. He couldn't get enough of her taste, her scent, the soft press of her thighs, and the live-wire reactions of her whole body.

He'd been dormant for so long, thinking life was all about sacrifice and trade-offs.

And then she'd run back into his life in slippers and a sleep shirt, and he'd been a goner. It had only been a matter of time from that moment that he would figure out everything had to change.

He was going to spend the rest of his life being anything but dormant. He was going to seize every day with her exactly as he was gripping her now: with lusty determination to make the God damned most of it.

New rule for life…weigh everything on the "but how does it stack up against making a meal of your woman" scale.

Because nothing beat the way January trembled as she neared her climax.

She'd be gasping his name right now if her mouth weren't full of cock.

He braced his thighs and pulsed his hips, thrusting gently to take over the rhythm as her hand and mouth fell out of synch.

She grabbed his legs, holding on tight as he pinned her hips and sucked on her clit.

Her whole body jerked hard as the orgasm hit, and he thrust his tongue deep to feel the clutching need he'd spun inside her.

"Good girl," he murmured as he peeled her off him.

She was sweaty and flushed. Absolutely beautiful. He sheathed up, then slid into her, lifting her hips to deepen the angle.

"I love you," she moaned as he worked his way out, then pulsed, teasing her entrance.

His cock swelled at the words. She held his gaze as he bottomed out.

"I love you, too." He captured her hands with his and pressed her into the bed, then dropped his face into her neck and snapped his hips into her again.

With all my heart, he added. *And for the rest of our lives.*

HE MADE love to her all night long. After the first time, they dozed, then he reached for her again. After that second time, they agreed he should leave, but then she nestled into the crook of his arm.

Dawn broke before he pulled on his jeans and she crawled out of bed to kiss him one last time.

"I'll see you this afternoon." It was a warm, earnest promise.

She nodded and opened the bedroom door—only to hear kids shuffling around. Her eyes went wide and she closed the door again.

Seth made a face. "Sorry," he mouthed.

She dragged him close. "Don't be sorry," she whispered. "I'm sorry."

"No, don't—"

"Because I think you need to go out the window."

He blinked down at her.

She was right.

Damn it. "Yes, you should be sorry." He tangled his hands in her hair. "Someone in the marina might see me."

"That's preferable to me explaining this to the kids before I have coffee."

She had a good point. "Right." He kissed her one last time. "You don't need to look quite so pleased with this idea."

She looked *very* amused. "Everything that is old is new again."

"Or everything that was once young is now old..." He waved her off. "I'll be fine."

"I'm going to go make a lot of noise in the kitchen." She opened the door, then stopped on the top step, turned back, and mouthed. "*Last night was amazing.*"

Every day was amazing, he thought as he shoved his way out the window.

Then he closed it, crab walked over to the antenna, and did the climb of shame.

———

January thought all morning that she got away with the overnight guest. But at lunch, August called, and as

January was mid-salad bite, Levi casually dropped that Aunt January had made up with Seth.

"She snuck him in last night," he said slyly. "And they played with my Dungeons and Dragons dice."

Summer snickered.

January inhaled a blueberry.

And on the screen, August gave them all an amused look. "Levi, it's important to share our things."

"I don't mind *sharing*," he said. "But they left the dice scattered all over the coffee table. And he left his sweatshirt on the couch! We're supposed to pick up after ourselves."

"Sorry," January muttered. It was all she had.

August raised her eyebrow from halfway around the world. The message was clear.

Call me back once you're alone.

"We like Seth," Summer said. "He's nice to you."

He was *very* nice to her. "Mm-hmm."

"So are you dating again?"

They'd zoomed right past that. But the old answer, *it's complicated*, no longer applied. It wasn't complicated at all. "Actually, when my house is finished being built, Seth is going to move in there with me."

"What?" August leaned into the camera, no longer patient. "We need the whole story."

January gave her an exasperated look. The whole story was not kid-friendly. But parts were. "Well, as you may have guessed, Seth and I have rediscovered feelings for each other. He's really important to me."

"But last week he made you cry." Levi frowned. "And you tried to hide it."

Well, damn. "Oh, sweetie, I'd hoped you didn't know that."

"Your face was all splotchy and he was too quiet when he came over."

"But he still came over," Summer said. "So we knew that he loved you."

It shouldn't have taken January longer to figure that out than it did the kids. She pressed her lips together and nodded. "He does. And I love him."

August changed the subject to back-to-school clothes shopping, and stayed on the call until the kids were done eating and had taken their dishes to the sink.

Then she gave her sister a pointed look. "Take me somewhere private."

January winced and grabbed the laptop. Downstairs felt more soundproof than upstairs, so she swept through the living room to grab the offending sweatshirt, then went to the office, carefully closing both doors on her way down.

"Okay, so...I'm sorry about having Seth over last night."

August blew a raspberry at her. "I don't care about that. I want to know how this all escalated so quickly!"

It didn't feel quick at all to January. "It's so hard to explain. But it feels...like this was inevitable? After Shaye came over, I had a crisis of confidence in...I don't know. Myself. Men. The world. Dad, definitely. And Seth just rode that wave with me."

"He's a good guy."

"He really is."

"And he's good to you?" August wiggled her eyebrows. "All night? Most of the night?"

January pulled on his sweatshirt. It smelled like him, and that was a good distraction from figuring out how to answer the question without sharing too much.

She popped her head out of the shirt and immediately buried her face in her hands. "He had to crawl down the antenna tower this morning because I wouldn't let him leave in the middle of the night."

Her sister laughed at her. "That good?"

"August, he's *so* good. So much better now than he was in high—"

Seth cleared his throat.

January squeaked and looked up. "What are you doing here?"

"I came in when you were putting on my shirt," he said dryly. He came around the counter and waved at August. "Hey."

"My kids know that you love my sister," August reported matter-of-factly. "So if you hurt her, I will be forced to—"

January clicked the end call button. She'd apologize later. "Hello."

"You're wearing my shirt." He smoothed his hands over her. "I approve."

"You overheard the wrong part of that conversation."

"Oh?" He gave her a wicked grin. "What context makes it better?"

She lowered her voice to a hiss. "There was nothing wrong with how we had sex in high school!"

"I guess I should be relieved to hear I've improved." He was enjoying this far too much.

"You know you have." They both had. They had maturity and experience on their side now.

"I know you always came first. Even then."

"That's true." Her face flamed.

"But what?"

"But now you always make me come *twice*," she admitted. "And that thing with your mouth…"

"What thing?"

"You know."

His lips curled wickedly. "But I want to hear you say it."

"The way you lick me now. Slow and deliberate. And when you go deep…it's amazing."

"Like I just can't get enough of your taste?"

Her face was genuinely a fire hazard now. "Yes."

He brought his mouth to her ear. "That's because I can't. Because you're the best I've ever had. The most delicious. And I'm hungry for you all the time. It's all I can think about when I'm in the sky. Getting back here so I can bury my face between your thighs."

"Seems distracting."

"You have no fucking idea."

She caught the front of his shirt and pulled him close. "You don't think I spend a concerning amount of my day daydreaming about licking a path down your abs and then taking you in my mouth?"

His eyelids hooded over his gaze. "Do you?"

"Of course I do."

"Well, fuck."

She laughed. "What?"

"I have to go meet my brothers to distribute scavenger hunt supplies, and I really just want to drag you across the road to the garage. We haven't fucked there yet."

"Go. We'll have time later."

"I don't want to. I want to stay here and bury myself between your thighs."

She laughed and pushed him off her. "Your brothers are waiting."

He found her mouth with his. This kiss was slow and heated, promising every wicked thing she might ever desire.

It would be so easy to stay in bed all afternoon. But they had the rest of their lives for this.

"Go," she repeated. "And then come back."

———

SETH WENT BACK to the marina that night, and didn't leave again. He told Josh the apartment was all his. He wasn't going to spend another night apart from January.

The next two weeks flew by in a whirlwind of wedding activities. The week-long scavenger hunt for Catie was a huge success—both with the bride and the town in general—and Seth and January were a big part of that, dropping geocache surprises in a new location each day as an optional, group participation component once the day's clue had been solved by the bride.

The new clue appeared in a different storefront each day, and the town played along on social media, with betting pools on how long it would take her each day.

The final day's clue took her out of town, to a cave on the other side of the peninsula—apparently an in-joke between her and Will.

The night before, Seth and January and the kids had hiked out to the cave and placed the ammo can for the geo cache.

It would be a good place to propose, he thought, as she climbed into the big-mouthed cave and posed for a photo with Summer.

If his brother's wedding wasn't a week away, he'd

have already done it. But he wanted to wait until the time around their engagement was wholly their own.

Soon.

"Levi, take a picture of Aunt January and Seth," Summer ordered in her most imperious voice.

"Please," added January.

Summer muttered a *please*, and then demanded her phone back so she could take one, too.

Seth laughed down at January. She looked up at him and sighed, but her face was soft and happy.

And when they looked at the pictures later that night, that one was his favourite.

Very soon.

THE NIGHT BEFORE THE WEDDING, it felt to Seth like half of the wedding guests were at the provincial park for the rehearsal.

Will and Catie had decided to get married next to the Search and Rescue Team's training centre where they fell in love. Twinkle lights strung between two large oak trees made a backdrop for the evening ceremony and a soaring white tent was being erected for the dinner and dancing that would follow.

It promised to be very fancy.

Tonight though, they were all dressed down. Catie was wearing a white eyelet lace sundress and a Bride-to-be bucket hat. Will was in jeans and a t-shirt that said, "I'll be Her Mister Anything."

Seth made a mental note to ask January what she thought about wedding-themed outfits. He was not sure it was either of their tastes, but he couldn't begrudge his brother for what obviously made Will dorkably happy.

Seth searched for his love as he finished hanging another string of lights.

Tonight, January was in his favourite jean cut-off shorts, with cowboy boots on her feet and a pretty pink peasant blouse on top. She was all business, running everyone through the order of speeches and the timings for the first dance, the cutting of the cake, and the midnight send-off.

Then the minister arrived, and they assembled in the Search and Rescue facility. The minister led Will and his brothers outside first, and they marched down the aisle. January and Kerry sat in the front row. Lila bounced on Kerry's knees, babbling happily when she saw her dad.

Then it was the bridesmaids' turn to practice walking down the aisle. Tonight they weren't playing the actual music, Catie had picked fun pop songs instead, and three of her SRT friends danced down the aisle first. Isla was last, standing as her maid of honour. And then it was Catie, and Seth—who had never considered himself a romantic before this summer—still felt all the air in the forest go still as Will caught sight of his bride-to-be.

For a rehearsal.

After joking and laughing all afternoon.

All the Type-A organizational details and Bro-mittee meetings aside, Seth got it. This was the night before the most important day in Will's life. He was bonding himself to this woman for life, and his brother wanted that to be as important an event as he could make it.

He wanted everyone to see just how much he loved her.

Catie thanked her friend Frank for walking her down the aisle, then handed a tissue-paper bouquet to Isla, and took Will's hands.

"Hey," she whispered.

"This is so fun," he whispered back.

And it really was.

They ran through the order of speakers, then it was time to practice their vows.

"Are we saying all the words tonight?" the officiant asked.

"Heck yeah," Catie said. "I've been practicing them for a week."

January choked on a laugh that sounded like *perfectionist*.

Will made a pointed comment about the peanut gallery.

And then they got back on track.

"Do you, Will, take Catie to be your lawfully wedded spouse?"

"I do."

"Please repeat after me." The minister lowered his voice to a murmur.

Will listened, his gaze locked on his bride's face. "I, Will Kincaid, take you, Catie Berton, to be my wife. I promise to love and comfort you, honor and support you, through whatever life throws at us. I will stand by your side, your loyal and loving partner, as long as we both shall live."

"And Catie, now you..."

The whole time, Seth kept his gaze locked on January. She was smiling. She could feel his attention.

Soon.

THERE WAS something else he needed to do, too, and he wanted her by his side when he did it. He asked Josh and

Bailey to help him clear a day off her schedule, then woke her up early with a travel mug of coffee.

"Will you come with me for another flight?"

She didn't hesitate. "Of course."

She didn't ask where they were going. They were quiet for the whole flight. She drank her coffee and slowly woke up as she stared out the window, looking down at the route he travelled so often.

When they landed, he helped her out of the plane, then locked up. It would be a while before they were back.

He led her up the dock, and stopped in front of the sign he'd planted in the ground almost half a decade earlier.

"It's time to take this sign down." He took a deep breath. "And list my house for sale."

She laced her fingers through his. "This is hard for you."

No hiding that. "Yeah."

He expected her to ask why. Instead, she glanced around, her tight hold on him never letting up. "Tell me about starting the business here."

"It was close to home, but not too close." He dragged in a breath. "And I could see the business potential up here. Up here...I could focus solely on the business. No distractions."

He liked the little smile that played at her mouth. Yes, she was the best kind of distraction.

"But it was lonely, too. I wouldn't have used that word, but it's what I was—until I found you again. So this is hard, but it's mostly bittersweet. Hard not to regret some things, but I don't want regret to overwhelm how happy I am with you now."

"Not lonely anymore?"

"Not even a little bit." He wrapped her in his arms. "I want to take you to my house. It's not much," he felt compelled to warn her.

She smiled. "But it's yours. Show me your life."

She was his life now. But it meant everything to him that she cared about what he'd had in that long stretch of absence.

Teegan, also in on the surprise, had left his truck for him. He helped January in, then held her hand for the drive to his house.

She gave him a warm smile as he parked, then followed him inside.

He tried to see it through her eyes. A squat bungalow without any landscaping. Clean and tidy, but absolutely basic, and a bit stale smelling now that he'd been gone for so long.

She trailed her fingers over his Craigslist-special table. "This is where you built your business?"

"Yep."

"That's amazing," she said softly.

Then she peeked her head into the galley kitchen. He still had a freezer of stew he needed to do something about. Maybe Linda and Teegan would take it.

"The bedroom is this way?" She pointed.

He grinned. "Yeah."

"You promised a nice big bed..."

The lusty desires of a thirty-seven-year-old woman were an amazing bonus to being in love.

He caught her around the waist at the edge of his bed. "I didn't just bring you here for sex."

She fluttered her lashes at him. "But you did bring me here for sex, too."

He couldn't deny that. Once he'd said everything he wanted to say, he was going to claim her in his bed. "Yes."

She bit her lip and turned in his arms. "Am I getting ahead of you?"

"A little." He dragged in a breath. "There's so much more that I want to tell you. I don't know what it's like for you, but bringing you here... It's revealing things to me that I didn't fully understand."

"Oh." She pulled him down onto the bed. "This is a really comfortable mattress, though."

He propped himself up on one elbow. "It's coming to our new house."

She smiled at that.

Our house.

"I want you to know why this is hard for me." He traced his fingertips over her shoulder and down her arm. "At some point, I convinced myself that I wasn't the right path for you. This house, my business here...it all represents that painful error. So it's hard, but not hard to give up. Hard to look at. Hard to think about. Because maybe if I had taken a different path, we would have been together from the very beginning, or gotten back together sooner."

"We can't live in the *what ifs*," she said softly.

"I know. I don't want to. I want to spell this out once, here, and then bury it." He took a deep breath. "Part of why I wanted to bring you up here and show you this small life I had built is to show you that *this* is the off-course path. I am not veering wildly away from a plan to come and be with you. I am getting back on course. And it may mean turbulent change. It will definitely mean a whole new ten-year plan for my business. But it will be a better plan, because I won't be purposefully keeping myself lonely anymore."

"Since we're opening a little capsule to put our *what ifs* into," she whispered. "I don't think we could have found our way back to each other sooner. We needed to live our separate lives first. Maybe because what we had wasn't meant for teenagers."

That burned hot in his chest.

She caught his hand and brought it to her mouth, kissing his knuckles. "I used to tell myself that we didn't love each other when we were young. But that's not exactly true, is it?"

He shook his head. "I loved you so much, it was too bright for me to see it as love. And you loved me—so much that you helped me leave you. Maybe you're right. Maybe that was a grown-up kind of love we couldn't appreciate at the time. You knew what I wanted, what I needed for my brothers, and you made that happen for me. You sacrificed more than I knew. And I already thought you'd sacrificed so much."

His voice cracked on the last line, despite himself.

Her eyes stormed in protest. "No," she pleaded. "Don't. Not that."

"I know. And it's not that. It's not *what happened*. It's the order it happened in. I've kicked myself for twenty years because I felt like I took away a choice."

"You didn't. I knew what I would do before I took the test. Before, during, after." She shook her head fiercely. "I didn't want a baby then. Don't carry that anymore."

"I was relieved. When we went to the clinic." It was a confession he'd been carrying for a very long time.

"I was, too." Her face was wet as she leaned into him and pressed her face into his neck. "I was, too. I have been so many times over the years. It was right."

He gripped her to him. "I love you so much. And I hate how much time we lost because I didn't have the words."

"Neither of us did." She kissed his face, and he tasted her tears.

"No, baby. God, please don't—" Which was a stupid thing to say. If she needed to cry, she needed to cry. Simple as that.

Soft sobs wracked her body as he kissed her mouth over and over again, loving her.

"January," he breathed.

She kissed him back.

"Marry me."

She went still.

It had slipped out. Not in the way he'd intended, although today was the day. It was just supposed to be later, on the other side of being done here.

But he was doing it now. His heart slammed against his ribcage. He rolled her back, just enough to get into his pocket, and then he slid off the bed.

The most ungainly start to a proposal ever.

She sat on the edge as he kneeled in front of her and held out the ring he'd picked out weeks ago. "Will you make me the happiest man in the world and be my wife?"

"Yes," she whispered—and then fresh tears slid down her cheeks. "Yes, I'll marry you."

He surged back up and caught her in his arms. "Then why are you crying?"

"Because I've had those two words *this close* to spilling out for weeks now." She pressed her forehead against his, her fingers soft on his cheeks. "But I didn't know if you were ready. I thought maybe you needed to wind down this part of your life first."

"I've been..." He laughed hoarsely. "It's been on the tip

of my tongue, too. I didn't want to rush you before your sister got home. I thought maybe I'd do it when we move into the new house. And then I knew I couldn't wait that long."

She chewed on her lower lip. "We might be too tired after moving all day."

He fought back another laugh, this one less desperately relieved, more deeply pleased at how adorable his future wife was. "Good point."

"Will you want a family?"

He tightened his arms around her. "I have a family."

She squeezed back. "And do you want to add to it?"

"If you do."

She kissed the corner of his mouth. "August guessed that we might want to start on a family before a wedding."

He tickled her sides. "You already talked to her about it."

"She's my best friend. I tell her everything."

"Do you tell her how much I like licking behind your knees?"

"What?" She howled with laughter, but then he pushed her over and showed her he wasn't kidding. He peeled off her jeans, then started at her ankles, sucking gently at the skin there, then worked his way up.

"Are you going to tell her how much you like it when I bite your inner thighs?"

She shivered. "Some things are just for us."

"What else is just for us?"

She arched her back as his mouth found her centre. "How much I like your tongue right there."

"Here?" He licked a slow path to her clit.

"Yes." She gasped and grabbed at his head. "Seth…"

"Let go, beautiful. Give it all to me."

"I love you," she breathed.

He groaned in response, his mouth full. Then he surged up her body, filling her, and it was his turn to breathe *love you love you love you* to the woman who turned his life inside out and gave him all the reasons to be happy again.

EPILOGUE

Six months later

THEY GOT MARRIED one year almost to the day of their reunion. It was a warm weekend in March, the start of January's midterm break from school.

Instead of spending the night before apart—they'd done enough of that for a lifetime—they got ready together, at home. January's dress hung in the window, waiting for the photographer to document it just so. While she waited to put it on, she helped Seth with his tie. Not that he needed it, after fourteen years of experience with dress uniforms.

"You nervous?" he whispered as she fidgeted in front of him in her slip.

"No." She smiled. "Excited. Can we show up early to our wedding? Is that a thing?"

"If there weren't so many people here, I'd—" He glanced out the door. "Ah, fuck it."

He pivoted her around, pushed their bedroom door closed, then pressed her up against it.

"Shh," he said, pressing his finger to her lips briefly before dropping to his knees.

"Seth!"

He pressed one big hand to her belly as he hitched her left leg over his shoulder, then tugged the gusset of her panties out of the way.

Her head thunked back against the door. His tongue was *perfect*, as always, and holy fuck, maybe she had been nervous—in a good way—because now she was already almost there, the wild coursing of adrenalin just as much an aphrodisiac as her fiancé's talented mouth.

Once he gave her a silent thigh-shaking, nerve-eradicating climax, she slid to *her* knees and took all of him into her mouth.

It was his turn to be very quiet.

And because of his very good idea, they were exactly on time for their wedding. They walked hand in hand down the path to the deck, where their friends and family waited.

She saw her sister first. Sisters, she corrected herself immediately. Because beside August stood Shaye, and they were both smiling.

It was a tentative relationship, but it was holding together.

Warm, happy tears pricked at January's eyelids. Then she exhaled quickly, sliding those thoughts straight into the *later* pile.

Instead of asking grown-ups to stand up with them, they had Summer and Levi as their maid of honour and best man. After their vows, August and Owen would sign the marriage certificate as their witnesses.

It was a perfect, intimate wedding in the place where they first fell in love, and then fell in love all over again.

Seth never let go of her hands, and when he slid her wedding ring on, his fingers shook. When it was her turn to put a ring on his finger, though, his hands had gone still. Sure, warm, and strong.

"I now pronounce you husband and wife."

He stepped in close, real close, and took her in his arms. Time slowed as he cupped the back of her head, swept his arm around her waist, and tipped her back.

"You may now kiss the bride…"

He already was.

And she loved him so much for it.

———

A week later, after a honeymoon spent at a luxury fly-in resort where Seth did zero fishing and a lot of seducing his new wife, they flew home again.

"Looks like we have a welcome home committee," he said through the radio.

She peered out the window, not seeing it at first, then there was a flash on the dock. Bright orange cards.

She pressed her hand to her chest. "Aww, it's Levi and Summer!"

And once they'd landed, the kids informed them there was an impromptu second reception happening that night, because "Mommy and Aunt Shaye have a surprise for you, and it deserves a party."

They barely made it to the end of the dock before the women in question came running out of the marina office to intercept them.

"Welcome home," August said.

"We did a thing," Shaye added.

Summer and Levi nodded in unison. "We told them."

"Did you tell them what the surprise was?"

"Nope."

August took their bags from Seth and set them on the steps to the deck. "Let's…just…"

"What is going on?" January asked.

But Seth was taller than her. He was taller than all of them, and he could see it.

In the week they'd been gone, January's sisters had replaced the faded marina sign with a newer, bigger sign.

He was grinning as they rounded the corner, happy for January to see her sisters working together and being proud—

Then he stopped dead in his tracks.

January bumped into him. "Oh," she breathed.

August looked back and forth between them expectantly. "Please tell me you like it."

Below the shiny new sign for Howe's Marina was another sign. Not a simple wooden sign like he'd once staked in the ground himself. A brightly lit banner with matching colours to the main sign that read, Fly North Aviation, operated by Kincaid Air Ferry.

It had been on his list of things to talk to the sisters about, but it hadn't risen to the top of his priority list yet. In part because he'd spent the winter focused on settling into a home with January. He'd earned a break after so many years of working non-stop.

But also because he hadn't wanted to insert himself too much into the marina. This was their space, a hard-fought, well-earned business they'd had to really struggle to make their own.

"I love it," he finally said, finding his voice. "It's…perfect."

"Welcome to the family," August said, throwing her arms around him and January together.

Summer and Levi piled on, then he felt his wife blindly reaching for her other sister, tugging Shaye into the group hug.

———

FOUR HOURS LATER, after a nap and a hot shower, they were back at the marina for the "We Have a New Sign for the Newlyweds" party.

August was grilling, a few new things she wanted to offer over the upcoming summer on weekends. The marina BBQ was back in business.

Shaye was talking with Jake Foster about the remodelling plans for the motel. Jake's wife, who was a paramedic who worked with Owen, was telling January something about their kids, which made Seth sweep his hand over the barely there swell of his wife's belly. She leaned back against him in a knowing way.

He tipped his glass of lemonade back happily and scanned the rest of the deck.

Campbell and Trent were there from the brewery. And all of Seth's brothers and sisters-in-law were in attendance as well.

It was a boisterous, happy party, so it took Seth an extra beat to realize there was a stranger in their midst.

Two people had a head start on him. Josh, who stood up so fast his chair tipped back and clattered to the deck.

And Trent Aitken, who had never seen a pretty woman he didn't want to chat up. "You look like you need a drink," he said, sliding over to the dark-haired young woman standing on the edge of the party.

She wore a puffy down jacket, which was a key indicator that she wasn't a local, because it was a warm day there, for the spring, and everyone else had arrived in hoodies. The expensive looking clothes visible underneath the winter coat also set her apart.

Glossy hair, perfect makeup.

She looked like she'd walked off the pages of a Banana Republic catalogue.

"I don't think we've met," Trent continued, even though everyone else had fallen silent. He introduced himself. "And you are?"

"Get away from her," Josh snarled at the same time as she said, "I'm here to see Josh."

Seth jumped between his brother and the other man, realizing just in time that Josh meant to push Trent bodily away from this woman.

"Whoa, hey," Seth murmured. "What's going on?"

Josh sidestepped him the other way, his soccer skills annoyingly effective in a party setting as well, and then he was between Trent and the newcomer.

She glared back at him.

"What the hell do you think you're doing here?" Josh asked, his voice low. If everyone else weren't so quiet one could hear a pin drop, it might have been for her ears only.

Trent grabbed his arm. "Hey, you can't talk to her—"

Josh shook him off, but his attention didn't leave the woman's face for even a second. His next words—meant for Trent, but still growled while staring down the woman —guaranteed that nobody would talk about the sign, or the motel renovations, or anything else for the rest of the evening. "Don't fucking tell me how to talk to my wife."

———

ALL THE KINCAID brothers have a swoon-worthy love story. If this was your first Pine Harbour book, or it has been a while, visit my website to explore the entire steamy and heartwarming series: www.zoeyork.com

ACKNOWLEDGEMENTS

Twenty-three years ago, I had an abortion. I was a little older than January, but not much. The young man who held me all night long after the procedure is now the father of my two sons. One of the many reasons I am grateful that I had an abortion when I was young is that it put me on a path to be *their* mother, the role I cherish more in life than anything else.

Very little about this book is autobiographical, but that tiny slice of it is mine.

Abortion is essential health care. At the time of publication, it's under attack in the United States in an unprecedented way. I can't imagine anyone who got through this book doesn't know how complicated it is to be pregnant when you don't want to be, but I wanted to name this personal piece. If you don't know anyone who has had an abortion (you do, though, but you might not *know*), then now you do.

Like every book, this one was a group effort. My editing team, as always, was a big support in the development and polishing of this book. Kristi Yanta who provided very helpful revision suggestions on the first draft, and Kim Cannon who came in clutch with the copy edits even as I re-wrote the ending of this book four days before publication.

Brighton Walsh helped with the blurb (thank you!), and Jennifer Cowan named Summer and Levi. (Another thanks as well to Melissa Lawhorn, who in that same reader poll suggested the runner-up options for the children's names, and I've tucked Isaac and Jemma away for future use!)

And The Viking and my little (now quite big) Viking boys, who have grown up knowing the word "deadline" to be sacrosanct. I'm done for the summer, my darlings. We can go get ice cream now.

ABOUT THE AUTHOR

Zoe York lives in London, Ontario with her young family where she writes romance novels set in the places where she grew up and fell in love herself. She's currently chugging Americanos, wiping sticky fingers, and dreaming of heroes in and out of uniform.

www.zoeyork.com

facebook.com/zoeyorkwrites

twitter.com/zoeyorkwrites

instagram.com/zoeyorkwrites